PLAYING STACY

Jenn Hype

Playing Stacy

ISBN-13: 978-0-692-53957-6
ISBN-10: 0-692-53957-3

Book design by J. F. Rountree
Cover photograph © Mihai Blanaru/ShutterStock.com

www.jennhype.com
press@jennhype.com

First Edition November 2015

Printed in the United States of America
10 9 8 7 6 5 4 3 2 1

For someone else
Just because

Chapter 1

Stacy

"Hey Joe, got a live one here," Officer Buzz Kill said to another cop as he pulled me into the police station. Adalyn, my old college roommate and best friend who had come to live with me only a month ago, had gone out with me to the opening of the new club Grind, where I might have gotten a little too tipsy, and then maybe gotten myself arrested.

Okay, maybe we were a lot more than just tipsy, but this cop that had me cuffed and dragging behind him, was seriously going overboard. So what if I had tried to prostitute myself to a stranger in front of him? It was his fault for being all sexy in his uniform. His chest and arms were so muscular that his shirt looked like it might tear at any second if he flexed too hard. He was like my own personal Bruce Banner. Yum.

"Get yourself a hooker, Chad? When I told you to get laid, I didn't mean pay for it. Probably not a good idea to bring her back here though. Kinda kills the mood, don't ya think?" Whoever this Joe guy was, he apparently thought he was hysterical as he stood there bent over, slapping his knee and laughing at his own joke. I had to admit, it was pretty funny, but it was at my expense so I decided to be offended instead of laughing.

"Hey, dickwad, I'm no hooker. Your buddy here, the one that's manhandling me right now, is just being an obnoxious douche. Apparently there were no real crimes being committed in the city tonight so he decided to spend his night screwing with me. And not in the way I'd prefer to be screwed with," I said with a wink.

Officer Man Panties yanked on my arm, not hard enough to hurt me, but enough to piss me off, and pushed me into an empty jail cell.

"What the hell? At least take off the cuffs. You're killing me here," I yelled, kicking the bars with the toe of my sparkly stilettos. "I mean, I like being in cuffs as much as the next girl, but it's not really worth the pain if I'm not getting any pleasure at the same time." Chad, aka Officer Killjoy, just glared at me while Joe folded over himself laughing. His laughter gave me a boost of confidence and I tossed a smug smile in Chad's direction, but he just growled and walked away.

I rolled my eyes at his retreating form and turned my efforts to the sexy cop he left me with. I tilted my head and stuck out my bottom lip in a pout. "Hey, stud muffin. What do you say you come help a lady out? I swear I'll make it worth your while," I asked Joe, throwing him a wink as he walked towards me, shaking his head, still chuckling.

"Are you sure you aren't a hooker?" He asked as he unlocked my cuffs. I glared at him as I rubbed my wrists that were aching from being restrained for so long. He threw his hands up in surrender and stepped back, locking the cell door again. "I didn't mean you look like one. You're way too hot to be a hooker, but you certainly have a mouth like one, with all that dirty talk."

"That's not the only dirty thing my mouth is capable of," I whispered as I licked my lips. His laughter was contagious and I couldn't keep a straight face any longer.

Chad walked back into the room a few minutes later and looked like he was going to say something to Joe, but changed his mind and stormed out. I supposed my tossing quips back and forth with his fellow officer wasn't exactly the night he had planned for me to have in the little cell I was sitting in.

"Okay, level with me here, Joe. What the hell is that guy's problem?" I asked, nodding at the door Chad had just left through.

"Who, Chad? Eh, he just takes his job and everything else pretty seriously. I've been trying to get him to lighten up since they partnered us two years ago. It hasn't worked yet, but I'm pretty persistent and I've managed to wear him down a little at a time." Joe pulled up a chair and perched himself on it right outside my cell, and I took a seat on the disgusting floor, stretching my legs out and crossing them at the ankles, leaning back on the palms of my hands.

"He takes his job seriously? I find that hard to believe seeing as how I was arrested tonight for no real reason. Can't he get in trouble for having me in here with no reason to hold me?"

The corner of Joe's mouth quirked up on the side and he looked at me like I had just asked the dumbest question he'd ever heard.

"You're clearly drunk, so if for no other reason, he can at least hold you for public intoxication. Sucks for you too because he just left for the night which means you aren't getting out of here until tomorrow."

I shot up to my feet and threw my hands in the air. "What does that have to do with anything?! He told my friends once I sober up then I can leave. Not that I'm so drunk that I couldn't hail my own cab, for goodness sake. Honestly, I think he was just mistaking my impressively outgoing personality for drunkenness. I can see how that would be confusing to someone who obviously wouldn't know a good time if it bit him in the ass."

"Well, regardless of how he interpreted your actions, he left without filling out any paperwork or informing anyone of why you're here. So yeah, technically I could probably let you go but if there is a part of the story that I'm missing and you really did do something wrong, then it's my neck on the line. So…sorry. You're stuck here until he comes back."

"When will he be back then?" I stopped my pacing and crossed my arms and started tapping my foot impatiently. The whole situation was so ridiculous. Joe just smirked at me and against my will I felt my shoulders relax and my face soften a little. There was just something about him that took the edge off of stress, like a natural sedative.

"9 A.M."

"What!? That's crazy! You have to call him. Make him tell you I did nothing wrong. You can't keep me here that long. I will seriously freak out on you right now. I can promise you that you have not faced anything in your career as terrifying as I am when I'm pissed off. This will be the longest night of your life. So pick up your damn phone and call Officer Numb Nuts and clear this matter up."

He never called Chad. Hours ticked by and though I was completely exhausted and very uncomfortable on the damp, dirty floor, Joe was good company. A couple of officers joined us a few hours later and they all told me a bunch of crazy stories from being on the job and I regaled them with my wit and sparkling personality. Honestly, the night kind of flew by and I completely forgot how pissed off I was.

Until Chad came back. Then it all came flooding back to me with a vengeance.

"Well, well, well. Look who decided to show up," I drawled, pacing back and forth like a captured wild animal.

"I work here. I have to show up," he retorted in a bored voice as he unlocked the cell door. I shoved past him, literally shoved him as I walked by, and demanded that they return my stuff. I needed my phone so I could call a cab or call Addy or call a hit man to murder this asshole. I let out a loud, very exaggerated groan when I saw that my phone was dead.

"You can make your one phone call on the pay phone," Joe mused, pointing to a nasty, slimy, ancient looking pay phone. I cringed at the thought of the types of people who had used that phone in the past. I was sure they had never sterilized it and I'd probably end up with Ebola or scabies or something. I knew it probably wasn't half as bad as the floor I'd been occupying all night, but I'd been drunk at the time and now that I was sober the thought of touching the greasy, disease-ridden phone made me want to go home and bathe in bleach.

A "working" girl who was seated a few feet away from me overheard us took pity on me and offered to let me use her cell. I wasn't being judgmental by assuming she was a prostitute, because believe me, she more than looked the part. It was, however, probably a little shitty of me to think that her phone was probably just as disgusting as the one hanging on the wall. She was all disheveled and a hot mess, and I didn't want to add to the horrible morning she was clearly having by adding insult to injury, so I gave her a reluctant smile as I took the phone from her.

After trying Addy's phone and not getting an answer, I tried Ian's. Ian had been one of my best friends since I was a kid, and he also happened to be one of the cities sexiest and most successful bachelors. He and Adalyn really did not hit it off when they'd met just yesterday, and when I'd been hauled off to jail last night she had been left behind in Ian's care. She was most likely very mad at me this morning, and I hoped she wasn't just avoiding my call as a result.

Ian answered after a few rings and much to my surprise, Adalyn was still with him. Very curious. I'd have to ask her about that later. Much later. After I'd showered a few times, making sure to exfoliate every inch of my skin until the grime of this horrid night was finally washed off of me. Then I needed to brush my teeth and eat something, all in that order and they all needed to happen soon before I ended up right back in that cell after being arrested for murdering Officer Man Tits.

No, he didn't have man tits, but I was exhausted and my ability to think of clever names to call him was suffering at that moment.

Chad had disappeared again, and I killed time waiting for Adalyn by talking to Joe and one of the other officers who had joined us during the night. Joe and I exchanged numbers and I was honestly kind of glad this whole mess had happened if it meant getting to spend more time with Joe. He was sexy as hell, though not re-ally my type, but our personalities were almost identical and I had really enjoyed hanging out with him.

Just as I was yelling at Adalyn for letting Officer Man Handle kidnap me, Chad walked back into the room, so I went back to making a spectacle. Ian had to drag me out of the precinct, limbs flailing and insults flying. Honestly, I wasn't even all that mad anymore, but I felt like I needed to keep up appearances. At this point Chad expected me to act crazy and I didn't like to disappoint.

After a hot meal, a long ass shower and four not-nearly-strong-enough pain pills later, I collapsed onto my bed. As my eyes became heavier and I started drift-ing off, I couldn't help but admit to myself that even though the night was high on my list of crazy shit that's happened to me, it had actually turned out pretty awe-some. I'd had fun hearing cop stories, made a new friend and as much as I hated Chad, I guessed I could at least thank him for giving me an awesome new anecdote for parties.

CHAPTER 2

CHAD

"What the hell are you still doing here, Joe?" I was changing out of my street clothes and into my blues, getting ready to start my shift when Joe walked into our precinct's locker room. Joe was my partner and was supposed to get off work at the same time as me last night. He had the day off today, but for some reason he was still here when I'd gotten in, talking to that crazy blonde, who I'd dubbed Bat Shit Crazy Stacy.

"I stayed and hung out with Stacy last night."

That got my attention and I jerked my head up and looked at Joe to see if he was joking. Based on his expression, he was serious. Stacy was a lunatic. Yeah, sure, she was smokin' hot, but that still wasn't worth hanging out at the precinct all night, still in his uniform. It's not like he was going to get laid while she was in lock up.

"Hey, she calmed down after you left man. She was like a totally different person. Eric and Gary joined us halfway through the night and hung out, so ask them. She's pretty awesome. We made plans to hang out."

"Listen, junior, you've been on the job long enough to know you should avoid the crazies, but in case you are too dense to know what you're getting yourself into, I'm going to give you a little tip. Stay away from the ones who act bipolar. You saw how she flipped out as she was leaving. You don't find her drastic mood swings a little telling?" I raised an eyebrow at him, daring him to dispute my astute observation.

"Pops," Joe called me, putting a firm hand on my shoulder, earning himself a death glare. Both the un-wanted nickname he'd given me and the invasion of my personal space were worthy of him taking one to the jaw. The little punk was obviously undeterred though, because he just kept on talking as if I didn't look like I wanted to kill him. "Obviously you are the cause behind those mood swings. I don't know what you did to get that girl to hate you so bad, but I doubt it was just putting her in jail for the night. She actually seemed to have a pretty good time, so maybe the issue here is you."

"You wanna say that again?" I dared him through gritted teeth. My frustration was real, but the threat to act on it was not. Over time I had just gotten in the habit of trying to intimidate people into staying at arms length. Joe had always been immune to my tactics, though, so he just shook his head and laughed as he walked away mumbling something about "hopeless."

Joe was a good cop, and most days I actually en-joyed his company, but my patience was running low after the fitful night of sleep I'd gotten and I knew he would get on my last nerve if he was working today. I was even more grateful to be patrolling on my own today because I knew not only would I be putting up with Joe's constant chattering on about stupid shit, but today that shit would have been about Stacy, and I was ready to just put that girl and this whole situation behind me and forget it had ever happened.

The day went by uneventfully. A couple of speeding tickets and one noise complaint was all the action I saw, and I was extremely grateful. I hadn't gotten any sleep the night before and I was still in denial about why.

If I admitted the truth, I would have to accept that I'd spent the night tossing and turning, fighting off dreams of Stacy. Of how her hands had felt on my chest when she threw herself at me when I'd arrived at the club. Of her warm breath on my neck as she whispered the cheesiest pick up line I'd ever heard, yet it still had made my cock twitch. Of how her soft body had felt pressed up against me when I pulled her out of the back of the patrol car, and the shivers that raked through me when her body slowly grazed mine as she stood.

No, I couldn't admit to any of that. Because I'd already resolved that Stacy was insane. Completely batshit crazy. The very little amount of time I had spent with her already told me enough to know that I needed to stay clear of her. My body's visceral reaction to hers, coupled with how much her over-the-top attitude irritated me, had me completely on edge. I was good at keeping my emotions in check, I'd honed the skill over the years.

Only I was finding that Stacy had an uncanny ability to challenge every piece of me, and whatever happened, I just knew I needed to be careful.

The next day mine and Joe's schedules were back in sync and Joe spent the whole day rambling on incessantly about Stacy. The worst part was that we were out patrolling, so I couldn't even get away from him. I tried to just tune him out, but after about the hundredth time I'd heard her name, I finally snapped.

"You know I don't give a shit about her, right?"

"What is your problem, man? I talk about all the girls I hang out with and it never pisses you off like this. You got a thing for this one?"

"Hell no!" I barked out entirely too quickly and much more defensive sounding than I'd intended. Joe raised an eyebrow at me as if to say he was calling bullshit, and I just rolled my eyes and shook my head. "She's just nuts, Joe. I don't normally know much about the other girls you spend time with, but I arrested this one, remember?"

"Yeah, for hitting on you," Joe snorted. "Who arrests a hot chick for hitting on them? That's messed up, man."

"I arrested her because she was drunk off her ass

and was going to end up doing something to get herself hurt if I didn't. She was trying to prostitute herself right in front of me!"

"She wouldn't have actually done it and you know it. Her friends were there and could have gotten her home safe. You didn't need to bring her in. You keep on lying to yourself all you want, but don't try and bullshit me. It would save you a lot of time and energy if you would just come clean with yourself about it."

"Fuck you man, there is no other reason. Quit trying to make more out of this than it was. You're the one who stayed at work all night hanging out with her, not me. You're the one who got her number and hung out with her, not me. So it's pretty obvious I'm not the one who wants to see her."

"Yeah, the only thing that's obvious is that if you keep denying you're attracted to her then you're going to have to get a much bigger crock to hold all that shit you keep spouting. And just so you know, Stacy and I are just friends. I actually really like hanging out with her and sex would just ruin that, so I have no intentions of stealing your girl."

I growled at Joe but didn't bother arguing. Not because he was right, but because apparently he'd made up his mind and nothing I said would convince him that I wasn't into Stacy. I didn't really care what he thought, and he was intentionally trying to get me riled up, so there was no point in feeding into his crap.

Every day that week Joe talked constantly about Stacy, but after that first day I'd quit complaining since it only seemed to egg him on. It was weird hearing him talk about the same chick so many days in a row, he never spent this much time with one girl. I spent the majority of the time inwardly berating myself for the jealousy I felt when he would talk about her. The way he described her made her sound a lot less crazy than I'd originally thought she was. In fact, he actually made her sound like she was a lot of fun.

Not that it mattered to me. I could care less. All I had to do was wait it out. Eventually Joe would get bored with her and I could go back to my normal life where I didn't obsess over women I didn't even know and didn't want to know.

By the time Thursday came along, at the end of our shift, Stacy was waiting for Joe inside the precinct when we got back. She was leaning casually against the counter, chatting up a few of the other officers. They were all cracking up and hanging on her every word. It was pathetic watching them stare at her like she was the only piece of ass that remained and it was their last day on earth. What the hell was it about this girl that got every guy she met wrapped around her finger?

Well she didn't affect me in the least, so there was at least one man left on the planet that wasn't caught under her spell. So what if there was a twisting feeling in my gut just from the sight of her with the other guys, it wasn't jealousy, it was just annoyance. Like when she stood on her toes to kiss Joe on the cheek when he walked up to her, for instance. The anger rising to my chest was only irritation at how much she distracted the guys from their work, and was most definitely not jealousy.

So when she turned in my direction and her lips turned up into the most beautiful smile I'd ever seen, I knew it was only because she loved to piss me off, and couldn't possibly be because she was actually happy to see me. Then when she walked up to me and stood so close that I could hear her breathing accelerate and watch the deep, piercing blue of her irises darken, I felt nothing at all. Nope, not a damn thing.

I didn't even feel the urge to run my fingers through her short blonde hair, or press my lips up against the soft and smooth skin of her neck where her rapid pulse was beating. The thought of running my hand up the back of her thigh and gripping her tight ass that was being show-cased beautifully in her sinfully tight jeans didn't do a thing for me.

Yep, nothing about her appealed to me. Nothing at all.

"Officer," she said sweetly, pulling me out of my trance. She was holding out her hand for me to shake, and it felt like a trap, so all I could do was stand there and stare at her hand extended in the air like it was a snake about to sink its deadly little fangs in it's next unsuspecting victim.

Only the way she was looking at me looked more like she would yank on my arm and pull me to her as she pressed her lips to mine as soon as I put her hand in mine. Or maybe that's just what I wished would happen, but either way, engaging with her in any way would be a mistake. So instead of taking her hand, I forced my legs to move and walked past her and into the locker room to change.

Joe ran in after me and I did my best to ignore him. "Chad, man, what's your problem? She was trying to be nice. Olive branch and all that shit."

"She's crazy, Joe. I figured it was a trap or something."

"You thought her shaking your hand was a trap? What the hell is wrong with you, man?" I pretended not to notice Joe looking at me like I'd lost my damn mind and hoped he would get bored and just walk away, but a quick glance in his direction told me he wasn't going anywhere without an explanation. When I still didn't say anything, he started in with a lecture. "Look, she's my friend and she's going to be around so you need to find a way to get over whatever hang up it is you have with her. You can't keep treating her like shit for no reason. I'm not saying you guys have to be best friends or even like each other, but you have to find a way to at least tolerate her and not act like a total asshole every time she's around."

"You know what? Screw you, Joe. You can be friends with whoever you want, but that doesn't mean they have to be a part of my life. It's not like you and I are great friends anyway, we're colleagues. So as long as she doesn't start tagging along while we're on the clock, then there shouldn't be any issues. Just go ahead and tell her to stay away from me, and I promise there won't be any issues."

I stormed off towards the showers, and this time Joe didn't follow. I wouldn't have been surprised if he punched me in the face the next time I saw him. What I'd said was really shitty and not at all true. I didn't mean to lash out at him, but I couldn't do what he was asking of me, and what was worse was not being able to explain why. Until I could figure out how someone who was still a complete stranger could so effortlessly pierce through walls I had thought impenetrable just by merely existing, then I at least needed some distance.

CHAPTER 3

STACY

"What the hell, Joe?" I asked as he emerged from the locker room, out of his uniform and now in jeans and a t-shirt. He held up his hand as if telling me to stop talking, then slipped his arms into a button down shirt and started to button it up as he spoke.

"I know, Stace. I don't know what his problem is. Just give it some time," Joe explained with an edge of irritation and exhaustion in his voice. He grabbed my arm and pulled me off to the side so that we weren't blocking the doorway.

"Time? What does that mean? Time for what? He acts like he hates me, or in the very least, looks at me and treats me like I'm the host of every communicable disease known to man. If anything, I should be the one who hates him after he fucking arrested me for no reason," I hissed, yanking out of Joe's grip.

"Just don't worry about it too much. It takes time for him to come around," Joe tried to assure me. "Let's just head out and get your mind off of it."

Right as we turned to leave Chad came out of the locker room, hair dripping wet and his shirt clinging to his entire torso, like he hadn't bothered to even attempt to dry off. He was still several feet away when he came to a halt, but I caught a whiff of his scent, and he smelled like soap with a hint of cologne. My stomach knotted, and I had to physically restrain myself from throwing my body at him and shoving my nose into his chest, just so I could breathe him in deeper.

I let my gaze drift down from his strong neck, all the way down to his jean clad thighs. There wasn't anything on God's green earth that could have stopped me from taking a long, slow perusal of his delicious body. Judging by how tightly his plain white t-shirt clung to every hard plane of his chest and abdomen, it looked to be a few sizes too small, and damn was I grateful. It was cruel, really, being able to see just enough of his taut body to make my legs weak, only to remember I'd probably never get to feel it up against mine.

When I finally let my eyes make their way back up to his face, his lips were pursed and his jaw was stiff, but his eyes...his eyes told an entirely different story. Everything about him, from the way his entire body tensed, to the tight, angry expression he wore, would have been intimidating if it weren't for his traitorous eyes. If I hadn't been looking closely, I might have missed how they widened just a fraction when he allowed himself the quickest glance at my perky chest that was being beautifully offered up to him beneath a very revealing halter top. And when his pupils dilated, I almost missed the flare of lust that was so fleeting I almost swore I'd imagined it.

I finally gained my composure, but when I opened my mouth to speak, he shoved past me and uttered a goodbye in Joe's direction as he stormed out the door. As irritated as I was with how incredibly rude Chad was every time we were near each other, I at least had to credit him for his consistency.

Chad's ability to so quickly judge and then disregard me, even despite his obvious attraction to me, had me doubting my read on the situation. I couldn't help but begin to wonder if the fervent intensity that resonated through the air when we were near each other was out of lust, or strictly from the pure and unabashed hatred growing between us.

Joe and I went back to his place and proceeded to get completely shit faced. He'd been a good sport, patiently listening as I ranted and raved like a lunatic about how much I hated Chad all night. He was my sounding board for all the ideas I'd been tossing out on how I could get back at him for being such a douche, even throwing in a few of his own from time to time. Of course, the drunker we got, the more ridiculous our plotting became.

I'd only seen Chad a handful of times, and we hadn't really spent any amount of time actually talking or getting to know each other. Yeah, he seemed like a giant dick, but truthfully I knew nothing about him. I recognized that his opinion of me was understandably skewed after the first night we'd met, but I found it hard to believe that a man who had undeniably witnessed some very crazy shit in his line of work wouldn't be able to look past a minor indiscretion. Surely he'd seen drunk people before, and it's not like he walked in on me having a gang bang with the Lollipop Guild.

The more I tried to figure him out, the more confused I became. It would have been easy to assume he was just sticking to a snap judgment, but my gut told me there was more to it than that. The fact of the matter was that his reasons were irrelevant. Not only did he automatically dislike me on a personal level, but he also found it a little too easy to ignore his attraction to me. And of the two, it was the latter that fueled my fire.

Joe seemed to find the thought of me trying to get back at Chad hysterical, but the joke was lost on me. He was also unrelenting, and a little too adamant that I would never be able to get a rise out of Chad, which piqued my curiosity. But when I couldn't get any real information out of him it only made me more determined, so somewhere around tequila bottle number two we decided to make a wager.

"So what do I get if I win?" Joe asked as he picked a card off the top of the pile laying strewn all over his kitchen floor where we currently had taken up residence. Yep, we were three sheets to the wind and playing Go

Fish. And we sucked at it. I wasn't even sure if we were playing it correctly.

"Do you have a knight?" I slurred and then hiccupped.

"I don't think there are any knights in a deck of cards, Stace," Joe slurred right back. His cards were facing outward and I squinted, trying to see what he was holding.

"Sit still, Joe, your cards are all blurry. I can't cheat if you keep spinning the room around in circles." Joe looked confused and glanced around the room, then slapped a hand down flat on the kitchen floor, like he was trying to hold the room still for me. "What about... you got a duchess?" I hiccupped again.

"Dammit, Stacy! You didn't tell me we were playing British Go Fish! I don't know how to play this version!" Joe yelled as he threw his cards down on the floor and fell back a little too fast, causing him to hit his head hard on the hardwood floor. "Dammit!" he yelled while I fell down next to him, giggling.

"So what do I win when you finally realize you're never going to get the upper hand with Chad?" Joe asked, locking his fingers behind his head and turning to look at me.

"I'll set you up with one of my hot friends."

Joe scoffed and turned back to stare at the ceiling. "I don't need you to help me get laid, I can do that on my own. What else you got."

"Ummmm… I'll give you a blow job."

"Hmmmm… tempting. Can't you just give me one now and think of something else for the bet?"

I punched his arm. Well, I tried to anyway, but I was too drunk to be even the least bit coordinated. "Dream on."

His head rolled to the side again and we grinned at each other.

"You think maybe we should try making out or something?" I asked Joe, following up my question with another hiccup.

"Why would we do that?" He had entirely too much incredulity in his voice and it irritated me. He made it sound like it was the dumbest idea I'd ever had, and I tried to punch him again when he smirked at me but completely missed that time.

"First of all, don't say it like the thought of sex with me would be punishment. I'm a great lay. And second of all…" I trailed off, trying to remember what we were talking about. "Oh yeah, second of all, I just figured since we get along so well, we're both really hot, and we spend so much time together, maybe we could have a friends with benefits kind of arrangement," I shrugged, wondering why it had taken me getting completely sloshed to even consider the idea of sleeping with Joe.

Oh yeah, I'd been entirely too distracted by Officer

Ass Hat.

"Stacy, if you needed an orgasm you should have just asked. You didn't have to concoct this whole plan of pretending to hate Chad so you could get me drunk and seduce me."

"Get over yourself."

"Okay, sure. Let's give it a shot," Joe said with a nonchalant shrug.

"Calm your pants there, buddy. Don't sound so excited," I said sarcastically. Joe chuckled and angled his body a little towards mine.

"Want me to kiss you on the mouth? Or were you hoping to test out our chemistry with me kissing you somewhere a little lower…"

"Ugh, I can't kiss you if you say douchey things like that. How do you get laid so often with game like that?"

"I'm not gonna waste my best stuff on someone who is practically throwing themselves at me. I reserve that stuff for girls who aren't a sure thing."

"That's not at all what's happening here. And you must have a really large bed." Joe raised a confused eyebrow at me. "I just don't see how you could possibly fit anyone else on it, what with how much room your ego takes up."

"Har har, just come here so we can get this over with."

I rolled my eyes but didn't give him shit for his

less than enthusiastic attitude considering I pretty much felt exactly the same. I briefly wondered if my drunken suggestion was a mistake since it was obvious we both felt like kissing each other was a chore rather than an enjoyable activity, but seeing as I was already halfway down the damn rabbit hole, I figured I may as well see it through.

I turned onto my side and lifted myself just enough to slightly hover over him. He threaded his fingers through my hair and pulled my face towards his, gently pressing his lips to mine.

It started off slow and soft, then a few seconds in I felt his warm, wet tongue on my lips eliciting an automatic response as I parted my mouth slightly, allowing him access. The instant his tongue touched mine I jerked my head back, breaking the kiss and pulling away from his body a little too quickly, because at that same time Joe was pushing me off of him, and our combined force threw me backwards. I rolled off of him and my head hit the floor with a hard thud.

"Ugh!" Joe yelled, scrambling to his feet, and falling over himself as he ran to the kitchen faucet. He was sticking his face under the streaming water while I started vigorously wiping my tongue with the back of my shirt sleeve.

"Do you have any bleach? I need to sanitize my mouth," I said between gags.

"It felt like I was kissing my sister!" He was taking in mouthfuls of water, gargling and spitting, over and over again.

"You don't have a sister," I said with my shirt still in my mouth as he slammed the handle

"Well even if I did, kissing her still wouldn't be as bad as that!" I would have been offended, but I was too busy crawling to the table by the couch to take a swig of beer and swishing it around in my mouth.

"That was the most awkward and least sexy kiss I have ever had. It even tops my first kiss in fourth grade when Billy cut my lip with his braces and accidentally drooled on my shirt. Seriously, seriously gross."

He tried to say something else but I was already up and running to the sink because it was closer than the toilet and I was not in the mood to clean up my own vomit off the floor.

"Seriously, Stacy? You're being a little dramatic. It wasn't that bad," Joe whined, handing me a wet rag when I finished retching.

"Shut up, it's just the tequila. Quit making everything about you. Now go away so I can throw up in peace."

"Okay, but can you at least move it to the bathroom? It's beyond disgusting that you are vomiting in my kitchen sink. I may never eat in here again."

I spent the next hour with my head in the toilet

and going through my well rehearsed break up speech with Mr. Cuervo in between bouts of vomiting. It was a speech I'd given often, and every damn time Jose just lured me back in, filling many, many nights with regret. I didn't regret the kiss though. As awful as it was, and it was seriously awful, it proved once and for all that Joe and I were just friends and that's all we would ever be. A tension I didn't even know was there lifted with my sudden revelation. Then with my stomach finally empty and my body achingly overcome with exhaustion, my head finally hit the floor and I was down for the count.

The following morning, I woke up on the bathroom floor with a towel folded under my head, and a glass of water sitting next to a bottle of aspirin on the bathroom sink. Without even counting them I tossed a hand full of pills into my mouth. I started to go thank Joe for being so thoughtful, until I caught a glimpse of myself in the mirror.

After cleaning myself up as best I could, I made my way into the kitchen where Joe was making breakfast. A few random people had joined us at some point during the night, two of them out in the pool and one passed out on the couch. It was really strange at first spending time at Joe's. There were always people in his house, most of which I almost never recognized, and they came and went like they lived there.

Every time I asked Joe about it he would just shrug and either change the subject or give some sort of vague answer. If it were anyone else I would have been a little too uncomfortable spending so much time at a house that had strangers constantly roaming around, but I felt safe with Joe and knew he wouldn't let dangerous people into the house with me there.

"Thanks for taking care of me last night," I said to Joe as I hopped up on a bar stool, grabbing a grape out of the bowl sitting on the counter and popping it into my mouth. Joe stopped stirring whatever was in the bowl in front of him and turned to look at me.

"I don't know what you're talking about. After you went to the bathroom to puke your brains out, I managed to crawl to my bed and pass out. I went to check on you this morning and you were curled up in a ball on the floor and I didn't want to wake you."

"Well, thanks for putting that towel under my head and sitting the meds out for me, at least." Joe looked even more confused and I paused, my hand halfway to my mouth with another grape, trying to figure out why he was looking at me like I had three heads. Then I realized Joe wasn't looking at me, but over my shoulder, so I turned to follow his line of vision.

"You're welcome," Chad said casually as he sauntered into the kitchen with a smug look on his face.

"For what?" I glared at him as he stood across from me on the other side of the counter, plucking the grape I was holding right out of my fingers and tossing it into his mouth.

"I always come to Joe's house Friday mornings for breakfast. He's usually already cooking by the time I get here, and when he wasn't I went looking for him. Found you in the bathroom." Chad walked over to the fridge and pulled out the orange juice, then grabbed two glasses out of the cabinet and started filling them both. When he handed me one of them I realized Joe had left the room and I was alone with Chad.

"Wait, so you're saying it was you who put a towel under my head and put the water and aspirin in there?" His cocky grin made me want to sucker punch him, but I was a little too stunned to even move. "I don't know what surprises me more...you doing something nice for me, or you not taking the opportunity to dump a bucket of ice water or something on my head."

CHAPTER 4

CHAD

"I have to admit; I was a little tempted. Believe it or not, though Stacy, I'm not a complete asshole." I was just teasing, but I could see guilt flash across her face. It made me feel like shit, because truthfully, when it came to her I really did act like a complete asshole. "I guess I just felt sorry for you. You were quite a mess. I couldn't in good conscience just let you lay there covered in your own vomit."

"Hey! I know I probably looked like shit but I was not covered in vomit," she huffed and crossed her arms. She looked adorable sitting there all defensive and pouty, and I realized I hadn't stopped smiling since I'd walked into the kitchen. She was sitting there with her mussed up hair and makeup smudges under her eyes, looking entirely too perfect than should be humanly possible after a rough night of drinking.

"It's okay Stacy, no need to be embarrassed. I didn't mind cleaning you up." I crossed my arms and leaned back against the counter, stifling a laugh as she buried her face in her hands.

"Oh my God," Stacy muttered before slamming her head down on the counter.

"Hey, it wasn't as bad as it sounds," I reassured her,

walking over to her. I leaned onto my elbows over the counter she had her head on so that I was eye level with her. I tapped her head gently with my index finger and she slowly lifted her head to look me in the eye. "I've been an ass, so I kind of owed you." Stacy averted her eyes, but not quickly enough, and I saw the disappointment flitter across her face.

I wasn't entirely sure where the disappointment was coming from, and it surprised me how badly I actually wanted to know. I didn't deserve to know anything about her, but I wanted to know all the same. I was on the precipice of going against my better judgment to ask her, but suddenly she was moving and I knew the window of opportunity had passed.

"Well, thanks," she whispered, sliding off the stool and turning away. I watched as she walked right out of the house, not bothering to look at me again.

Two weeks had gone by since seeing Stacy at Joe's that morning. Joe had been unusually tight lipped, so I had no idea how she was or what she was up to. I itched to ask about her, but knew no good would come of it, so I let it go. Not hearing about her or seeing her hadn't prevented my thoughts from all too often turning to her, though it wasn't as constant as it had been in the beginning.

Joe and I had standing plans to meet at Petey's a

couple nights a week, which was a local bar located a couple blocks from the station that all the guys at our precinct frequented. It had become generally populated solely by cops and other law enforcement over the years, so it was a good place to kick back and relax.

Most of the time when I spent my entire drive to Petey's filled with dread. Joe was a talker and his constant droning on about things I couldn't care less about made me want to drown myself in a bucket full of battery acid. This time, however, I was actually looking forward to it. Joe was still his normal self on the job, but conversation lulled a lot more often than usual, and he'd not been frequenting Petey's as much as normal.

I sensed that his absence was and lack of constant jibber jabber was all in relation to Stacy. Joe was always very forthcoming, but unless I came out and asked the question, I probably would never know. I didn't know how to phrase it without making it sound like I was trying to bring her up, so I just kept to myself and I found that for once in my life I was...bored.

Since Joe hadn't met up with me the last few times I went to Petey's I was a little surprised to get his text asking me to meet him there. An hour later I was already perched on a stool, sipping a cold beer when I saw him come strolling in out of the corner of my eye.

I turned to face him and saw the feisty blonde I'd spent the last two weeks trying not to think about. Stacy hadn't spotted me yet and I seized the opportunity to thoroughly drink in her presence. The entire room seemed to shift on it's axis as the entire room became as entranced by her as I was.

Something about her just commanded attention, and I realized just how much in denial I had been over the last couple weeks. My memories did her little justice. She was wearing tiny little black shorts, a white tank covered by a denim jacket, and tan heels that did dangerous things to her already long legs. I forced myself to turn away before she caught me ogling her, and studied the label on my beer bottle while internally berating my cock (who I had affectionately nicknamed Sarge) for not being able to control himself.

Joe interrupted my thoughts, taking a seat next to me and slapping me on the back casually. Stacy stood on the other side of him but in the perfect position for me to be able to stare at the outline of her lacy bra that showed through her tight fitted tank top.

Joe motioned for the bartender, getting himself and Stacy a drink. Joe was strictly a beer kind of guy, and I assumed he Stacy probably drank some kind of girly frou frou crap, though I didn't know for sure because I was too busy trying not to stare at her chest to hear what he ordered.

It surprised me when the bartender handed her a beer as well. I would have easily pegged her as the type of girl who always drank some kind of fruity crap. My assumption most likely stemmed from the way she was dressed. She leaned back with her elbows against the bar, pressing the bottle to her lips, and everything about her came across as casual. She was the exact picture of femininity, all soft curves with legs for days. Yet something about her seemed so relaxed, making it obvious how comfortable she was in her own skin.

If she had any makeup on, it was very little. At first glance there was nothing extravagant about her, though it was obvious her beauty came easily. It was easy to picture her looking just as stunning first thing in the morning as she was standing there in a little dive bar, managing to both perfectly fit in and completely stand out at the same time.

I shook myself out of my trance just in time to see she'd caught me staring.

Fuck, my head was all kinds of screwed up when she was around.

It was like she did some kind of telepathic witchcraft voodoo shit on me or something. I never lost this much control, no matter how attracted I was to someone sexually. I'd never had trouble controlling myself in or out of the bedroom.

Maybe I was just drunk already?

No, that didn't make sense. I was only about halfway through my second beer. It would take at least a few more to get me even a little tipsy, and even drunk I'd always been able to keep myself in check.

I could feel Stacy's eyes on me, and fighting the urge to look over at her again was damn near impossible. I finally lost the battle and risked a glance, immediately regretting it. Another officer from our precinct had made his way over to Stacy and was chatting her up. I couldn't hear what they were saying but he must have been laying it on thick because Stacy laughed and put her hand on his arm. A powerful surge of jealousy and possessiveness surged through me before I could think better of it.

Out of nowhere I felt the urge to jump up and yank him away from her, but before I had the chance Joe was waving him off. Joe leaned down and asked if I wanted to join them at a table, but I waved him off, thankful for a little space between me and the vixen that was quickly brainwashing me.

I watched as she walked over to a table with Joe. He pulled a chair out for her and she smiled up at him, but when she looked up and her eyes locked with mine, her smile fell. Without warning her eyes went dark and her expression turned serious. All of my senses kicked into overdrive, and suddenly everything happening around me was in both fast forward and slow motion at the same time. The room fell silent, but simultaneously grew so loud I thought my ears would bleed. My heart started to race while, though it felt like it had stilled entirely.

Everything became a contradiction and I couldn't make sense of anything.

I needed some air. I needed to just clear my head for a minute. Stacy and Joe were obviously dating or fucking or…something. Hell, I didn't know, but they'd been spending a lot of time together recently, and he hadn't even mentioned that he was bringing her to Petey's, like it was just a given that wherever Joe went, Stacy went. I'd never seen Joe spend so much time with one person, and most certainly had never seen him bring a girl to Petey's, which told me she was a serious part of his life in some form or another.

I tossed back the last of my drink and snuck out the back door that opened to a small alley right behind the old building. The sun had just gone down and there was only a small street light at the opposite end of the building that illuminated the back of the bar. I'd have to talk to Pete about that, this wasn't very safe for his staff.

As I took in the alley, taking advantage of the distraction by mentally taking notes as to how Pete could improve his security back here, I heard the back door open. I assumed it was Pete or one of his staff just bringing out the trash or something, but when I turned around I came face to face with Stacy.

I'd come out here to get away from her. I didn't want her to follow me out here. Why was she out here? She should be back in there with Joe.

"I wanted to see you," she whispered, her voice low and shaky. Even with the uncertainty I could hear in her words, her voice was like silk. Seductive and enticing. "I was caught off guard that morning at Joe's and didn't really thank you for taking care of me the way I should have. I was waiting until the next time I saw you again, but you ran off tonight before I had a chance."

"It's not necessary, Stacy. You didn't have to follow me out here; it was no big deal. I owed you anyway." Stacy shrugged and took another step towards me.

"It's probably better this way, being able to talk to you in private. I never know how you're going to react when I'm around you. But now I get the feeling you're avoiding me, Chad. Why is that?"

She took another step and was suddenly standing entirely too close. My dick was yelling me to push her against the wall and kiss her, while my mind was warning me to get the hell out of there. I didn't have much of a chance to decide which direction to go before Stacy had completely closed the distance between us, standing only inches from me. So close I could feel her warm breath against my face.

"You need to go back inside," I growled in warning. Was I warning her or me? I wasn't really sure, but one of us needed to go back inside. Whatever was happening or was about to happen just couldn't happen. No happening right now. The opposite of happening needed to happen.

Stacy raised her hand tentatively to my face, hesitating right before touching me. Her eyes were asking permission, but she didn't wait to see if I would give it to her. She trailed a finger down the side of my cheek and along my jaw. I caught her wrist with my hand and gripped it tightly, holding her arm away from me. Her eyes widened in surprise, but only for a split second. Her blue eyes turned to black as they glazed over, and all the reasons why I was trying to avoid her dissipated, only to be replaced by an insatiable hunger.

I yanked on her wrist, spinning her around and pinning her back against the brick wall of the building. I pressed my body up against hers, letting her feel my arousal hard on her thigh. It was almost pitch black where we stood against the wall, but even in the shadows she was stunningly beautiful. Any remnants of self control I was struggling to hold onto vanished when she licked her lips and let out a moan as I pushed myself into her harder.

I grabbed her other wrist and held both her arms pinned above her head before forcefully pressed her lips to mine. It was bordering on painful, how violently I kissed her, and I started to pull back until I heard her whimper in pleasure. I began to grind myself between her legs, eliciting a very loud moan that gave me the opportunity to slide my tongue between her lips.

We continued warring with our mouths and bodies,

each of us battling for control, eager to unleash our pent up lust for each other. Stacy half heartedly struggled to pull her arms away, but I kept them firmly held in place.

I ripped my mouth from hers and aggressively kissed down her jaw and to her neck, sucking and biting as I went. It occurred to me that I was being rough enough that I would most likely leave a mark, and the thought only made me more desperate to taste her.

And fuck, she tasted amazing. I wanted to memorize every inch of her with my tongue, and there was a good chance that I would end up doing just that right out there in the middle of the alley.

I let go of her wrists and she thrust her hands around my neck, pulling my mouth back to hers roughly. I ran my hands around her waist and cupped her ass tightly. Understanding my intent, Stacy quickly wrapped both legs around my waist as I braced us against the wall with one hand, sliding the other up the back of her shirt, moaning at the feel of her soft, warm skin.

Her hands moved from my neck to the zipper on my jeans. I pulled back just enough to give her access, and began biting and sucking on her ear as she fumbled with the button to my pants. After a few seconds I grunted in frustration and pulled my hand her from shirt and yanked my pants open in one swift, violent move.

Just as Stacy moved to thrust her hand into my briefs, the back door opened and one of the bartenders walked out, snapping me back to reality with a vengeance. Stacy and I jumped apart quickly, as if an electric current had just jolted us away from each other. We were mostly blocked by some stacked crates, and with how dark it was; the bartender didn't even notice us.

The moment was over, though, and like a fickle bitch, sanity used the interruption as an opportunity to backhand my libido. It took all of two seconds to build back the walls that crumbled beneath Stacy's touch, giving self preservation a short enough window of time to commandeer all other thoughts. Logic and reason erased the feel of Stacy's body against mine long enough for me to start damage control.

Stacy started smoothed her clothes as I zipped my pants back up. After the bartender went back inside, I grabbed Stacy's hand and led her back over to the door we'd exited out of, opening it and shoving her inside before closing the door and leaving.

I'd let my guard down and made the mistake of kissing her, and although I was going home with the worst case of blue balls, I was still thankful we had been interrupted before it went any further. Later I would take the time to kick my own ass for losing it back there, but right then the only thing I could think about was going home and taking a very, very cold shower.

Chapter 5

Stacy

What. The. Fuck. No, no it wasn't possible. There was no way in hell that I'd just had the most passionate, earth shattering, panty incinerating kiss with Chad. I must have dreamed it, because it makes zero-fucking sense that he would shove me back inside the building and slam a door in my face after a kiss like that.

I had to have stood staring at that door for a solid ten minutes, going over the last five minutes again and again in my head, trying to figure out at what point my sanity checked out and let my vagina start calling all the shots.

Because my vagina, she didn't think things through. I thought for damn sure I'd taught her to behave herself, but she really pulled out all the stops tonight. It was like she'd been lying in wait, prepared to pounce as soon as she was close enough to Chad. And pounce she had. And now? Now she was throwing a temper tantrum, and I didn't know who was angrier - my vagina or my ego.

He always looked devastatingly sexy in his uniform, but damn. Chad in a tight black t-shirt and jeans was just enough to start a riot in my pants. It took everything in me not to tear off my clothes and jump on his lap right when Joe and I walked in the door. So you can see how easy it was to become entranced by his tight ass as he'd walked away. Yep, just one glance at his retreating form was enough to hypnotize me.

Enter vagina - and suddenly she was barking orders at the rest of my body, preparing for a hostile takeover. Then before I knew what was happening, the rest of my traitorous body joined forces with my vagina and marched my ass right out that door, leading me to what could only be described as the massacring of my self esteem.

When I saw him standing in the middle of the dark alley, looking ominous and just a tad dangerous, my vagina started gloating about how awesome she was to make me follow him. I noticed a tattoo peeking out from the sleeve of his t-shirt, and the shadows on his face made him the poster boy for all things bad...or naughty...or both. Knowing he was a cop just made the entire scene before me even more delicious. He was the best of both worlds, and I felt my mouth start to water, just thinking about how amazing it would be to run my tongue up the contours of his chiseled arms.

My vagina was feeling pretty smug right about then, and even I had to concede that maybe she'd made the right call on this one. Sure, it would most likely backfire on me - and boy, had it - but I mean, why the hell not? Life is short. So what if I was harboring some serious animosity towards the man? He was too damn delicious to not be tempted, and his random act of kindness weeks back at Joe's had my opinion of him so murky that I couldn't think straight.

So when he pinned me against the wall and held my hands above my head, my vagina did a little victory dance in the form of creaming my panties. I was so turned on that the world got fuzzy, and my vagina was throbbing so hard that she started issuing death threats, saying if I didn't give her some relief then she would murder me in my sleep.

And I believed her.

Death by vagina. Hysterical. My headstone would read:

Twenty-six years should have been enough

For Stacy to learn not to mess with her muff

She had it coming, so don't feel distraught

Karma's a bitch. - Sincerely, her twat

That moment, pinned up against the wall with Chad's mouth on me...it had been life altering. Then some idiot I wanted to strangle ruined my chances of having hot alley sex. If I had balls, they would have been blue.

What would the female equivalent of blue balls be? I spent another few minutes staring at that damn door that had slammed in my face, mulling over what to call my lady hard-on I was sporting. I finally settled on "cliffy" - or clit stiffy - before remembering why I was standing there in the first place.

Damn that asshole and his propensity for humiliating me. Never in my life had one guy made me feel so desired and disposable at the exact same time. Seriously! I knew he felt what I felt during that kiss. Because I really felt it…felt it grinding all up in my nether region.

I wasn't sure what Chad's problem was, but I was way past the point of putting up with his constant rejections. He was clearly attracted to me, so at that point it felt like he was really going out of his way to make me feel like shit. So what was the whole point in being nice to me at Joe's? Was it just a game? Maybe he just wanted to get me to let my guard down long enough for him to strike again.

Well played, Chad, well played. He had just dropped the gauntlet and blew the air horn and whatever other metaphors there were for starting a war. He had done them all.

Game on.

"Your partner is a dick," I snapped as I plopped down on the empty bar stool next to Joe. Some guy sitting to the right of me gave me a questioning look, and normally I would have at least flirted with him a little because, well, I was a relentless flirt, but I wasn't in the mood. Joe was too busy flirting with some bimbo to hear me, so I got up and walked to the other side of him where she was standing.

"Excuse me, Bambi, can you shoo along now please? I'd like to talk to Joe."

She just stood there staring at me like I'd just asked her to explain the theory of unifying gravity and quantum mechanics. (No, I'm not a genius. I just watch a lot of Big Bang Theory.) So I started with shooing her with my hands until she finally got the hint and left, but not before calling me a bitch.

I looked at Joe to see if he was mad about me scaring away a potential lay, but he was just shaking his head and laughing.

"What did he do now?"

"Rejected me. Again. I don't know why either, because I know he went home with a serious case of blue balls. If he hadn't been hard as rock while he was dry humping me then I'd accuse him of being gay. What kind of guy passes up the opportunity for hot, dark alley sex?"

Joe coughed on his beer and I started smacking his back. "Wrong pipe, buddy?"

"Stacy, that was a whole lot more information than I needed. Chad's my partner and I did not need to hear about him dry humping you. That's an image that I never, ever wanted to have in my head."

"Oh, get over it, prude. He's hot, I'm hot. Don't act like the thought of him nailing me up against the wall with my legs wrapped around his waist doesn't turn you on. Twenty bucks if I grabbed your crotch right now you would be rock hard."

"First of all, there's a decent chance at any given time during the day that if you grab my crotch my dick will be hard. I'm a guy with a healthy sexual appetite, so I think about sex a lot. Second of all, you're right, that does sound pretty hot. Need me to finish the job?" He wiggled his eyebrows up and down at me.

"Shut up," I laughed as I playfully punched his arm and yanked his beer out of his hand, taking a swig. It felt like I'd known Joe for years even though we'd just met about a month ago.

"No, I don't need anyone to finish the job but myself. I'm going to head home and spend some quality time with Gerard." He raised his eyebrows in question. "My vibrator," I clarified for him. He just gave me a nod of understanding and waved bye as I made my way out of the bar and toward my car.

My ego had taken a serious hit tonight, and that didn't happen easily. I had no idea why Chad was fighting his attraction to me so hard, but no matter what he did now, I already knew the attraction was there. I'd just have to use it against him. How I would do that I wasn't quite sure yet, but one thing I was certain of was that I was going to humiliate him as much as he had humiliated me tonight.

This bitch was on a mission.

CHAPTER 6

CHAD

Fuck, I was exhausted. Right when I was supposed to be done with my shift, they called all available law enforcement to a bar brawl that had made it's way out to the street. When I arrived, over fifty big ass bikers were in the middle of the fucking street, beating each other's faces in. If I wasn't already fried from my eighteen-hour shift, then having to restrain men twice my size who looked like they could unhinge their jaw and swallow my head whole would definitely have done me in. It took thirteen cops, two fire trucks and three ambulances, but three hours later, despite the four news crews drawing attention from the rest of the block, we managed to calm down the scene.

I still didn't know what caused the fight and I could fucking care less. The more I knew, the more paperwork I would have to do. Right then, all I wanted to do was go home, piss for like an hour because I hadn't been able to stop for more than two minutes at a time all day, take a hot shower and pass out on my bed.

I hadn't gotten more than a few hours of sleep at a time since kissing Stacy that night at Petey's over three weeks ago. The more I thought about her the more pissed off I got about not being able to stop thinking about her which made me even more pissed, and so went the cycle. I found myself wishing constantly that I could go back to the night I took the call that ended up turning my life upside down. I was already supposed to be off work. When the call came in about a stolen purse, I was right down the street and it sounded like a quick job, so I volunteered. Still regretting that one.

Joe had been my partner for over two years now. He knew more about me than pretty much anyone, and while he drove me fucking crazy most days, I couldn't deny that he was a good friend. I'd die before telling him that, but it was the truth. Sure, everyone at the precinct knew about my past, but no one talked about it. It was the constant elephant in the room, but I'd grown to ignore it.

Joe had gone with me to my dad's parole hearing. I had told him over and over not to come, even threatened his life, but he showed up anyway. Afterwards we went back to Petey's and he just sat there in silence while I drank my weight in liquor, then listened intently while I revealed the whole sordid story in my drunken stupor.

We had never talked about it again. Joe was nosy and pushy and annoying as fuck, but the fact that he never brought that day and everything I'd confessed back up and we were able to go on pretending as if it hadn't happened was really what cemented our partnership. I could trust him. That was important out in the field.

He'd managed to get me to open up about other

things a time or two, always careful never to bring any-thing up twice, but for the most part our friendship was a casual, surface level type of thing and the heavy weight-ed conversations didn't happen very often.

"Don't forget about the party tonight, man. This shit's gonna be awesome. There is gonna be some hot ass, plenty of pussy for you to choose from." Remember how I just said Joe was fucking annoying? That stupid shit he just said to me? That's why.

"Do you have to talk like a fucking teenager who just learned how to work his dick for the first time? I enjoy a hot piece as much as the next guy, but there is more to life than sticking your dick in anything that will let you."

"Okay pops, I'll tone it down." His mocking tone and dumb as shit nickname annoyed the piss out of me, and I was already in a seriously bad mood. I was only four years old than him for Christ's sake! I wanted to turn and give him the look that usually made the rookies shit their pants, but Joe had always been immune to it. I'd done everything I could to put the fear of my wrath into him since we'd been partnered up, but he was stub-born and too cocky for his own damn good.

"Call me that again and I'll put my fucking boot up your ass. And don't worry, I'll be there. I just need to run home and grab a shower first. I smell like sweat, cigarettes and biker balls. Seriously, why did that guy not have any pants? Where did they go? Who sees a bar brawl and thinks 'hey, I want to hop in and join this mess, but first, I should take off my pants.' What the fuck is wrong with people anymore."

Finally, we pulled into the station. Normally I would change out of my uniform there and either head to the gym or Petey's afterward, but I couldn't wait to get home and rip off my gear before I could be forced on another call.

Joe called out some smart ass comment in my direction as I practically ran from the cruiser to my car, but I couldn't hear him. All I could think about was finally getting to relax for a night and not have to worry about hairy biker balls for once. Sometimes I couldn't believe this was my life.

Parties at Joe's place were usually pretty awesome. His house was pretty big and sat on a decent amount of land just outside the city. A year back I'd bought a little fixer upper not too far from him, so the distance between us wasn't too bad. It was far enough from the city though, that we both ended up buying vehicles. Driving in the city was a bitch, but it was too expensive to take a cab that far to work every day. Not to mention there were times when we got called in for emergencies and needed to be readily available.

Joe loved any excuse to have a party and his house was well equipped for them, too. His backyard came equipped with a large, heated in ground pool and the back of his property was lined with trees that gave privacy.

If I'd known Joe ten years ago when I was still into all the juvenile bullshit then I probably would have enjoyed his parties a lot more, but even then I'd never been much of a partier. My life had never been easy enough for me to just fuck off and be selfish. And if I were being totally honest, I'd have to admit that sometimes the constant flow of naked chicks at Joe's house was actually pretty pathetic. Personally, I'd never really been into girls who just gave it away like sex was a form of currency and your affection could be bought with it.

I'd never really had a long term relationship, and never really wanted one, but I still didn't want to spend any amount of time with a girl with such low self esteem that she just spreads her legs for any guy who will give her the smallest amount of attention. It was one of the reasons I'd been so put off by Stacy at first, when she'd thrown herself at me and all but offered herself up on a silver platter the instant I'd gotten out of my cruiser. Only the more time I spent with her, the more I was starting to feel like my initial assumptions about her were most likely way off.

Aside from the debauchery, Joe's parties always

had a seemingly endless supply of good food and beer. He had inherited the house and a ton of money from his parents. I didn't know exactly how much money, but I did know he really didn't need to work. I asked him once about it, and though it clearly made him uncomfortable and he didn't elaborate, he just shrugged and said he loved being a cop and that it wasn't about the money. He earned a hell of a lot of my respect that day.

Not to mention I got to reap the benefits of his wealth anytime I wanted, not that I would ever take advantage. One of Joe's quirks was his open door policy. Literally. He never locked his doors. For a cop he was seriously a dumbass, but he had always refused. There was almost always someone at his house, even if he wasn't home. It was like a fucking halfway house. I knew one day I'd walk in and there would be homeless people squatting in his living room.

By the time I made it over to his house, the party was in full swing. I was only about an hour late, but half the people there were already blitzed, and there were at least six nude people in the pool, which I seriously hoped contained a lot of chlorine.

There was a big bonfire going halfway between Joe's house and the woods that lined the back of his property. I saw about ten people I recognized, and about twenty that I didn't. That wasn't unusual for his parties. Joe made friends everywhere he went, and it was on rare occasion when I'd actually get to meet one of them twice. Did I mention that most of his friends were female? Yeah, the male to female ratio was always severely skewed whenever Joe was involved. The ladies fell for his charm and boyish good looks every time without fail, and the guys appreciated Joe's laid back personality and the constant flock of women that surrounded him.

I made a couple rounds, saying quick greetings to the people that I knew, then made my way into the kitchen to get the hamburgers and hot dogs out of the fridge. I always manned the grill at Joe's parties. It made it easier to avoid small talk with people I didn't give a shit about, plus I was damn good at it. I grabbed a bottle of beer and made my way over to the grill, supplies in hand.

As I lit the match and got the grill fired up, a petite little brunette approached me. I'd met her maybe a couple of times before hanging around Joe. She was one of the few who had been around more than once. Shit, what was her name? Lisa? Lilly? Laney?

"Hey there, handsome," she purred as she stroked my arm. She was pretty stunning up close with olive skin, straight, dark hair that hung all the way down her back and dark chocolate eyes. It wouldn't surprise me to find out she was a model; she was that beautiful. And I bet she was a firecracker in bed. The little ones always were.

"Hey yourself, kitten." Kitten was my go-to nickname when I didn't know a girl's actual name.

"Hey Leelah! Grab me a beer while you're over there!" A friend yelling her name saved my ass from having to spend all night trying to remember what it was.

"Well, it's good to see you, Chad. I'm going to go over to the fire and roast some marshmallows. Come find me later if you find you're in the mood for something… sweet." She winked and walked away. Before you ask, of course I looked at her ass when she left. What hot blooded male wouldn't?

I pulled my eyes off of Leelah's tight ass and started to turn back to the grill, but stopped halfway when my eyes met with the face of the blonde I hadn't been able to get out of my head for weeks.

CHAPTER 7

STACY

I knew Chad was going to be there. I'd been dreading seeing him ever since Joe invited me to the party. I'd pathetically spent the entire day reminding myself over and over that he was an ass and that I hated him. It was my lame attempt to prevent me from doing something stupid again, but as soon as I saw him I knew it had been a waste of my time. Apparently what I should have been preparing myself for the jealousy I would feel when I saw Chad flirting with another girl.

I told myself it was just because I'd hoped to even the score tonight, and the slut bag was standing between me and revenge. Yeah…I'd never been really good at lying to anyone, especially myself, and seeing him stare at her ass as she walked away only made me angrier. Was I the only one that felt something the other night when we were kissing?

I could have sworn I felt sparks ignite when his body was pressed firmly against mine. I mean, it didn't feel as strong as when I'd stuck my metal hair clip in a light socket when I was six, but I still felt a pretty strong jolt. And I remember Mr. Lopkins, my seventh grade science teacher, saying that a strong electrical current could result in heat, and it was pretty damn hot when we were kissing.

And the look he was giving me? Whew, talk about smoldering. It felt like there was a direct connection from his eyes straight to my lady bits, and the electricity passing between us was giving me twinges in all the right places. Forget sticking a fork in me, because those flames he was shooting in my direction had me way past done.

It wasn't until Chad smirked at me that I realized I was actually fanning myself. Next thing I knew Joe was running over to me and throwing me over his shoulders. With a loud thwack to my ass, he jogged toward his pool while I bounced around like a rag doll. "Saw you fanning yourself and thought maybe I could help you cool down."

"I will seriously kick your ass if you throw me in that pool! Don't even think about it. Besides, based on the looks of everyone else in there I'm clearly too over-dressed to be swimming," I yelled, squirming and kicking, trying to break free. Joe chuckled and sat me down on my feet, but I still punched his arm anyway.

"Dammit, Joe! Do you have a bionic arm? That fucking hurt," I whined as I tried to shake the pain out of my hand.

"Nope, I'm all man baby," he said with a cocky flex of his arm. I leaned up to kiss his cheek and made eye contact with Chad again, who had apparently been watching the little show. He looked away as soon as he saw me notice him, but I could have sworn I saw his jaw clench.

Hmmm, maybe I wasn't the only one feeling a little jealous.

The thought of Chad being jealous was enough to give me hope. I mean, hope for my plan, of course. Hope that I would be able to pull off my plan. You know, the plan to...what was I planning again? Oh right, revenge. That plan.

A group of Joe's friends called him over, so I headed towards the house to grab a drink. When I walked into the kitchen a group of guys were sitting at the table playing poker, two of which I remembered meeting at the precinct that night I was arrested.

I grabbed a bottle of water and walked over to the table, standing behind Eric, one of the officers I knew, and watched a few rounds. Eric introduced me to everyone at the table, and despite a few of them paying more attention to my tits than my conversation, they all seemed like decent guys.

I was in the middle of teasing Eric about how horrible of a player he was when Chad walked in with a plateful of hamburgers and hot dogs. I followed the guys over to the food and made a plate and piled the works onto a hot dog, taking much too big of a bite. I grabbed a napkin and started wiping the mess off of my face when

I noticed everyone staring at me.

"What?" I asked with a mouthful of hot dog.

No one answered me, so I just shrugged and followed them as they retreated to Joe's living room. Everyone found seats around the room, and one of the guys clicked on the television, changing it to some sort of sports game. I was too busy trying to discreetly look to see if Chad had followed us into the room, then immediately chiding myself for being disappointed when I didn't see him.

After a few minutes we all fell into easy conversation, and I even managed to forget Chad was nearby somewhere. I kicked my feet up on Joe's coffee table and grabbed Eric's beer out of his hand, taking a swig. He was sitting on the couch next to me, and feigned offense at my stealing his beer.

"Gonna arrest me for stealing your beer?" I joked, earning a chuckle from the guys.

"Hell no, I was there the first time you got arrested, remember? I have no interest in making you an enemy like Chad did." I elbowed him in the side lightly and he doubled over, clutching his side and wailing like I'd broken his rib.

"Such a drama queen. And for your information, Chad became my enemy for being a giant dickwad. I don't know how you guys put up with Officer Tight Ass all the time. And I don't mean 'tight ass' as in he has a tight ass. Seriously, does that guy ever let loose?"

I took another drink of Eric's beer and froze when I noticed none of the guys were laughing at my joke. Instead they were all looking over my shoulder, and I knew without turning that Chad was standing behind me. They didn't look like they were afraid of him, per se. More like they were afraid that some kind of bomb was going to go off.

I leaned my head back on the back of the couch, far enough to be looking straight up at Chad, who stared directly down at me. He looked angry, but I saw his mouth twitch and knew he was holding back a smile.

"Speak of the devil himself, here he is," I held the beer bottle up in the gesture of a toast and sat up. I sat the bottle down on the coffee table, stood up and rounded the couch, ready for our face off. Chad turned to face me, but stood still as a statue, and I just couldn't help myself. I bent at the waist and looked around him, putting my face right up to his butt. I put a confused look on my face and pretended to be searching for something.

"What the hell are you doing?" He barked out, sounding extremely annoyed.

"Oh, I was just trying to help you out but I don't think I can. You'll probably need a surgeon." He sneered and lifted one eyebrow. "Well, I was going to try and help you remove that giant stick from your ass, but it's so far up there that I think it will take the help of someone more qualified."

His jaw ticked and I winked at him. I could see him struggling with a response, but he didn't have time to think of one because suddenly the room erupted in laughter. I should have been pleased with myself when I saw him trying to conceal the embarrassment I'd caused him, but instead I just felt like shit. It's not that it wasn't true what I'd said, he most definitely had something stuck up there, but I knew teasing him wasn't going to help him loosen up. I'd only made it worse.

I wasn't sure how to recover the situation, so I went with an oldie but goody—flattery and sarcasm. "How about this, Officer Panty Melter, we were just thinking of starting back up the poker game. Why don't you join us? I'll even take it easy on you, that way you have a chance of winning."

Chad didn't answer right away, so I got up and headed towards the table. "C'mon guys!" I turned around to find them all still seated, their eyes darting back and forth between me and Chad. I put my hand on my hip and cocked my head. "Don't tell me you all are afraid of losing your money to a girl."

At that challenge, the ruckus started back up as they clamored out of their seats and followed me back to the table. I wasn't surprised that Chad didn't join us, but he did stay and quietly observe as I wiped the floor with the men. A couple hours later I was fifty bucks richer and half buzzed.

"Alright, boys, time to ante up. I don't want to hear any grumbling or nonsense about how I must have cheated or some shit like that. Take it like a man and just admit you got bested by a girl." All the men simultaneously groaned, and I just chuckled wickedly as I gleefully pocketed the money they each handed me.

When I finished draining their wallets, I looked up at Chad and found him studying me intently. He was leaning against the wall, his arms crossed over his chest, and he was trying his damndest to hide the smile threatening those gorgeous lips of his. I watched as he took a long drink of his bottled water. It was such a mundane action, and if it were anyone else I would have looked away without another thought. Only this was Chad, and watching his Adam's apple bob as he swallowed made my stomach clench. Without warning, the memory of having that delicious mouth on mine assaulted me, and my legs started moving towards him before I could think better of it.

"Bet you're glad you didn't join in right about now. Guess it's a good thing you were too chicken shit to play," I said in a low voice while I trailed a finger from just below his chest up to his neck. Chad growled low in his throat and pushed my hand away, and quickly made his way out the back door. The sun had long gone down and most of the party goers had made their way to the bonfire in Joe's backyard, trying to keep warm as the night had grown chilly.

I started to follow him, annoyed that he was blowing me off once again, but stopped in my tracks when I saw him already laughing and joking with the little brunette slut he'd been talking to when I first arrived. Jealousy rocketed through my veins and I couldn't help but wonder what the hell was so wrong with me that he could so easily flirt with her, but blow me off every chance he got.

After a few minutes they went their separate ways, but the anger and confusion warring inside me spurred me into action. All I could think about was how I needed to get Busty McFakeTits to back the hell off. I glanced back at Chad to make sure he wasn't looking and trailed behind her as she walked up to a group of girls standing a few feet away from Joe. I wasn't entirely sure what I was going to do, but I was pretty good at coming up with evil plots on the spot, so I figured I'd wing it.

Inspiration struck me as I stepped up close to Joe, only a couple of feet away from Shorty McSlutPants. I kept my voice hushed as if I was trying to whisper, but made sure I was talking loud enough for her to hear.

"I can't believe Chad gave me the clap, Joe. It's fucking bullshit. He wore a rubber and everything, but it tore, and when I told him about it he just laughed and said 'that's what you get for being such a slut.' He is such a dick."

Joe choked on his beer and I patted him on the back, then made sure he made eye contact with me so I could wink, letting him know I was up to something before he said anything to screw up my plan.

"He said there's this cute little slut with dark hair that's here tonight that he's going to give it to next. He's sick, Joe. I don't know how you put up with him."

I heard her let out a disgusted noise and tell her friends she was leaving. I smirked at Joe as I watched her storm off. Joe finally let out the laughter he'd been fighting hard to hold in and I joined in.

"What was that about, Stace?"

"Chad wanted to screw that girl that just left and I wanted to screw his chances of screwing her," I said with a shrug.

"That sounds a whole lot like jealousy. I thought you wanted to get revenge? Might be difficult to do when you seem to have developed a little bit of a crush on him."

"Shut up, I do not have a crush on him. I hate him. Nothing has changed. I just wasn't going to pass up the opportunity to mess with him."

"You keep telling yourself that, Stace. I think that kiss at Petey's fucked up your head. Maybe you should just bow out before you end up getting hurt."

"First of all, that kiss didn't do anything. Yeah, it was hot and I was pissed at him for acting like such a dick but that's just because I haven't gotten laid for too long and getting rejected pissed me off. There are no actual feelings there. Second of all, the only one who would end up getting hurt is him. Quit acting like I'm some delicate little pansy ass twat. I'm the one who does the heart breaking."

Joe didn't even bother responding, instead giving me a quick head nod and walking away. I had gotten too defensive. I should have played it cooler. I hadn't meant to react that way, but his accusation of me feeling something for Chad threw me. There was no way I felt anything for him except disdain, the guy was all asshole. There was no kindness in him, nothing worth falling for. Sure, he was sexy as sin, but that wasn't enough to make me actually fall for someone. I'd never even been in love, and Chad would definitely not be the guy to change that.

"I heard that," Chad whispered in my ear from behind me, startling me out of my thoughts. I jumped and let out a little squeak, then smacked his arm for scaring me.

"Heard what, asshole?"

"Heard you telling that chick that I gave you Chlamydia," he said with a smirk as he took a drink of his beer.

"Oh yeah? Then why didn't you speak up and defend yourself?"

"Because I don't give a shit what people think, and

it was kinda cute seeing you get all jealous over me."

"I was not jealous! I was just…I just wanted to…" I growled at my inability to explain myself. I'd never been at a loss for words in my life, and it me feel vulnerable and exposed. I wanted to tell him that I just hated him and enjoyed screwing up his night, but he probably would have just found it humorous that I was going out of my way to mess with him. Plus, I wasn't entirely sure that Joe wasn't maybe a little correct in what he'd just said to me.

Suddenly I froze when I realized if Chad heard what I'd said in front of that girl, then he'd probably heard my conversation with Joe. I clenched my fist and opened and closed my mouth several times, still not able to get so much as a squeak out, before growling again in frustration.

Chad just chuckled and walked off, seemingly uninterested in even hearing an explanation. He seriously could care less that I was spreading rumors that he had an STD. He was so infuriating! Nothing got to him, and it shouldn't matter to me, it shouldn't. But it did. Like it or not I couldn't shake this guy off, and since Joe and I had become so close I was going to have to be around him fairly often. I needed to either find a way to not let him get to me, or find a way once and for all to get him out of my system so I could just move on.

Problem was, I'd go weeks without seeing him and

think I'd gotten myself under control, only to completely unravel as soon as he was within fifty feet of me.

Suddenly I just wanted to be anywhere but at that party. I felt bad for leaving without telling Joe goodbye, but I couldn't be near Chad. I needed some space from him so I could get my shit together. I felt like I didn't know who I was any more, he had my head all twisted and I hated how much it was changing me. I had already wasted too much energy on someone who obviously hated me just as much as I hated him. Though, he didn't seem to hate me very much when he was kissing me.

Screw it, I just needed to leave. I practically ran to my car, and in the twenty minutes it took me to get home I had two missed calls and four texts from Joe.

Where did you go?

Your car is gone. Are you coming back?

Why did you leave?

Please answer me so I know you aren't dead.

When I got inside my apartment I text him back and told him I was home safe and to leave me the fuck alone. I really didn't want to be alone, but I was too frustrated to be good company, which would only lead to someone asking questions. And talking was the last thing I wanted to do. I contemplated going out, maybe finding a random and letting out some frustration, but that just didn't feel right. I didn't want some random guy tonight, and I felt like I needed more than just sex. It wasn't just pent up sexual frustration that was nagging at me, it was whatever hold Chad had on me that I couldn't shake.

After showering and throwing on a ribbed tank and some boy shorts, I fell back on my bed and stared at my ceiling. Obsessing. Replaying every minute that had passed since the night I met Chad, trying to figure out where things had gotten so complicated. I finally passed out around two in the morning, no closer to figuring anything out, and feeling more frustrated than ever.

After a fitful night of sleep, I finally gave up and got up at an ungodly hour of the morning. Adalyn was always at work nowadays, so I hadn't even had a chance to talk to her about any of this. I was too embarrassed to talk to Carrie about it. The way I was behaving was so out of character for me, and I knew she'd give me shit about it and I was not in the mood.

Despite my lack of sleep, I had so much pent up energy threatening to burst out of me that I couldn't just sit still in the apartment any longer. The sun was barely up so there weren't going to be any places open, but I needed to get out, needed to move. I threw on some shorts, a sports bra and long tank. I borrowed Addy's running shoes and a hooded sweatshirt. I hated working out and I didn't even own a pair of gym shoes, but suddenly the thought of running sounded very appealing.

I threw my phone and keys in the pocket of the hoodie, and as soon as my feet hit the pavement outside, I took off. Did people run in this part of the city? I guessed it didn't matter since there weren't many people outside yet anyway. I knew Carrie, my life long friend and Ian's little sister, ran at the park that was a few blocks over because there were jogging trails, so I headed in that direction.

By the time I made it to the park I was already struggling to breathe and had a line of sweat dripping down the back of my neck. It was a chilly morning and my lungs were on fire from sucking in the cold air so harshly. It felt like I had run ten miles already, though I doubted it had been more than a mile by the time I stopped in the middle of one of the trails and bent over, putting my hands on my knees, trying to catch my breath.

It felt like my lungs were frozen, and no matter how deeply I tried to breathe, I felt like I couldn't get enough air in them. I felt like I was suffocating, and suddenly I started to feel woozy, so I ran to the bushes on the side of the trail and dry heaved. Nothing came up because I hadn't bothered to eat anything before I made the stupid decision to jog for the first time in my life, so my stomach felt no relief after the heaving finally stopped. I collapsed to the ground, knees bent with my head hanging between them.

"Stacy?" I looked up and through my blurry vision I

could barely make out the details of Carrie's face. "What are you doing out here? Were you attacked?" She sounded really worried as she leaned down to get a closer look at me.

"No, why would you think I was attacked?"

"Um, because you look like you've been running? You're panting and all sweaty and sitting in the middle of a running trail?"

"I decided to go for a jog."

Carrie barked out a laugh. "Ha! Good one. Seriously, what are you doing out here?"

"I seriously was jogging," I said defensively.

"Well if it wasn't because you were running from a mugger, then why were you jogging? You hate exercise. Where did you even get those shoes?"

"They're Addy's, I borrowed them." Her nose scrunched up at the mention of Adalyn, but she recovered quickly.

"Have you eaten?"

"No."

"You can't go running for the first time in your life with no food in you. I'm surprised you didn't pass out, especially with how cold the air is this morning. Your nose is all red and your legs must be freezing. You're not dressed properly at all."

"Shut the hell up, Carrie, no one asked you. Not everyone gets up at the ass crack of dawn to go outside and torture themselves like you do, so I didn't exactly have all the gear needed for a run."

"So why are you running in the first place?"

"Can I explain it over breakfast? I'm starving and I might actually pass out if I don't get food, or in the very least some caffeine, very soon." Carrie grabbed my arm and helped me stand up. I teetered for a moment before catching my balance, and then gave my eyes a moment to adjust, blinking a few times to try and clear up my line of vision. "But if you give me shit then I'll never tell you anything ever again."

Carrie sat and listened patiently while I went over every detail since that night at the club where Chad arrested me. She didn't interrupt to ask questions, and she didn't even tell me to lower my voice when I would get worked up during certain parts and yell out expletives like a crack head with Tourette's. When I finally finished my rant, I was breathing heavy and my body was flush. It wasn't from the running, because I'd long recovered from that, though I could tell my underworked muscles were going to be punishing me later.

I waited for her to lecture me or give me some kind of advice. To criticize me or express her disappointment in my lack of self control. Instead, she just said "hmmm," and then took a drink of her coffee.

"Hmmm? That's it? Hmmm? Are you fucking kidding me? You aren't going to tell me how stupid or immature or ridiculous I'm being? You aren't going to lecture me about how childish it is to have a vendetta towards someone I barely know, especially since he's a cop? You aren't going to tell me that it's time for me to grow up and stop playing games and start putting more energy into trying to settle down?"

Carrie just smiled over her coffee mug and she looked so smug I almost knocked it out of her hands. "Why would I say any of that when you obviously know all of it already? Besides, I don't feel that way."

I stared at her in surprise for a minute, trying to figure out if she was screwing with me. Carrie didn't play games, she was a straight shooter, but that response was so out of character for her I thought maybe she'd had a personality transplant.

"You don't feel that way? What the fuck does that mean? Of course you feel that way. That's the same shit you say to me every time I get myself into trouble or wake up in some random's bed and have to walk outside to figure out where I am so you can come get me. And now I tell you that I'm losing my shit over some dick head cop I don't even know, and you decide for the first time in your life to not feed me the same bullshit crap you have practically every day since we met?"

Carrie just shrugged and took another sip of her coffee. "I don't know what to tell you, Stacy. You're an adult and can make your own decisions. I'm done butt-ing in since for one, it's really not my place, and two, it never does any good anyway. But yeah, I don't think all of that necessarily applies in this situation."

"Okay, we'll come back to that epiphany of you not wanting to harp on my life choices later, but for now let's skip right to the part where you said my current situation is different somehow."

"It's just different this time, Stace."

"What the hell does that mean, Care? The one time I actually want you to tell me what to do and you decide it's time for me to leave the nest and find my wings? That's bullshit. You love telling people what to do. This is your chance to do it without me getting pissed and threatening to throat punch you. So come on, lay it on me."

"No."

"No?"

Carrie let out an exasperated sigh and scrunched her eyebrows together, staring into her coffee mug like she was trying to see if the meaning to life was hidden in her cup.

"You're going to get mad."

"No I won't, I just told you I wouldn't get pissed."

"Okay, but…"

"Oh my God, seriously, spit it out Carrie."

"You like this guy, Stacy."

Okay…that was not what I thought she was going

to say. I held up one finger, indicating for her to hold on a moment, while I stared at the ground and took deep breaths, reminding myself that I just promised only two seconds ago that I would not throat punch her. When I finally calmed down and looked back up at her, I gave her a nod, indicating for her to continue.

"I've known you forever, Stacy. I know you better than I know myself. You've never gotten this worked up over a guy. Ever. In my honest opinion? I think you like that he doesn't put up with your bullshit. I think you like that he doesn't just fall for your hot body and over the top flirting like every other guy. It sounds like he's actually a pretty decent guy, and I think you're just trying to find ways to convince yourself that he's an asshole so that you can just hate him. You want to hate him because you really don't want to like him. But I think it's too late, because I think you already like him, and that scares you. And instead of being real with him and putting yourself out there, you've villainized him and turned him into the enemy. This ridiculous bet you made with this Joe guy, claiming you only want to get even - it's just an excuse for you to get closer to him without putting your heart on the line. I don't think you actually want to hurt him. I think you're just afraid he's going to hurt you."

I didn't even know how to respond. I just stared at her with my mouth gaping open, struggling to find the words I needed to argue and tell her she was wrong. I wanted to throw things and cause a scene. I wanted to shout at her and tell her how off base and ridiculous that little speech was.

But I didn't. I just sat there trying to understand why I was so angry. Angry at Chad, angry at her, angry at myself. So instead of yelling and taking out my frustrations on her and the random strangers in the coffee shop with us, I closed my eyes and fought back the tears that had started to well up. I felt so out of control, and it was terrifying not knowing how to fix it. But mostly I was terrified that she was right.

CHAPTER 8

CHAD

I only stuck around about another hour after Stacy bailed from Joe's party. I kept finding myself looking for her and feeling disappointed when I couldn't find her. I knew I should be angry at her for cock blocking me, but as much as I could probably use a good lay, it wasn't really what I wanted. I didn't sleep around a ton, nothing like Joe who had a different girl in his bed almost every night, but I didn't have trouble finding someone for a night if the mood struck me.

Problem was, since the night I met Stacy, I hadn't wanted to sleep with anyone. Every time I thought about sex, Stacy railroaded my thoughts. It was like she had taken over my brain. Even when I would jerk off in the shower I couldn't keep my mind from wandering to thoughts of her. Her body, her taste, her smell. I tried just distracting myself from thinking about sex entirely, but it didn't keep me from thinking about her.

So three days after Joe's party, I found myself at the gym taking out all my frustrations on the punching bag. Someone walked up behind me and tapped me on the shoulder, and it startled me, causing me to turn around quickly and take a swing at them.

"Shit!" Joe yelled as he took an uppercut to the jaw.

"Shit! I'm sorry man. You snuck up on me and it was instinct, I was in the zone. Shit. I'll go get you some ice."

The front desk gave me an ice pack and I made my way back over to Joe, who had taken a seat on a bench off to the side. I expected him to be pissed and was about to offer to let him take a swing at me to even the score, but as I handed him the ice pack he started cracking up. Like, seriously losing his shit laughing. Everyone in the gym turned to stare at us.

"What the fuck is your problem? Everyone is looking at us. What did I miss that's so funny?"

"You didn't miss. You have pretty good aim, actually," Joe said gesturing to his chin.

"I'm sorry man, seriously. I'll give you one free shot," I said as I opened my arms in gesture.

"Shut up, I'm not going to hit you. You're the one with all the pent up anger, not me. If taking one to the jaw will snap you out of whatever shit storm that's happening in your head right now then I'd gladly take another." Joe rotated his jaw and popped his neck, trying to stretch out after the jolt of getting punched.

"There's nothing going on with me, I'm just working out."

"Stop with the bullshit, I know you better than that. You only beat on that bag when something's really weighing on you. I'm here if you want to talk about it, but I'm not going to keep offering up my face. Although, it might give me more of an edge to have my face busted up. Make the girls think I'm a badass."

"Well if you think it will help you get laid then I'd be happy to punch you in your face any time. Just say the word."

"Screw you, I don't need help getting laid. I think you're the one who needs help. Is that what all the frustration you're taking out on the bag is from? You need some pussy? There's probably at least two chicks at my house right now. You can head over and take your pick. Or take both, whatever."

"I don't need to get laid, and even if I did, I wouldn't settle for your sloppy seconds."

"Well good luck finding a woman in a 20-mile radius who I haven't been with."

"You're disgusting. One day your dick is going to rot and fall off."

"Don't say shit like that! That's not even funny."

I laughed as I walked towards the locker room, shaking my head at Joe's perpetual horniness. As I stood under the steaming hot water of the shower, I had to admit to myself that he was right. I didn't usually feel the need to let out any aggression unless something was really bothering me. The problem was forcing myself to admit what was causing my anger to begin with.

I hated feeling angry. After seeing my father beat

the shit out of my mom for so many years I began to hate the emotion. So despite all the times when my temper would flare or I would start to get pissed off, I always found a way to tamp it down. I wasn't sure how long my dad had been beating my mom, but I first witnessed it when I was ten. He only took it out on me when I tried to intervene. I would have thrown myself in front of him every time to protect my mom, even when I was little, but she had begged me and made me promise over and over not to do it again. I hated agreeing to it, but the fear in her eyes when he hit her wasn't nearly as bad as the fear I saw in them when she watched him hitting me.

Keeping my anger in check wasn't easy, and was something I battled with daily. I refused to turn into my father and I lived in constant fear that one day I would snap and lose control like he did. I didn't know what caused him to beat her. He wasn't a drunk so he couldn't use that as an excuse. Maybe if I knew his reasons I wouldn't be so afraid of becoming him, but since I refused to talk to him I would probably never know.

I'd learned to detach myself from people and most situations that had the potential to make me angry, and while it had been a lonely life, I hadn't hurt anyone. For the most part I could see everything and everyone from a very objective standpoint, and could prevent myself from getting emotionally invested. Until Stacy, that is.

Never in my life had someone gotten to me like her.

It wasn't that her actions made me angry, it was my inability to control my attraction to her. She was a wild card, unpredictable, and that made her risky. Her smart mouth would be a constant source of trouble for her and I didn't need anyone coming in to my life and muddying things up. I'd worked hard to keep myself and my life stable, and there was no way that Stacy's involvement in any capacity wouldn't rock the boat.

She had been trying to push my buttons and get a rise out of me since the very moment I first saw her, which was red flag number one. Then her ostentatious flirting and bickering were red flag number two. Her following me out into the alley when I was trying to gain my composure, only to realize how little control I had when I was around her, was red flag number three. Then to round things out to red flag number four, she had acted like a jealous girlfriend at Joe's party and scared off a potential date.

Four red flags. Four. With any other woman if there was even one then I'd drop them like a bad habit. So what the fuck was wrong with me that I couldn't get this crazy chick out of my head?

After I got dressed and got my crap packed up, I walked out of the locker room and spotted Joe a few feet away, talking up a couple of girls whose workout clothes were so small they may as well have been jogging in their bathing suits. When he spotted me I saw him gesture to the girls to wait and then jog over to me.

"Hey man, you heading out?"

"Well I'm not going to hang out at the gym all damn day." Joe ignored my sarcasm, as usual. Nothing I said ever fazed him.

"Well, hey these girls were telling me about this new bar that has a live band playing that is supposed to be pretty good and they invited me to go, but they want me to bring someone else since there are two of them."

"Thanks, but no thanks, man." I patted him on the back and started to walk away, but he ran up to me and stopped me again. He wasn't going to let this go, I could already tell.

"Come on, Chad, they're hot. And you could use a night out. It's a low key type of deal, it's not some huge club or anything. At least show up and then if you aren't interested in one of them, I'll charm my way into getting them both to come home with me." Joe winked at me then turned and winked back at the girls. His cockiness knew no bounds. And honestly, I had no doubt he'd be able to convince them both to go home with him.

I really wasn't in the mood to go out, but Joe had been putting up with my shit for weeks now, so I figured I owed him. Plus, I wouldn't mind a distraction if it would help get Stacy off my mind. I reluctantly agreed and Joe said he'd text me directions, and told me to meet him there at eight.

I watched him run back to the girls and they both looked over at me, openly appraising me, most likely deciding if I met their standards to be joining them for the night. They both grinned at me, and Joe turned around to give me a thumbs up. Dumb ass.

CHAPTER 9

STACY

My conversation with Carrie had been eating at me since I had gotten home. I kept trying to tell myself that she was way off, but the more I thought about it the more I worried she might be pretty close to nailing the issue on the head.

After a long, hot shower and several pain killers, my legs finally stopped aching. It took a couple days for me to not need the assistance of pain meds to be able to walk, but I had to admit, the running felt good. If I did it regularly, it probably wouldn't have been so awful.

Adalyn walked in right as I was putting a movie in and sitting down on the couch with a big bowl of popcorn.

"Who is this random whore in my apartment? Should I call the cops? Oh wait...is that you Addy? It's been so long I forgot what you looked like. Do you even still live here?"

"Shut up, Stacy. I'm sorry I've been gone so much for work. You should be happy that I love my job so much. I owe you for helping me get it."

"Yep, you do. So sit your ass down and spend the day with me veg'ing out on the couch watching movies."

"Deal. Just let me go change real quick."

Six hours, five energy drinks, several bathroom breaks and three bags of popcorn later we finished the third movie in our marathon.

"Don't test my gangsta. I will cut a bitch up."

"Do you even hear yourself right now Stacy? What are you even talking about?" Adalyn asked, shaking her head at me. I was too hyped up to say anything, so I just hopped around from foot to foot, punching the air like a boxer on crack. I was fired up and ready to test my bitch slapping skills.

"I've never seen someone constantly try to instigate violence like you do. What would you do if someone ever actually challenged you? Have you ever even been in a fight?"

"Yes, I've been in tons of fights. Okay, yeah, I was only like eight years old, but that doesn't matter. Adrenaline would kick in and I'd beat a bitch. I've got spunk."

"Every time we watch this movie this happens. I am never watching Fight Club with you again. There will never be a female fight club, so give up on that dream right now. And if you don't sit your ass down and stop bouncing all over the living room then I'm going to lose my mind. You've already knocked over a lamp and spilled my drink."

"Geez, Adalyn, freaking chill," I said, plopping down onto a pillow on the floor, a little winded from my impromptu workout. "You've always been jealous of my bad assery."

Ignoring her eye roll, I got out my phone.

"Who are you calling? Is it Chad?" She asked wiggling her eyebrows up and down.

"I'm not calling anyone, bitch, I'm texting. Don't act like you know me." I'd spent the day getting Adalyn caught up on the past few weeks and everything that had happened with Chad. She started to lecture me, but once I told her what Carrie said to me, she shut up and nodded her head and said "Good for her. It's exactly what I would have said."

"Stacy, I wish I didn't know you so well. I also wish you would leave that poor man alone."

"That 'poor man' is an asshole and deserves everything he gets. But regardless, he's not who I'm texting. I'm texting Joe."

"Oh, tell him I said hello," she said in a perky, singsong voice. She'd met him a couple times briefly, and like the majority of the female population, she was instantly smitten by his charm.

"Tell him yourself, bitch. I don't have time to pass on your messages like some secretary. An evil plot is afoot and I need to finalize some deets," I told her giddily, my fingers tapping away on my phone.

Adalyn groaned and threw her head back pretending to be exasperated, but I knew she secretly loved my shenanigans. "I hate your evil plans. They always backfire and I end up having to bail your ass out of trouble."

"Calm your tits, Addy. This evil plan is foolproof. Joe is going to help me with Operation Take Down Officer Pissy Pants."

"Not only are you planning something evil, but you also gave it a name and found a co-conspirator? Wow, Stacy, I'm impressed. You are taking crazy bitch to a whole new level."

She didn't mean it as a compliment, but I took it as one anyway.

I was all worked up from watching Fight Club and since I couldn't actually kick anyone's ass, I had finally decided how to handle Chad. I needed to follow through with my original plan. He had seriously been an asshole to me and even if him not putting up with my shit was a bit of a turn on, he didn't deserve me. That meant putting the plan to get even with his sorry ass back into action.

Truthfully, Joe hadn't seemed too on board with the whole teaching Chad a lesson thing lately. Ever since that drunken night at his house when we jokingly made a bet, any time I brought it up he acted uncomfortable and changed the subject, but I was persistent.

Hey, you know what Chad is up to tonight?

Yes, but I don't think I should tell you…

WTF? Why???

He's been especially difficult to put up with since you guys kissed and I think seeing you will make it worse…

Screw you! You knew the plan when we started this. Did you think he was going to be all rainbows and sunshine? You can't back out on me now.

Seriously? Still sticking to the whole 'this is just a part of my evil plan' thing? Fine…but if he asks then you better not tell him I told you where we were going to be or else.

"Alright, put on something cute, we're going out," I told Adalyn as I hopped to my feet and headed towards my room.

"Ughhhhh…. why?"

"Well, since I haven't seen much of your face lately we're going out and you don't have a choice. I'll kick your ass if you try to argue with me." Adalyn fell back again with a groan and smacked her hand over her eyes. Typical response, so predictable. "Suck it, Addy, I need a wingman."

"Okay fine, but please tell me you aren't going to do something stupid again like get arrested."

"No promises," I said as I disappeared into my bedroom to get dressed. Adalyn followed me, still whining.

"Last time you had an evil plan you ended up crashing an event we weren't even invited to and I broke the heel to my favorite pair of stilettos running out the door to our getaway car while the angry mob chased after us."

"Yeah, that really was an awesome night. But no,

this is just a low key bar with a live band."

"But Joe and Chad will be there?"

"Yep."

"So this could potentially turn into another disaster? Should I go ahead and call Ian and tell him to be ready for our call when we have to go bail you out of jail again?"

"Seriously shut it, Addy. First off - don't try to use me as an excuse to call Ian. Secondly - we're just going to have some fun so lighten up. And go put something nice on for once. I'm not going to be seen with you dressed like a bum like you usually are."

"Screw you, twat, I don't dress like a bum, I just like to be casual. There's no law that says I have to spend three hours getting ready every time I decide to leave go somewhere."

Adalyn kept on rambling, but I'd already zoned her out. I was too distracted thinking about how much I was looking forward to seeing Chad tonight, and then trying to convince myself that it was only because I was in the mood to stir up trouble. Either way, it was going to be interesting.

I shot off a text to Carrie, inviting her to come along, even though her and Adalyn still weren't exactly chummy. Right when she text back saying she would be there, Adalyn popped her head out and said she had to go to work. I was happy she had a job she loved, but I was looking forward to spending some time with her, too.

Oh well, there would be time later. For now, I had an ego to destroy.

CHAPTER 10

CHAD

I wouldn't admit it to Joe, but I actually liked this bar. It was a good size, so the bar was far enough from the dance floor that you didn't feel too crowded. It was split into two areas, one that had the stage for bands and the other filled with pool tables and dart boards. I sat on a stool at the bar, keeping one eye on the game on the TV behind the bar and another one on the door. Joe must have been feeling guilty, because shortly after we'd gotten here he had confessed and told me he'd invited Stacy. I wanted to pound his face in at first, but when he genuinely pleaded with me to try and make the effort to be nice to her, I caved and promised I would play nice.

Joe was chatting up a girl on the dance floor when Stacy walked in. The familiar urge to put up walls and get defensive tugged at me, but I fought it back down, wanting to keep my promise to Joe. When Stacy spotted me, I could see uncertainty overcome her. It caught me off guard, making me realize how little I really knew her. I instantly felt like a dick for being the reason she was doubting herself, and managed to force a smile and give her a short wave.

Relief washed over her and she headed my way, another girl close behind her. I downed the rest of my beer and asked the bartender for another, trying like hell to ignore how my heart rate picked up as she neared.

"Hey Chad, good to see you. This is my friend Carrie. Is Joe here?" She scanned the room and found him easily, a smile tugging at her lips when she saw him flirting with someone. Her tone was casual and friendly, but you could hear how forced it was. Maybe Joe had the same talk with her about getting along as he'd had with me.

Her friend was a petite little thing with long, brown hair. She had incredible posture, which I realized was a strange thing to notice, but despite how stiff she was standing, she didn't seem tense. Something about her gave off an overly confident and almost regal vibe, and I wondered how she and Stacy knew each other, because as far as first impressions go, they couldn't possibly have very much in common. Especially when you took in how conservatively her friend was dressed, which was in stark contrast with Stacy's deliciously revealing outfit.

We stood there a few minutes in uncomfortable silence, and Stacy said "Well we're…" at the same time I said "So how about…" and we did that awkward "no you go" thing a few times, before I finally put the uncomfortableness to an end and spoke up.

"There's another area over to the right, more like a pool hall with darts and separate bar. You guys want to head over there and get us a table while I grab Joe?"

At least if we were playing a game it would give us a distraction. The forced niceness between us just felt... wrong.

Joe was balls deep and working hard on picking up the blonde he was flirting with, but when I told him Stacy was here he bailed without so much as a hand wave in the blonde's direction. She scowled at him and huffed as she stomped in the opposite direction, but if the way these types of situations went for Joe in the past were any indication, she would be back and trying to flirt with Joe again by the end of the night.

Joe and I fought our way through the crowd that had doubled in size since we'd first arrived, and made our way to the girls, where they already had drinks and were racking up the pool balls.

"Hey, hey, hey ladies, be careful with my balls," Joe joked. I rolled my eyes, Stacy laughed and her friend blushed.

"Get your ass over here and show me how well you handle that big stick," Stacy teased back. I almost spit my beer out of my mouth. I made the mistake of looking at Stacy as I was coughing, and was rewarded with a wink. Dammit. She knew she'd caught me off guard and that wink had Sarge immediately standing at attention.

I couldn't tell you where the urge came from, but before I knew it, I joined in on the juvenile wordplay. "Nice rack," I added with a head nod in Stacy's direction. I watched as her eyes widened a fraction in surprise. Her surprise quickly morphed into an easy smile, and the way her face lit up playfully made something in my chest ache.

Carrie impressed us with a more than decent break, which segued into Joe making jokes about his own balls again. He wasn't going out of his way to flirt with Carrie like he would most girls, but that could be due to how uninterested she seemed in anything he said. Outwardly, everything about Stacy's friend came across as uptight and prudish, but something about the ease of her movements and casualness in her tone made me think there was more to her than met the eye.

The game continued on in much the same fashion with everyone focusing more on who could come up with the best sexual innuendo, rather than the game itself. An hour later the table was still covered in half the balls we started with and we were all laughing so hard our cheeks hurt. Even Carrie, who'd been fairly quiet for the first half of the game, starting to chime in with her own quips.

I couldn't remember the last time I'd had that much fun, and wondered at what point in the night my guard had completely dropped without me even knowing it.

The conversation was light and easy as we made our way to an empty table, asking the waitress to bring us all another round of drinks. Stacy was sitting to my right, her chair much closer than necessary, but like hell was I going to complain. The table was round and we were the only four occupying it, but somehow we'd both managed to scoot our chairs within inches of each other without being conscious of it.

I could feel the heat emanating from Stacy's bare leg that was almost touching my denim clad one, and every time I shifted my face even a fraction in her direction I was immediately engulfed in her scent. But despite how intoxicating her smell and bare skin was, I couldn't help but notice that she wasn't nearly as affected as I was.

Granted, we were so close at that point that if we turned to look at each other at the same time our mouths would almost be touching, which made eye contact difficult, but it was more than that. She seemed distracted, and though she contributed to the conversation from time to time, it was obvious that her thoughts were elsewhere. It pissed me off how much it bothered me that she was so close, but clearly so far away, because I shouldn't really care what the hell she was thinking about. Yet I couldn't keep myself from discreetly studying her and trying to figure out how to bring her back to me.

I saw her eyeing the dart board and couldn't resist the opportunity to bring her attention back to me. "You up for a round?" I whispered close enough to her that my lips lightly touched the outer shell of her ear, making sure to breath softly on her neck as I spoke. A shiver ran down her body and I grinned, pulling away, but only slightly. Now that I was so close to her, it took everything in me not to close the distance and suck on her neck, which made putting the distance back between us too fucking painful.

"Oh, I'm always up for a round. I could go all. night. long," Stacy whispered back, not missing a beat. I discretely rearranged my semi in my pants as Stacy got up and headed towards the dart board. Or, at least, I thought I had been discreet. Stacy glanced back at me over her shoulder, and the smug look on her face told me she at least knew the effect she'd had on me, even if she hadn't seen it. I sidled up next to her and she handed me my darts, saying, "Ladies first." I waited for her to step up, but she nodded in my direction, indicating she was suggesting I throw first.

"Ladies? If you need me to prove to you just how man I am, just say the word," I said, brushing my erection against her ass, before getting in place to take my first shot. I pulled my hand back, but right as I went to release, Stacy pushed her tits up against my side and whispered in my ear. "Oh, you may be a man, but that doesn't mean you can hit my bulls eye."

"Dammit!" I yelled when my dart completely missed the board. Stacy was giggling like a fiend, and I couldn't help but join in. Her laugh was so beautiful, and my chest constricted, reminding me that I couldn't let my guard down with her. I wanted to - I wanted to just enjoy this carefree side of her, but I wasn't ready to let go completely. At least, not yet, anyway. "I'll get you for that," I growled, and not so casually grinded against her when we exchanged places.

Stacy took a few seconds to compose herself before lifting her hand to throw her dart. I was going to do something to throw her off, but she stopped mid-throw to face me. She opened her mouth to say something, but then closed it, quickly turning back and throwing the dart towards the board. Bulls eye.

"Impressive," I said, genuinely meaning it. I looked out of the corner of my eye and saw her taking a sip of her drink, so I took my chance and threw my dart quickly, not wanting her to distract me again. I only got the outside of the board, but at least I'd managed to hit it at all that time. I was usually pretty decent at darts, but apparently she only needed to be in the room in order to distract me.

She had a smug grin on her face when she stepped back up to throw her next dart. I stood back and crossed my arms, not even attempting to try and throw her off this time. Another bulls eye. I uncrossed my arms and looked her over. "You play a lot of darts?" I asked, stepping up to take my turn. That time I came pretty close to the center, but still not as accurate as Stacy.

"No," she responded, shrugging. "I just have really good aim. I see something I want, and then I go after it, and I never, ever miss." Her voice was a seductive whisper, and if she hadn't been standing so closely, I wouldn't have even heard her. The way her eyes darkened at the statement told me we were still talking in innuendos.

"Never, huh? You seem pretty sure of yourself." I took my last shot, not really even bothering to try at that point. "Maybe we should make this interesting."

"Oh, it's not interesting enough for you already? Is getting your ass kicked in darts boring to you?" She was shaking her head as she stepped up to make her last throw. "Tell you what, I hit the bulls eye and you have to do whatever I want."

"That's pretty vague, care to narrow that down a little?"

"Nope," she responded quickly, sticking her bottom lip out, giving just a little pout. "What's the matter? You scared?"

I thought it over for a minute, and I can't lie, I was a little scared about what it would be she asked me to do. Stacy was so unpredictable, and while I'd hoped it would be something sexual, I realized that was more wishful thinking than anything. My luck she'd end up asking me to arrest some asshole ex-boyfriend or something.

"Alright. As long as it's not illegal, I'm in. Hit

me with your best shot." I was going to wait until she turned back around and sneak up to distract her, but she never took her eyes off of mine. Without even looking, she pulled her hand up and threw. Landing right on that damn bulls eye.

Son. Of. A. Bitch.

"How the hell did you pull that off?" I asked, not even trying to hide my surprise.

Stacy just winked and headed off towards the bathroom, leaving me stunned. She turned back one last time before she walked in, and it took everything in me not to follow her in there and push her up against the wall. I'd never had the desire to have sex in a dirty bar bathroom, but it didn't really matter right then, because all I wanted was to feel her up next to me. The flirtatious banter and casual brushing up against one another from the last couple hours had been incredible foreplay and I was entirely way too worked up.

I was leaning against the wall, my eyes never leaving that bathroom, and hoping she would hurry up and come back so we could continue the foreplay, when all of a sudden one of the girls from the gym earlier stepped into my line of vision. Dammit, I'd forgotten all about the original reason we were at the damn bar.

She was already a little tipsy, but not drunk yet. If she thought for a second that she was going home with me, then she was sorely mistaken. Not only was I not at all interested, but I didn't fuck drunk chicks. I needed them to be coherent enough to understand that it's just one night, nothing more, and more importantly I needed to know they were aware enough to willingly consent. I didn't need to get laid bad enough to ever feel the need to take advantage of someone.

"You wanna dance?" She whispered in my ear as she pushed her tits up against me. Her breath smelled like vodka and her words were so slurred I almost didn't understand them.

"Not really my thing," I answered, taking a swig of my beer, scanning the room for Stacy and hoping the sloppy slut trying to stick her hand down my pants would be gone by the time she came back. I took a step to the side to try and go around her, but she stepped along with me and pushed me back against the wall with her grabby little hands.

"That's a shame. I bet you would feel amazing pressed up against my body. I've been dying to feel you all night," she whispered as her hand tried to find my crotch again. I grabbed her wrist and spun her around. She let out a little squeal and I got in her face, which of course she took to mean I was going to kiss her, so she closed her eyes and puckered her lips. I opened my mouth to tell her to leave me the fuck alone, but a flash of bright blonde hair drew my attention away and I saw Stacy's delicious body step out of the bathroom and start in my direction.

I completely forgot about the woman I was pinning up against the wall, too mesmerized by the easy sway of Stacy's curvy hips. It wasn't until Stacy's gaze met mine and she stopped a few feet away that I realized how it must look, me pressed up against another girl. The look on her face gutted me, and I watched the look on her face turn from hurt to angry, before it morphed into something else entirely.

Jealousy. An hour ago I would have reveled in watching her be jealous over seeing me with another girl, but after seeing this entirely different side of her it only made me feel like shit. It dawned on me that Stacy was the first girl I had ever had this much fun with, and the way her body tensed as she took in the picture before her told me it was probably the last time it would happen, too.

My attention snapped back to the girl whose hand I still had pinned above her head when I felt her hand start rubbing my semi hard cock, which had only started to harden at the sight of Stacy. I quickly dropped her hand, which she promptly used to wrap around the back of my neck and yank my mouth down on hers. I was so caught off guard that I hesitated for just a second before ripping my face away from hers. I quick took a step back and searched for Stacy, fully expecting to see her plotting my murder, only to find she wasn't standing there anymore.

I looked around frantically, ignoring drunk girl shouting at me to come back, and finally spotted her on the dance floor talking to Joe. No, not talking…yelling. I watched as Joe threw his hands up in the air, and the only words I could make out were him saying "I'm sorry," before Stacy turned away from him and grabbed the closest man she could find and started grinding on his leg. He didn't seem too put out, because he put his hands on her waist and started rocking with her to the beat.

I watched for a few beats of the song, deciding what I should do. It would have been better for everyone if I had just walked away and cut my losses, but seeing the asshole grind his crotch against her ass and his eyes glaze over just made me see red. He whispered something in her ear and she threw her head back in laughter, and I just lost it.

Next thing I knew I was moving towards Stacy, not even bothering to apologize to all the people I roughly knocked out of my way to get to her. She didn't notice me approaching, seeing as how she was too busy letting some asshole suck on her neck. When I was finally right up next to them, I grabbed the asshole by the collar of his shirt and threw him off of her. I knew I had no right to be acting possessive over her. I'd been a dick to her since we'd met, and one fun night was going to make up for that, but seeing someone else touch her filled me with so much blind rage I couldn't think straight.

"What the fuck, man? What is your problem?" He yelled at me while the people he'd knocked over when I threw him helped him stand. He stormed over to me and stepped into my personal space, his face red from anger, and probably embarrassment from being thrown across the room like a rag doll.

"Better think twice before you get in my face, buddy. You're gonna regret it."

A crowd had started to gather, watching the spectacle we were causing, and I felt Joe step up next to me but I didn't take my eyes off of the dickhead that was nose to nose with me now. I bumped his chest with mine and growled.

"One last chance, buddy. Walk away," I warned, my fists clenched tightly at my sides.

"Or what?" He challenged, making the mistake of raising his hands and trying to shove me back.

I didn't bother answering, instead I just punched him right in his face. He stumbled backwards a few steps, then like the idiot he is, he came at me again. I stepped to the side as he swung at me, causing him to miss me entirely and stumble forward. He turned around to come at me again, but before he could make a move I gave him another punch to his face. He was scrambling all over the floor, but stood in the same place, unmoving.

I could feel hundreds of sets of eyes on me, but I never took mine off of him. I just watched, predicting his next move and dodging him each time he took a swing, then rewarded him with another punch to the face. This happened several times before Joe finally stepped in and restrained the guy. He was panting and wobbly and spitting blood as he cussed at me.

I watched as Joe pulled him to the door and said something in his ear. Most likely telling him he was lucky I just punched him instead of arresting him for assaulting a police officer, even though I technically started it.

Joe came back and yanked on my arm so hard I almost took a swing at him, but I snapped out of it in time, luckily. I would have felt really guilty if Joe had to take a hit to the face twice in one day from me. I was out of control, and I knew I needed to get it together. I looked over at Stacy who was standing a few feet away from me, looking terrified, her mouth hanging wide open in shock. I wanted to go to her and try to explain, but I had no idea what I would say, so I just shook my head and walked to the back of the bar where I had seen an entrance to some kind of outdoor patio people had gathered to.

I heard the band pick back up as I walked over to the railing lining the once busy patio that was now empty. Most likely everyone had gone back inside to witness the fight, and I was so fucking grateful to have a moment alone. I gripped the edges and took deep breaths, trying to calm myself down.

What the fuck was the wrong with me? Why would

I react like that?

Because I'm my father's son, that's why.

No. No, I couldn't think like that. I wasn't him. I didn't just go around beating people senseless. I gave that guy an opportunity to walk away and he chose to keep lunging at me, so he had some fault in what happened, too.

Dammit! These were just excuses. There was no way to justify my behavior, no matter the reasons behind it. Violence could always be avoided and I knew better than anyone that there were better ways to handle issues than by raising your fist. Even flashing my badge to get him to back off would have been a smarted decision, yet I'd gone all caveman and lashed out just because some random guy was touching a woman who didn't even belong to me.

I was unraveling. I was starting to feel desperate. I couldn't lose control, I just couldn't. I had to figure out what the hell was going on with me and fix it. Fast. Before everything fell apart.

"Dammit!" I yelled as I slammed my hands down on the railing. I felt a hand gently touch my shoulder and I inhaled sharply. It was Stacy. I knew without turning around that it was her. I could smell her, sense her. The warmth from her hand shot now familiar sensations straight through my body, gathering in my chest. "What do you want Stacy?"

"What was that back there, Chad? Why did you do that? He wasn't doing anything wrong. I was the one who asked him to dance. Did you think he was forcing me or something?" She was speaking in a low, soothing tone and I could hear the concern in her voice, maybe even mixed with a little bit of guilt. Did she feel guilty for flirting with that guy to make me jealous, or did she feel guilty for using him not knowing I would go bat shit crazy and beat his ass?

I shook my head but didn't answer her. How could I? I wasn't sure why I had done that myself, so how could I explain my actions? It was inexcusable, and knowing she was there to witness me lose it like that filled me with shame.

"Chad," she whispered, moving to my side and gently sliding her hand from my shoulder to my cheek, tugging my face to the side so she could look at me. My body was shaking, and I told myself it was from the adrenaline, and not because her touch felt so right. I gripped the railing even harder to try and hide it, and had to force myself not to look away from her eyes. Eyes that reflected back at me all the same conflicting emotions that were threatening to crack me in two. "Chad," she whispered again before she leaned up on her toes to press her lips to mine.

Her lips were soft and gentle at first, tender and forgiving, like she was trying to express that she wasn't mad about the scene that had just taken place. As if it didn't bother her that I'd just beaten a man for seemingly no reason. I wanted to pull away and ask what was wrong with her. Ask her why she wouldn't be furious with me, or terrified of me, for doing something so irrational and violent. But I couldn't.

A calm washed over me, and I pulled my hands away from the railing and shoved them into her hair, cupping her face in my palms as I relaxed into the kiss. Stacy responded by placing her hands over mine then ran them over my shoulders, down my back and then around my waist. I tugged her face even harder against mine and turned us so her back was up against the railing. The kiss deepened as need and desire took over, our touches becoming frantic and desperate.

I finally forced myself to break the kiss, both of us gasping for air, our foreheads pressed together.

"What are you doing to me, Stacy?" It was a rhetorical question. I didn't really expect her to answer, obviously. "You need to stay away from me," I said, pushing myself away from her. I felt the loss of our bodies touching all the way into my soul, and it took all my willpower to not reach out for her again.

"Wait…what?" Sadness and confusion marred her face and it broke me just a little, but not enough to stop me from doing what needed to be done. There was no way to explain it to her without going into the details of my past, and that was just something I didn't talk about.

I wasn't entirely sure I was doing the right thing, but what I did know is that Stacy deserved better than what I was ever going to be able to give her. Years of working towards being the man I was supposed to be, and in the brief amount of time I'd known Stacy, it all had gone to shit. I couldn't stand who I was becoming, but I was certain that if I continued down this path that it would end up destroying us both.

"I'm not good for you. I can't control myself around you. It's dangerous. I'm dangerous. It's just not a good idea. Please, Stacy, I'm not asking - I'm telling. Nothing between you and I is ever going to happen."

I started to walk away, but Stacy grabbed my arm, stopping me. "Chad, wait. I don't understand. I know I may have not made a very good first impression, and I know we seem to butt heads a lot, but I thought we were getting along back there. I thought we were having fun. So why is it that any time I'm near you, you push me away? Am I really so horrible that you don't want to get to know me at all?" The hurt in her voice betrayed the playful tone she was forcing, and I watched her face struggle to maintain stoic, even as her lower lip quivered.

I wanted to pull her into my arms and tell her all the reasons I did want to get to know her. I wanted to tell her that she made me laugh, when it was damn near impossible for anyone to make me do that these days. I wanted to tell her that it terrified me how little control over myself I had around her, and how I wished I could just give in and just give her all of me. I wanted her to know that she was the sexiest, most enchanting woman I'd ever met, and that no other woman I'd ever met had ever been able to penetrate my tough exterior like she had.

But all that would do is make it harder for her when I finally did walk away, because commitment and love just weren't things I was capable of. For a very brief period of time back when we were joking around, I thought maybe things could be different. That I could be different. But then I went and lost it on that guy she was dancing with, and just remembering how it felt seeing his hands on her made me want to punch something again. So, I knew what I was about to do was right. It would hurt like a mother fucker, but I didn't have a choice.

I yanked my arm out of her grip and turned to glare at her. She inhaled sharply and took a step back. I wasn't intending to scare her, but I needed to make a clean cut - completely sever the tie that was tethering us together. She might not know it, but whatever was going on between us was destructive, and it would destroy us both. It didn't take a genius to see how much her presence fucked with my mind, so if that meant I had to be the bad guy to get her to stay away then that's what I would do.

"Don't touch me, Stacy. I'm not a good guy. The only reason I was even nice to you tonight was because

Joe begged me to try, but I can't do it anymore. It's not worth it. I have no interest in spending any amount of time with you."

"Chad don't, I know you feel it…"

"No!" I yelled, interrupting what I knew she was going to say. I wished there was a way to do this without completely lying, but I had to make sure I completely burned this bridge. I wouldn't have the willpower to stay away from her, so I needed her to hate me. It was cowardly and weak, but I was desperate. "The only thing I feel towards you is physical attraction, but I can get those needs satisfied anywhere and by much more attractive women. Why would I settle for you? The only reason anything has happened between us at all was because you were convenient. Right place, right time. You're too much work, though, so now I'm telling you to stay away. I don't want you, so don't embarrass yourself further by trying to convince me otherwise."

It looked like she was about to cry and if that happened, I wouldn't be able to keep up this facade of not wanting her. So I turned and walked away, with each step that took me away from her leaving a piece of my soul behind with it.

Stacy deserved someone stronger, someone who could appreciate her and cherish her without his demons getting in the way. I'd never hated myself more than I did in that moment, knowing that the man she deserved would never be me, and hating how much I wished I could be that man for her.

I had to talk myself out of turning around and going to her to take it all back, but the more distance I put between us, the more I knew I was doing the right thing. I barely knew her, so letting the attraction between us take me down a dark road I may never recover from wasn't worth it. When things went to shit, she would recover just fine. No doubt she would be able to find someone who would treat her right and she would get her happily ever after, while I would be left trying to regain control over myself.

The more I tried to tell myself I was right, the more I felt things spiraling out of control. All I knew was that it wasn't normal how badly I yearned to possess her, to be able to call her mine. I craved her like an addict craved their next fix, and it was dangerous. She was dangerous. So it didn't matter that every time I looked into the depths of her eyes it felt like my heart tethered to hers just a little tighter. And it didn't matter that every time her soft skin brushed against mine it felt like she was filling in all the cracks where my soul had broken over the years.

No, all that mattered was that every reaction I had to her was entirely too intense, and too irrational. Every time I breathed her in I felt myself unravel just a little bit more, and if I wasn't careful then all it would take is just one quick tug, and the tattered threads that barely contained my inner demons would rip to shreds. And then there would be no turning back.

CHAPTER 11

STACY

I was not going to cry. I would not give that asshole the satisfaction of seeing just how much is words really hurt. He was lying, I knew he was. I wasn't imagining this pull between us, it was there and he was just fighting it. I didn't know *why* he was fighting it, but I didn't deserve to be treated that way no matter his reasons. I was fucking done.

Joe emerged a few minutes after Chad had stormed off and he tried to put his arms on my shoulders but I shrugged him off.

"Don't fucking touch me!"

"What the hell, Stacy? What's the matter with you? Chad just stormed out of the bar and wouldn't talk to me, and now you're freaking out about me touching you? Tell me what's going on," Joe pleaded as he ran his hand through his hair.

"Your partner is an asshole."

"No shit, but that's nothing new. What happened out here, Stacy?"

"Why did he attack that guy, Joe?" I asked, deflecting his question.

"I don't know, Stacy. Chad has…" he trailed off like he was trying to figure out the right words to say.

"Chad struggles with his temper. He bottles everything up and that's part of what makes him kind of an asshole sometimes, but I've never seen him snap like that. Not in the two years I've known him. He's never just completely lost it. One minute you guys seem to be getting along great, the next minute you're yelling at me about some girl he's with and then I turn around to see him punching some guy. Did you guys get in an argument? Did that guy say something to Chad?"

I didn't answer right away. I was thinking back to everything that happened leading up to him attacking that guy. When I got back from the bathroom he was practically fucking some chick up against the wall, so I went to yell at Joe like it was his fault that I was acting like a jealous girlfriend. And then yeah, I acted like a selfish bitch and started grinding up on a stranger to make Chad jealous, but I didn't think he would care enough to haul off and pound someone's face in? Why would it matter so much to him when it took all of two seconds of me being gone for him to find some random whore to hit on?

"I don't know, Joe, nothing happened. I thought we were getting along, like, for real getting along, and when I came back from the bathroom he was... I shouldn't have done it, but I was trying to make him jealous. It's stupid and immature, I know, but I never thought he'd attack someone just because they were dancing with me. It happened so fast. I followed him out to the patio and asked him if he thought that guy was forcing himself on me or something, but he didn't say anything. I just...I don't understand."

"I think it's time we call off this bet, Stacy. I thought it was a good idea at first. I only encouraged it because I thought maybe you could help Chad to come out of his shell. Every time you guys are near each other he would get all riled up, and I stupidly thought that meant that you could get to him in a way other people never could. But if this is the result of that, then I think it's time we just let it go. It's obviously not good for either of you."

"Fuck you, Joe! It's not my fault he went psycho on that guy! And this isn't about the stupid bet. I thought that we...back there when he was...dammit, I don't know! I thought things had changed, but the shit he said to me before he left...you don't have to worry about getting me to stay away from him, because I don't ever want to see him again." I tried to walk away, but Joe grabbed my arm and pulled me back to him.

"What do you mean? What did he say?" His face was serious, and it was like a knife to the gut, because it was apparent that his concern was more for Chad than me, though I didn't know why. No one was explaining anything to me and I was getting really fucking sick of being kept out of the loop.

"It doesn't fucking matter. He made it very clear what he thought of me, and not a damn word of it is worth repeating. Let him think whatever he wants, because I'm done. Don't worry - bet off."

I tried to yank out of his grip, but he stopped me again. It was a good thing there weren't any weapons close by, because I probably would have stabbed him if it meant him letting me go.

"Just stay the fuck away from me, Joe. I'm sorry but I need some time. He's your partner and I don't want to keep putting you in the middle. I'll contact you when I'm ready to talk again. Tell Carrie I left and give her a ride home."

I yanked again, and that time he let me go. I felt like shit for bailing on Carrie and pushing Joe away, but what I said was true. He was right in the middle of all this bullshit and I could see it was tearing him up. I just needed a break from all the bullshit, even though it was a little late at that point. No matter how much distance I put between between us, it was too late to keep myself from becoming just one more casualty in the cruelness of Chad's assholery.

I didn't see Chad or Joe for the next few weeks. Joe had kept his distance like I'd requested, and while I was thankful, I really fucking missed him. Adalyn was never home and I had to keep myself from tracking her down so I had someone to talk to about everything that was happening. It wasn't fair for me to distract her when she'd finally found something she was really passionate about.

Having so much time alone in my thoughts gave me the freaking awesome ability to constantly overthink everything that had happened over the last month. It was self inflicted torture at it's best. Carrie had tried several times to reach out to me, and when I didn't respond to her texts or calls, she started showing up. She gave up on me too, though, once she realized I wasn't talking.

I didn't embarrass easily, but I did have pride, and he'd managed to stomp all over it. I should probably have been hurt, felt rejected or shameful over how much I was letting him get to me, but I couldn't. That just wasn't me. I didn't get hurt. Angry? Yes. Vengeful? You bet. Psychotic? At times. Hurt? Never. I was pretty sure I didn't even have tear ducts. There had been a few times in my life where I thought I might cry, but nothing came out. I just wasn't a crier.

I wasn't cruel, I didn't enjoy hurting people. But I did know who I was and what I wanted and I didn't apologize for it. I had learned long ago that you can't please everyone. No, nothing traumatic happened to me. Everyone expected me to have some tortured past that made me into the person I was. Honestly, it was just me. If something happened in my life to influence my personality, then I was either too young to remember or blocked it out entirely.

Even in grade school I remembered being this way. Almost every day my mom would have to come to the school because I was sitting in the principal's office. It wasn't my fault my teachers were dumbasses. Even at eight years old I knew they were stupid, and I wasn't afraid to tell them. I argued more with the adults in my life than the kids in my class.

Unless someone was being bullied. I had no tolerance for that. I couldn't even tell you how many fights I was in when I was younger. Of course once I got a little older and learned to fight with my words, then I stopped using my fists. Plus, beating up boys wasn't any fun because they never hit back. So I learned how easy it was to wield my words into a weapon, and man, could I do some damage.

Don't worry, I used my super power for good. For the most part. Although I guess it's debatable on whether or not the things I did could be considered 'good.' Most people would probably say it's better to take the high road, walk away, brush things off. I say those people are idiots. I can't change people, but I sure as shit didn't have to put up with them either. I had no qualms with speaking my mind to any asshole who deserved it. I was like the female child equivalent of Batman, only without all the gadgets. A young vigilante, teaching bitchy girls and shitty boys lessons on a daily basis.

I knew my temper got the best of me sometimes and

my reactions could be harsh. That's the thing with using words to hurt people. Sometimes your words came out before you could stop them, and words can't be unsaid. It had certainly made it difficult for me to sustain any kind of long term relationship. I wasn't opposed to dating exclusively, but I found as I got older that men looking to settle down wanted a more 'mature' woman who would act demure and polite. So yeah...not me.

At some point I'd lost sight of who I was. Ever since meeting Chad, I didn't even know myself. I was starting to understand things about myself that I would have rather never known. Like, how part of me feeling lost was because I'd always spent my life taking care of other people and right now the only person who needed taken care of was myself. I didn't know how to help myself, I wasn't used to making myself a priority.

Also what Joe had said to me kept looping through my mind. He said Chad struggled with his temper, and the way he said it implied there was so much more to that statement. Was that the reason I was so infatuated with him? Why I kept pursuing some kind of relationship with him, even an unhealthy one? Did I sense something in him that needed fixed? After seeing that scene he made in the bar, I realized that whatever demons he was fighting were probably more than I could handle.

But if he was hurting, if he was struggling, then shouldn't someone fight for him? With him? It didn't matter. He didn't want me. He might have been fighting his attraction to me, but that didn't mean he wanted anything more. He didn't need someone to fix him and I couldn't force him to let me in. And even though I didn't believe for one second that he meant those things he said to me, the fact that he said them at all was cruel enough. He had chosen his words with the specific goal of hurting me, and it worked.

And this game I'd been playing, trying to get a rise out of him. That wasn't me, either. I didn't screw around with people, so maybe what Carrie had said to me was right. Maybe I had just been looking for ways to be near him. Maybe I was settling for any kind of reaction from him because it was better than nothing. But when we were playing, joking around like normal people, I wasn't even thinking of the stupid bet. I was actually enjoying our playful banter, and had actually kidded myself into thinking he was enjoying himself, too.

All of these thoughts ran constantly through my mind and I seriously thought I was going to go nuts if I couldn't find a way to make them stop. So after weeks of only interacting with people at work, I decided I need to figure my shit out. Something about Chad was drawing me to him and fighting it wasn't working. I needed to get to know him, find out if what I thought was happening between us was real. And if once he knew me he still didn't want me around, then maybe it would be easier to walk away.

I just had to find a way to get him to give me a chance to be real with him for once.

CHAPTER 12

CHAD

It had been weeks since the incident at the bar, though it felt like years. Time was literally moving in slow motion. I was a fucking zombie most of the time, and after screwing up several times at work, my Captain finally "encouraged" me to take a "vacation." It was the first time I had ever taken time off work in the ten years I'd been a cop. But my head was all over the place and I knew it wasn't safe for me to be out in the field when I was a mess like this, so I couldn't even be angry about being stuck at home. I was a danger to myself and to my partner, and as much as I loathed the idea of sitting around, stuck in my own head being unproductive as shit, it was the responsible thing to do.

I couldn't get Stacy out of my head. I had to constantly fight the urge to reach out to her, explain why I'd been such a dick to her at the bar. She had come out there to comfort me, even after I'd acted like a total asshole, and I'd treated her like shit. Nothing I'd said was true. It was more than a physical attraction for me, but how realistic was that anyway? I barely knew her. The only thing I really knew about her was how out of control I felt around her. And that's what terrified me.

Then when I thought about everything I had said to

her, making her feel like she meant nothing to me and that the connection between us was all in her head… Man, I was a piece of shit.

Finally, I decided enough was enough, so I text Joe and asked him to meet me at Petey's. I'd been cooped up in the house for too long and I needed some air. I knew I had some apologizing to do, which was part of why I'd been ignoring his calls and texts, but it was time to stop being such a pussy and face what had happened.

When I got to Petey's, Joe was already sitting at the bar, nursing a beer. He gave me a head nod when he saw me approach and I asked the bartender for a water. Joe looked at me questioningly when I didn't order a beer, but I'd been fucked up for weeks now and getting drunk wasn't going to fix it. I needed to keep my head clear and hope that eventually I could figure my shit out.

"Glad to see you're alive, man," Joe said dryly, turning to face me.

"Yeah, I'm sorry. I'm sorry about a lot of things. You know this isn't easy for me…apologizing and admitting I was wrong. But I've been a complete dick lately and you've been the one on the receiving end of most of my shit and I just wanted you to know…I'm sorry."

Joe didn't respond, just gave another head nod. I was thankful he wasn't going to drag out this emotional shit.

"You know you and I are cool, and I think we both

know I'm not really the one you should be apologizing to."

"I know," I sighed, wishing Joe was angrier with me. I deserved to be yelled at, I didn't deserve to be treated with the respect he was giving me. "She told you what happened?"

"Nope."

"Then how do you know I need to apologize?" I regretted the question as soon as I'd asked it, knowing it sounded like I was trying to pretend I had no blame in the situation, but that's not how I meant it.

"Oh, I don't know, maybe because I thought hell would freeze over before I ever saw Stacy cry, yet when she left that night after you took off it was fucking easy to tell she was fighting really hard not to break down. And then, I don't know, maybe the fact that she hasn't talked to me or anyone else in weeks because she's so fucking depressed, even though she'd die before admitting it. I'm trying hard not to assume the worst and go off on you, but I'll tell you this. You either apologize to Stacy or fess up about what happened. And if it's half as bad as I think it is, you can expect me to punch you in your fucking face. I love you man, but you can't treat women the way you've been treating her."

I didn't bother responding. I had no excuses or arguments, everything he said was right. I planned to apologize to Stacy, I just hadn't figured out how yet. If I stood any chance of earning her forgiveness, I had a feeling I'd have to do something pretty spectacular, and grand gestures really weren't my thing.

"I think it's good that you're taking some time off. Not that I don't wish you were out there with me, but you work too hard. I tell you that all the time. You deserve some time away from all the bullshit we deal with."

"Trust me, I'd rather be out there dealing with someone else's crazy shit than be stuck with mine in my house with no escape."

I didn't have to explain. Joe knew what I was referring to and for once, I was glad to have someone who knew everything so I didn't have to feel so alone in it all. Even though we never discussed my past, it was still a relief of sorts to be in the company of someone who truly understood.

"I deserve a hell of a lot worse from you after all the bullshit I always put you through. You're a good friend, and I'm...well..." I rubbed the back of my neck nervously, hoping he didn't give me shit over what I said next. "I love you, man."

Joe spit out his beer and the bartender ran over with a towel, mopping up the counter. "I'm sorry, man, I love you too. You just took me by surprise," he said with a grin and slap to my back.

"Alright, enough of this bromance shit. Now that I've officially lost my man card, I need to ask a favor of you. I'm sure she doesn't want to hear from me and will probably end up kicking me in my nuts as soon as she sees me, but I need to get ahold of Stacy. I was hoping maybe you could give me her number so I could get in contact with her."

Joe narrowed his eyes and looked at me like he was trying to figure out if I was serious or not. Seeking out Stacy to apologize definitely did not sound like something I would normally do, but I'd never fucked up this bad before, and even though Stacy and I could never be more than friends, I didn't like the idea of her hating me.

Joe took my phone and programmed her number in and said he needed to head out. I stayed behind a few minutes, trying to work up the courage to call her. I wussed out and decided to send a text instead.

Hey Stacy, it's Chad. Any chance you could meet me at Petey's?

I waited and waited, staring at my phone, my stomach in knots like some fucking teenage girl. Finally, twelve minutes later she responded.

Sorry, kinda busy tonight. Maybe another time.

I briefly considered looking up where she lived and stopping by her place, but if she didn't want to see me then acting like a stalker wasn't going to make anything better. I wanted her to know my apology was sincere, so I'd just have to wait until she was ready to give me a few minutes.

I left a five on the bar as a tip since I'd only had water and headed for my car.

When I pulled into my driveway I noticed a light on in my house, which was strange because I always turned out all the lights every time I left the house. Of course, I'd been so out of my mind lately that there was probably a good chance I just forgot this time.

I shrugged it off and unlocked the front door, but as soon as I pushed it open I heard a noise from the kitchen. I didn't have my gun on me, which was another habit I usually never broke. So I slowly made my way toward the kitchen, hoping the intruder wasn't armed.

As soon as I was close enough to steal a glance around the corner, I saw Stacy standing over the stove, stirring something.

"What the fuck, Stacy!?" I asked a little too loudly, and she jumped back, causing her to splatter whatever it was she was stirring and burn her hand.

"Dammit!" She yelled as she moved to the sink and put her hand under the faucet.

"What are you doing here? How the hell did you even get in?" I asked as I walked over to the cabinet behind her and pulled out a small emergency kit.

"Maybe you don't know so much about me. Maybe I have a criminal past and I used to break into people's houses all the time," she answered with a shrug.

"You used to break into houses and cook for people?" I smirked at the thought of Stacy being a criminal. She was wild, but not sneaky about it. I turned off the faucet and pulled her hand into mine, examining the area where she was burned.

"Yeah, maybe I did. Maybe I was really poor growing up and had to break into houses for food, and my penance was cooking it and leaving them left-overs so I didn't feel guilty."

"Why wouldn't you just shop lift? It'd be much less risky."

"There weren't any stores within walking distance," she replied softly, obviously distracted from my fingers rubbing across her hand lightly. Her skin was only slightly pink from the burn, but I was enjoying the excuse to touch her.

"So you only broke into houses close to you? That's even riskier. Someone could have recognized you."

She didn't respond, still staring down at my hand on hers. I couldn't help but smile at how distracted she was with such a small touch, but also couldn't ignore the stirring in my pants just from feeling her soft skin against my calloused hands.

"Stacy?"

"Hmmm?" She asked, finally tearing her eyes away from our hands and snapping out of her trance. "What did you say?"

"Nothing," I chuckled and let go of her hand. The

loss of contact made my stomach clench and I immediately wanted to reach out and take her hand back in mine, but managed to fight back the urge. "What are you doing here, Stacy?"

"Cooking," she replied dryly, like I was a dumbass for asking such an obvious question.

"Okay, but why are you cooking in my house? And how did you get in?"

"Does it really matter? I'm here now, and I'm making you spaghetti. Nothing fancy, I'm a horrible cook. It's pretty much the only thing I know how to make, so I hope you like store bought pasta sauce and noodles that are slightly undercooked."

I walked over to the stove and looked at the sauce that was about to start burning after being left on the stove for so long and at too high of a temperature. I turned off the stove top and moved the pot to a different burner. I wasn't an amazing cook, but my mom had taught me young how to take care of myself and I'd been living alone for so long that if I hadn't learned how to cook a few dishes I would be living off take out and microwave dinners.

"I love spaghetti, and soft noodles are for sissies. And if you won't tell me how you got in my house, will you at least tell me why you're in my house?"

Stacy sighed and looked down, as if she'd forgotten the answer to my question and could find it hidden somewhere on my tile flooring. Watching her fidget with her hands and shift her weight from one foot to the other was adorable, reminding me yet again that the tough as nails persona she portrayed wasn't all there was to her.

"I just didn't like how we left things at the bar," she mumbled so low I almost didn't catch it.

"I know…I wanted to apologize for that. It's why I asked you to meet me at Petey's. I didn't realize you were waiting for me at my house or I would have run home sooner." I winked and realized for the first time in over a week that I didn't feel like I was suffocating.

"I didn't know you were going to contact me or I would have just waited instead of breaking into your house like a crazy person. But I was afraid you were going to refuse to see me, so I may have had some help in getting in here."

Joe. That asshat.

I couldn't even be mad at him though. Seeing Stacy in my house, in my kitchen, looking so vulnerable…it made me realize how lonely my house had always felt. I'd never brought a girl home, and having Stacy there just felt…right. Maybe it was time to stop fighting whatever was causing the magnetic pull between Stacy and I. Maybe giving in and spending some time with her to see if I'd even enjoy her company wouldn't be the mistake I'd been convincing myself it was. Maybe if I stopped fighting my feelings then I'd stop feeling so out of control around her. Maybe….

CHAPTER 13

STACY

I wasn't sure what I'd been expecting to happen when Chad got home and saw me in his kitchen, but I was fairly certain I did *not* expect him to be laughing and joking with me. That easiness between us at the bar weeks ago returned, and I found Chad was actually really easy to talk to once we both cut out all the bullshit. He seemed so relaxed and just…happy. I suddenly wished I could get a picture of him like this so I could show Joe. He'd never believe me.

It took some convincing to get Joe to go along with this plan. He was a little mad at me for being such a bitch to him and then blowing him off for so long. After apologizing and explaining as best I could about why I was approaching Chad with a whole new set of motives, he reluctantly agreed to help. He seemed a little skeptical of whether or not my intentions this time really were sincere and not part of some hair brained scheme to hurt Chad, but he must have heard something in my voice that assured him I was being genuine, because he was surprisingly supportive.

When Joe texted me and said Chad was on his way to meet him at Petey's, it didn't give me much time to figure out my plan. If things with Chad weren't so rocky,

I probably would have been standing in his kitchen with nothing but an apron on, but since I was trying to make amends I figured things would go over better if I dialed things down a bit.

So in a very un-Stacy like fashion, I threw on a simple pair of jeans, paired with a fitted pink sweater and boots. It didn't do much to help my confidence to dress down, but I wanted to show Chad I could be down to earth. Every time he'd seen me up until this point I'd been dressed up and had my over the top personality on high gear. I thought that maybe if I toned it down he would feel more comfortable around me.

Joe told me where the extra key was hidden, and I was very surprised when I first walked in. His house was small but extremely tidy. I half expected to see pizza boxes and empty beer cans littering the floor, but it was almost a little alarming how clean it was. At first I thought maybe he just spent a lot of time alone here and cleaning was something for him to do, but I doubted that was the case. I saw all the girls that eyed him every time he was out anywhere. It was definitely a far fetched dream to think he didn't spend a lot of time with women.

I quickly decided to put a pin in that thought. I did not need to start acting jealous about Chad spending time with women. We weren't dating, hell we weren't even friends. He could do whatever, or whoever, he wanted in his free time. I was only there to make amends, see if we could reach some kind of truce so that we could be near one another without him nearly killing someone, or me nearly tearing off all my clothes.

I'd had to stop at the store for the supplies I needed to cook, and I had contemplated just bringing food already made since I was so terrible at cooking, but figured it was the gesture that would show how hard I was trying. Once I was inside his house though, I suddenly felt really lame for making such a simple dish that I would probably screw up anyway. Hopefully I just didn't catch his house on fire.

What was most unexpected was Chad rubbing my hand, trying to comfort me. His rough, calloused hands made my skin burn in an entirely different way than the splattering sauce had. Just a simple touch ignited my entire body and he sucked me in like a moth to a flame. His plain white t-shirt was snug against his broad chest, and the tender movements of his hands combined with his manly smell made me almost spontaneously combust. Chad was ruggedly handsome. He had a shadow of a beard from not shaving for at least a few days, his hair had grown out a little longer and I wanted badly to run my fingers through it.

Chad excused himself to freshen up while I finished up the spaghetti. Thankfully he had saved the sauce before it burned. When we sat down to eat though, the noodles were more than just slightly undercooked. Had

I even turned the water on? I expected Chad to tease me about it, but instead he sweetly tried to force himself to eat the food anyway. I finally took pity on him and chucked the food and suggested we order pizza.

Chad had insisted he do the clean up since I cooked, but considering we didn't even eat what I made, I figured it was my job to clean up the mess. So we ended up compromising and cleaning up together in comfortable silence, our hands occasionally brushing and other various body parts casually touching as we moved around each other in the small kitchen. Every time we made contact a zing of electricity would shoot through me, and several times I could have sworn I saw it affecting him as well. I told myself I was imagining things and tried hard to not get carried away in how good it felt to be near him.

After the pizza arrived we sat on his couch eating right out of the box, flipping through channels and not really settling on one specific show. When we couldn't find anything good on, Chad switched it to a soap opera channel and muted it and we spent the next several hours making up our own captions for what was going on. When our stomachs started to hurt from laughing so much, I yanked the remote out of his grip to find something else to watch. I saw Chad raise an eyebrow at me out of the corner of my eye, but he didn't say anything, just let me flip through the channels.

It was late and nothing was on, so I eventually gave

up with a huff. As much fun as I was having, I couldn't help wishing that the distance between us on the couch was smaller. I wanted to be snuggled up next to him, my head on his chest. I couldn't remember ever feeling that way about a guy. The intimacy of such an act usually made me uncomfortable, but I found myself wanting to be in his arms.

Glancing at the clock I realized it was after one in the morning, and as much as I wished he would make a move or ask me to stay, I knew that's not why I had shown up at his place and figured it was better to just leave before things went south. It seemed like every time we got close to each other is when shit would hit the fan.

I stood up to leave and turned to him, avoiding his eyes as I spoke. "Thank you for not kicking me out when you came home tonight, Chad. I had a really great time. It's um, it's getting late so I should probably…"

He yanked on my arm, pulling me down onto his lap and cut me off with a kiss. I immediately sank into his arms, wrapping my hands around his neck. His hands were tangled in my hair and I started gyrating my hips, the feel of his hardness underneath me fueling me and causing me to quicken my movements. My hands started roaming, eager to feel every hard line of muscle on his body from his chest down to his abs and around his back. The kiss grew hungrier and he bit my bottom lip hard as I tugged on the hem of his shirt and lifted it over his head.

I started trailing kisses down his neck and all over his chest. I noticed a few tattoos spread out over his otherwise perfect stomach, but I couldn't tell you what they were and I didn't stop to examine them more closely. I couldn't stop even if I wanted to. I wanted to taste and lick every inch of his body. His skin was smooth yet somehow rough at the same time, and I couldn't get enough.

I stopped long enough for him to pull my shirt over my head and his hands immediately pulled down the cups of my bra, exposing my hard nipples. He flicked one between his fingers and I moaned as he pulled the other into his mouth, licking and biting until I felt like I would explode just from his mouth on me.

I threw my head back and pushed my hands into his hair, pulling his mouth harder against my chest as he let out an appreciative moan. I knew he'd like it rough. I put my hand on his chest and pushed him back against the couch and slithered down his body until I was on my knees in front of him, and I started to undo his belt buckle.

"Wait, Stacy. Maybe we should slow down," he said as he put his hands over mine, stopping my movements.

"You've got to be fucking kidding me..." I mumbled under my breath as I stood up and fixed my bra, grabbing for my shirt that had been tossed aside.

"No, Stacy, listen it's..."

"Just stop right there," I snapped, holding my hand up to prevent him from saying anything else. "I get it; you don't want me. You said it before, no need to say it again. I hear you loud and clear this time, so don't worry, I'm leaving."

"Stacy, that's not what I was going to say," he said sternly as he tried to get between me and the door.

"Save it, Chad. This is the third time you've done this to me. I can only take so much rejection before I have to start putting the blame on myself. Coming here was a mistake. I thought…I thought we could be friends, but I don't think I can do that now. I can't just pretend I don't feel something for you, and I can't keep going through this humiliation every time you push me away." I turned away, trying to blink back the tears that were threatening. I'd spent more time fighting back tears since meeting Chad than I had in my entire life, and I'd be damned if I was going to let now be the time I finally broke down.

"Stacy, stop…"

I was out the door before he could finish. I had parked down the street so he wouldn't see my car when he first got home, and I didn't stop running until I reached the driver's side door, thankful for not having worn heels. I yanked the door open and heard Chad yelling my name and knew he had come running after me. I started the car and hit the gas and took off, not bothering to look back to see how close he was.

He'd humiliated me for the last time. I realized to-night how much I truly liked Chad, and I had even con-vinced myself for a while tonight that maybe we could have some sort of future together. I felt like a fool and now that there was a safe distance between us, I gave in and let the tears fall. For the first time in as long as I could remember, I cried. And it felt horrible.

CHAPTER 14

CHAD

Stacy took off right as I reached the bumper of her car. I stood in the middle of the street cursing at myself for being such an idiot. I don't know how long I stood there doing that, but when porch lights started to come on and a couple neighbors started yelling, I finally retreated back to my house, slamming the door behind me.

I should have realized what stopping her was going to look like. I'd not only walked away from her twice in the middle of a heated moment, but the last time I had gone as far as to tell her I didn't want her. Of course she would assume that me stopping her would mean I was about to say the same damn thing.

But that's not what I was going to say. I hadn't meant to pull her onto my lap, but when she said she was leaving instinct kicked in and my body just reacted. Then once her mouth was on mine and her hands were all over me, I realized how much I really wanted her, needed her. More than I needed to breathe. But I also didn't want her to think that sex was all I was after and that she didn't mean more to me than one night of pleasure. I wanted to take things slow, not cease them entirely. The whole night with her had been such a damn surprise, and just hanging out and laughing with her had been so easy.

It was the happiest I'd felt in years, sitting next to her, joking and letting my guard down for a few hours. It had changed something in me, made me want to let her in.

Yeah, she was wild and a little on the crazy side, but there was more to her than that. And if I was being totally honest with myself, I was the one who had been acting crazy for most of the time we'd known each other. Something about her called to me and I became a different person when she was near. I'd been fighting it so hard that it had cultivated into anger in her presence, but after the bar and taking the time to reflect on everything that'd happened since meeting her, I realized that I was the issue, not her. So when I found her in my kitchen, despite her having broken in, I was relieved. It was my second chance.

And I'd ruined it. She was there, in my house, in my arms, and it felt amazing. It felt right.

"Fuck!" I threw my fist into the drywall, busting a hole and making a mess. Thankfully I hadn't hit a stud or my hand would have been paying dearly for that outburst. Though I would much rather have been dealing with a broken hand than the pain in my chest right that moment.

I went back and forth over whether or not to chase after her. I wouldn't have to go after her at all if only she'd given me a chance to explain why I'd stopped things, why I wanted to slow things down. I didn't blame her, I couldn't after how I'd treated her. From the moment I'd met her I had been pushing her away.

I didn't understand it at first. Attractive women hit on me often enough, but the reaction my body felt to her had made something snap in me. It was as if my mind instinctively started pushing her away as a defense, but I hadn't just pushed her away, I'd been mean about it.

She'd come over tonight to make amends, even though I was the one who needed to apologize. I had to find a way to make it up to her. This couldn't be over. Even if she hated me and never wanted to talk to me again, she at least deserved to know that I wasn't pushing her away because I was rejecting her. I was pushing her away because I wanted her so badly and scared shitless of screwing up. And maybe, just maybe, if my luck hadn't completely run out, she might forgive me and I'd get a third chance.

CHAPTER 15

STACY

I'd been in a funk since the night at Chad's house, but I refused to act like a whiny chick about it. So what, he didn't want me, big deal. His loss.

That's what I told myself over and over again, even though it never did any damn good. I was just in denial. It fucking hurt having him reject me again. I'd been even bitchier than normal, and it was starting to seep into all aspects of my life.

Chad had called several times since our last blow out and I sent him to voicemail each time. When he started texting I considered changing my phone number. I had no desire to talk to him. Then to my surprise, he actually sent me flowers to my work. Lilies, which were my favorite flower, so either it was a coincidence or he'd actually taken the time to do some recon about me.

It was hard not to give in, almost physically painful to fight the urge to reach out to him and thank him, but I couldn't let myself do it again. I couldn't keep giving him all the power just to watch him use it to hurt me.

A few days after the flowers, his calls and texts started slowing down, and as much as I was actually enjoying how hard he was trying, I knew it was for the best if he just gave up. There wasn't anything he could say or do that would make me put myself out there again for him. Then when the contact ceased entirely, the sinking feeling in my gut about destroyed me, but I fought the urge to let it consume me.

I lost that battle the morning the stupid fucking alarm went off at work.

I was the first one to work one day and I entered the damn code wrong, which made the alarm start blaring. I didn't know the stupid password for when the security people called, so ten minutes later the cops showed up. And because I have the shittiest luck in the entire world, it was Joe and Chad that got the call to come to my office.

To say things were awkward would be an understatement of epic proportions. When they walked in and Joe saw me, he turned right back around and walked outside, without even saying a word to me. I'm sure he assumed something ugly was going to go down between Chad and I, considering I'd told him everything that had happened, but I was over it.

Okay, maybe not over it, but at least numb to it. Or at least I thought I was, because now that Chad was standing in front of me, only a few feet away, the piercing ache in my chest felt like a fucking ninja had shoved a samurai right through my chest cavity. I felt like all the air had been sucked out of my lungs, and seeing the look of vulnerability on Chad's face nearly killed me.

I opened my mouth to say something, but quickly shut it. I honestly had no idea what I would even say, it was just so quiet and awkward that I wanted to break the silence. Chad started to take a step towards me, but I backed up, shaking my head.

"You haven't returned any of my calls or messages. I got the delivery confirmation for your flowers, but I didn't hear from you. I asked Joe what your favorite flower was, and he had to do some investigative work to find out, but he said lilies. I thought maybe he got it wrong when I didn't hear from you, but…"

"Just stop," I snapped, wincing a little at the harshness of my own voice. He tried to take a step towards me again, but I met it with a backwards one of my own, this time looking him in the eye. I always felt so damn vulnerable around him and I was sick of it, so even if it meant pretending, I was not going to let him see how much his being there was hurting me.

"I guess Joe didn't know this is where you work. When the call came through I panicked. I was worried something bad happened here so I took the call. He's probably going to be pissed at me, but I…"

"Seriously, just stop!" Something inside of me just snapped. I didn't want to hear that shit. I didn't want him being nice and caring and pretending like he gave a shit about me, because he didn't. Maybe it was a game to him or maybe he was fucking crazy, but it felt like all he ever did was toy with me and I couldn't do it any more. "Just leave."

Pain flashed in his eyes, but was erased quickly by anger. "Fine," he bit out at me. Then without a glance back he walked out the door.

My day only got worse from there. By lunchtime I was almost to my breaking point.

"Stacy, a word please?" I didn't even try to hide the groan as I tossed my head back and trudged towards the office of the dentist I worked for. I plopped down on the chair in front of his desk that was covered in charts and papers. How he ever got a damn thing done I had no idea, the man's office was a mess. He was a decent enough guy, but somewhat of a push over. Usually he didn't bother to call me out on my shit, but like I said, I'd been bitchier than normal.

"I don't know what's going on with you, Stacy, but if you can't snap out of it then I'll have to force you to take some time off." I was laying back in the chair with my arm draped dramatically over my eyes. Even without seeing him I knew he was cringing, nervously waiting for me to lash out at him. It almost made me feel a little guilty that a grown man would be afraid to have what most would consider a civil conversation.

"Is this about that little shit this morning? He's fucking ten years old and he was crying like a little bitch. All I was doing was cleaning his teeth and he acted like I was ripping his fingernails off with pliers. And his mom was in the corner babying the shit out of him, so yeah, I lost it."

I was a dental hygienist and while even on a good day it was still pretty hard for me to keep my opinions to myself, today had been an exceptionally ridiculous one. After dealing with two patients this morning telling me how much they hated the dentist and then having that little twerp crying the whole time, I just kind of lost it.

"Alright buddy, quit acting like a whiney baby and shut it. If you're going to cry over a stupid cleaning, then I'll just give you a reason to cry. You see this sharp instrument in my hand? I'm being really careful with it right now, but when I hear little girls crying like you are it makes me jumpy, and I'd hate to accidentally stab...I mean poke you with it."

His mom had been pissed when I said that, but I wouldn't have had to threaten him if she would have just slapped him across the face like any good parent would do. He was seriously being a little shit, and personally, I felt I'd taken it easy on him. But apparently Dr. Doofus (the affectionate nickname I'd given my dentist) thought losing the family as patients because of my little outburst was a big deal.

"Stacy, I get complaints about you on almost a daily basis and for the most part I let it go, but you threatened a little kid. That's just not okay, and the worst part is, I'm not even sure whether or not you would actually do it. If you don't get control of yourself then I'm going to have to up my malpractice insurance. You've worked here for years and you're good at your job, even though you're horrible with people, but some things I can't just turn a blind eye to."

"Ughhhhh, I know, but I'm not bad with all of the patients. Just the ones who are idiots or annoying. Is it my fault that the majority of people fall under one of those categories?"

Dr. Doofus, or Dr. Daniels by his real name, had known my family for years. I grew up coming to his office and he hired me right out of school, but he was getting up there in age and his exhaustion was obvious. I felt myself actually feeling a little guilt, and shocked the shit out of both of us when I said, "I'm sorry, I promise I'll work on it."

It was hard not to laugh when his jaw dropped open. I was pretty sure he'd never heard the word 'sorry' come out of my mouth, but as much as I hated it, he was right. It was time I grew up and started behaving appropriately for my job.

The rest of the day was excruciating, having to paste on a fake smile and grit my teeth so I didn't spout off when a patient made a big deal about refusing to swallow their own spit. They swallow it all damn day, but because they're in a dental chair, all of a sudden the thought of swallowing their own damn saliva is disgusting? Yes, it would my pleasure to stop eighty thousand times during your cleaning just to suction up your saliva. It's not ridiculous or inconvenient at all.

By the time I made it home that night I was exhausted. Being nice and pretending to like people was more work than scraping last week's dinner out of their teeth and it drained me. Adalyn was at work...again. Her and Carrie had made up and were all buddy buddy, so I'd hardly talked to either of them in days, but we all had plans to go shopping the next day and I was grateful because I was in serious need of some girl time.

I was so pissed at Addy and Carrie for thinking I couldn't keep the secret they were planning for Ian. Apparently they'd been working on some elaborate plan to surprise Ian with some new product that was loosely based off of him, and they were going to do a big reveal at an upcoming charity event we were all invited to attend. After a few hours shopping and pampering courtesy of Ian's black Amex, though, I felt a lot better. Ian had insisted on treating us all for the event, and Adalyn really struggled with spending his money even though they were doing it like rabbits, but like hell was I going to pass up a girly day funded by my ridiculously rich friend.

We retreated to our favorite coffee house for some

caffeine after having fully exhausted ourselves from shopping. A guy near the door kept eyeing me, and as much as I appreciated the attention, I really wasn't in the mood to flirt. My ego was still bruised and despite hating myself for it, I was still feeling hung up on Chad. He really was attractive though, so when he flashed a stunning smile at me and headed my way, I decided maybe a little flirting was exactly what I needed.

Without even glancing in Carrie or Adalyn's direction, he walked right up to me and held out his hand. "I'm sorry, I couldn't help but notice you from across the room. It might sound like a line, but you are just so beautiful, I couldn't not introduce myself. I'm Scott." I gave him my hand and instead of shaking it, he kissed it, which felt a little cheesy to me, but sweet I supposed.

Then after several intense seconds he seemed to finally notice I wasn't alone as he glanced at the girls, then leaned down to loud whisper in my ear. "If you're going to shoot me down, can you at least do it gently? Don't want to embarrass myself in front of your friends here." His tone was playful and while he was extremely attractive, it was more in a pretty boy, Wall Street kind of way. He was obviously confident I wasn't going to shoot him down, though, or he wouldn't have bothered coming over.

We chatted a few minutes after Adalyn and Carrie introduced themselves, and after I gave him my number he said goodbye, promising to call the next day. I wasn't holding my breath. He was charming enough, but I hadn't felt very much of a connection, so it would shock me if I never heard from him.

Adalyn and Carrie headed back to the office to finish up some things for the charity event and I headed home. I wasn't even in my door before my phone lit up with a message from an unknown number.

I couldn't wait until tomorrow but didn't want to come on too strong, so I thought maybe a text message would make me seem less eager. ;-)

I laughed and shook my head, genuinely surprised at just how much charm this handsome stranger possessed, even through text. I decided to let him sweat a little bit and threw my phone on my bed, heading for the shower. An hour later, I'd almost forgotten about his text entirely, and when I went to look at my phone I had two more messages from him. He was coming across a little needy in my opinion, but it still felt good to have someone eager to pursue me.

Put a guy out of his misery and let me know I didn't scare you off.

Or if I did, at least give me a chance to show you I'm not some creep. ;-)

Maybe some girls would like the forwardness, but I tended to enjoy a good chase over blunt honesty. And his use of emojis was kinda weirding me out. I was half tempted to just ignore his texts entirely, but then chided myself for being so judgmental. Maybe my problem was that I never gave the good ones a chance, instead only ever going after the assholes like Chad.

Takes a lot more than a few text messages to scare me off. But you can make it up to me. I need a date for a big charity event the day after tomorrow. How would you feel about being my arm candy?

Scott agreed and we ended up spending the next couple of days texting back and forth with playful banter. It was only through text, but he seemed like a laid back guy and had a good sense of humor. At least, it seemed like he did because he didn't act offended when I'd send him inappropriate gifs.

Still, I couldn't help but think of Chad every time I thought about Scott. It was pissing me off. I even felt guilty at times for talking to another guy which was bullshit. Chad and I had never even dated! I was getting on my own nerves, so thank God I hadn't seen Carrie or Addy since we'd went shopping. I would have driven them crazy.

The night of the charity event Scott picked me up, and I had to admit, he looked just plain sinful in his black three-piece suit. Too bad I felt absolutely nothing when I looked at him, other than an appreciation for such a gorgeous specimen of a man. When he put his hand on my lower back to help me into his Audi I expected to feel butterflies, but...nothing. I felt comfortable near him, but no sexual tension. It was like being with Joe. Maybe my libido was broken.

Scott was great company. He was a gentleman and polite to everyone, and I was genuinely enjoying my time with him. I kept trying to talk myself into wanting to sleep with him, which was a fucking ridiculous thing to try and force, but anytime I tried to picture it I still felt...nothing. Every woman in the entire room was eyeing him like they would strip naked in front of the crowd if he'd give them the slightest bit of attention, yet here I was on his arm with my vagina dead to the world.

It was like Chad had caused the apocalypse of my sex life and my vagina had gone into some kind of self-preserving hibernation. Or like my sex drive had climbed into itself like a turtle that had been startled. I wondered if my ovaries had dried up and disintegrated from lack of use. Or if my G-spot was even still alive, or if it had lost hope and just gone into retirement. I hadn't even used Gerard in weeks. Was I even capable of an orgasm anymore? Just the thought of trying to find out made me cringe.

I understood why lonely women bought cats. When your pussy shrivels up and dies like mine apparently had, then you just go looking to replace it. Maybe I could look into a pussy transplant. Could you go to the ER and tell them your pussy was dying?

There was once a time when I felt like my loins were literally on fire. I actually walked up to a fireman in uniform and asked him to put out the fire in my pants with his big hose, which of course, he did. But now? It was a freaking ice box. I was sure if I went to see a gynecologist, when they went to do my exam a bat would fly out, since my vagina had turned into a cold, empty cave.

Maybe there were vagina mechanics? Maybe they could jump start my libido. Lube me up and hook me up with some new spark plugs. I could flash my headlights and help them blow a gasket while they cleaned out my rear exhaust. They could give me a full throttle body servicing and hook me up to some jumper cables to get my engine going.

Okay, I never really realized how much men compare sex to cars. There is no way it's a coincidence that practically every car term can be used as some kind of double entendre.

I remembered watching a TV show once about a woman who had a condition called Persistent Genital Arousal Disorder, where she was constantly in the state of arousal, like an orgasm that would build for days. They compared it to restless leg syndrome, but for your vagina. I was so jealous. On the show she was miserable and embarrassed because she would have spontaneous orgasms, but I thought that sounded fucking awesome. Anyone who would take that for granted was just an ungrateful bitch.

Can you imagine how much something like that would mess with a guy's head? Men wouldn't even have to try to get her to orgasm. They'd think all you had to do was look at a clit and a woman would just go toppling over the edge. The let down they would feel when they had to actually earn an orgasm would probably be devastating to their ego.

What would the opposite of that disorder be? I'd have to Wikipedia that shit when I got home, because I was sure I had it, whatever it was. All of my sex organs joining together and going on strike was bullshit. Forming a union and treating me like the enemy wasn't going to help, because I would have easily given them whatever they wanted if it meant they would just go back to work. Problem was, every time I would beg and plead for my sex parts to just tell me what the hell they wanted so I could put an end to the temper tantrum my vagina was currently having, they just ignored me. It was such a slap in the face, being treated like I hadn't spent the majority of my life trying to stimulate and please them daily.

I deserve better than this, dammit! I was mentally yelling and shaking my fist at my vagina, which signaled the beginning of the end for me. I was going to have to find a way to survive in this post-orgasmic world I had found myself in.

I was still cracking myself up at the expense of my dearly departed sex life as Scott and I joined Carrie in the ballroom. We took our seats and I kept one eye on the door, waiting for Adalyn to walk in with Ian. It was truly amazing what she had pulled off for him in such a short amount of time. Her creativity and artistic abilities had always impressed me, and the product she had made for Ian's company was just proof of how much talent she really had.

I couldn't wait to see Ian's face when he walked in, and I sat with my knee bouncing up and down as we waited for them to enter. Everyone had taken their seats and after about fifteen minutes past the time the presentations were supposed to start, I started to get worried. Where were Adalyn and Ian? The speakers on stage were concerned as well, sharing hushed whispers between themselves.

Suddenly the doors burst open and Ian appeared, yelling for me and Carrie. I started to jump up and run to him, because even with his dramatic entrance aside, there was panic written all over his face. Something was wrong, and Adalyn wasn't with him. But before I could get to him, someone pulled him up on stage.

Adalyn was supposed to speak first. She had worked hard on her speech, poured so much into it. It was clear Ian had no idea what was happening and the person talking was doing a great job of butchering all the hard work

Addy and Carrie had put into the comic they were presenting. It took everything in me to not just yank Ian off the stage, but luckily I didn't have to, because at the first opportunity he was running down the steps. I looked at Carrie and knew without asking that she was thinking the same thing as me. We jumped up and ran to the exit, Scott close behind us as we met up with Ian at the doors.

There was fear and desperation in Ian's voice as he gave us the CliffsNotes version of what happened, which apparently was his ex Maggie all by raping him, only to be interrupted by Adalyn when Maggie's tongue was shoved down Ian's throat. If I wasn't so worried about what Adalyn must be thinking and feeling, then I would have strangled him right there. How the hell could he do that to Adalyn?! I saw the pain in his eyes, and knowing how great of a guy Ian truly was, I didn't doubt that it was all a misunderstanding. Regardless of how shitty he was feeling, though, Adalyn was still out there somewhere alone.

We all rushed outside to our cars and it wasn't until I went to get my keys out of my clutch that I remembered I hadn't driven. I had completely forgotten Scott was even there, and I instantly felt guilty for him having been sucked into this shit storm.

"Scott, I'm so sorry. I know I haven't been great company and then all of this drama...thank you for coming with me. If you don't mind running me home so I can get my car, I'll find a way to make this up to you later." I gave him a tight, forced smile, because right then it was all I had to offer. All I could think about was getting in my car so I could start looking for Adalyn.

"No way, Stacy. You aren't driving when you're upset like this." I started to argue with him, but he interrupted me before I had a chance, which was probably a good thing because when I was stressed I was mean and I honestly didn't have time to be apologizing for my bitchiness. "I'll drive you. When you find Adalyn she's going to need you to be there for her, and you can't do that if you're in the hospital after wrecking your car."

"Scott, that's so sweet of you, and I really appreciate it, but I can't ask that of you. We don't even really know each other. I can't let you drive me around looking for my friend. It could take all night."

Scott didn't even respond, he just opened my door and I slid in. We sat quietly as I instructed him different places to go to in hopes of spotting Adalyn, but after hours of driving and still not seeing her, I was starting to lose it. Ian, Carrie and I had been in constant contact either by phone or text, and they were having just as bad of luck as I was. I tried to keep myself from thinking the worst, but the longer I went without hearing from Adalyn, the more worried I got.

Around five in the morning is when I started to really get worried. Scott took me back to my apartment to wait in case she came home while Ian and Carrie still traveled all over the city trying to spot her.

I'd been trying Joe's cell phone all night but he wasn't answering. I didn't know if it was because he was pissed at me for all the shit going on with Chad or if he was just busy, but I was starting to panic. Just disappearing without a plan or telling anyone where she was going wasn't like Adalyn. Even in the darkest time of her life, when she'd been raped in college by her asshole ex-boyfriend and his shithead group of friends, she hadn't run away like this. All I could think was that she had to be in a ditch somewhere, because she should have come home by now or found a way to reach me.

Scott drove me to the police station. Bill was working and said Joe was off duty. I tried to file a missing person's report but he said it was too early, she hadn't been gone long enough. Joe still wasn't answering his phone, even when Bill tried calling him, so I knew he wasn't just avoiding me. I decided to take a chance and drive to Joe's house with the hope that he'd be home and willing to help us.

I knew Adalyn was an adult and was probably fine, but she had no money, no phone and was emotionally distraught. To top it off she was in New York City, where one wrong turn could take you to extremely dangerous places and she didn't know the city all that well yet.

Scott followed my directions to Joe's house, but

when we got there; Chad's Jeep was in the driveway. I hesitated after he put the car in park on the street out front of the house, but despite how much I desperately did not want to see Chad, this wasn't about me. Adalyn could be in danger or hurt or worse, and my pride would have to be put aside.

I was faintly aware of the fact that Scott was following close behind me, but my brain was swimming with so many emotions it was hard to think about anything other than finding Joe and getting out as quickly as possible, hopefully managing to avoid a face to face with Chad. I raised my hand to knock, even though the door was never locked. I reached down and opened the door instead and stepped in.

My feet were killing me and I realized I was still in my gown from the event. I'd been freaking out so badly for the last several hours that I never thought to change my clothes. Suddenly standing in the middle of Joe's dark living room with people I'd never met scattered around, I was acutely aware of how ridiculous I must have looked in my formal attire.

I squinted my eyes to see if the one of the sleeping bodies scattered across the living room was Joe, but none of them were. I made my way out back when I heard people in the pool but I didn't spot Joe there either. It wasn't unusual for Joe or other houseguests to still be up partying this early in the morning. Or late in the night, depending on how you looked at it. Luckily, I still hadn't seen Chad. Maybe they had gone somewhere in someone else's car?

I approached Joe's bedroom and when I went to turn the knob I could hear moaning from the other side. I knew Joe didn't care if people witnessed his sexual acts, but I still felt bad to interrupt. I stood outside the door for several seconds trying to decide if I should wait. Realizing Scott was still standing behind me I turned and asked him to wait in the car. It was bad enough me having to walk in and bear witness to whatever devious acts were happening behind Joe's door. I didn't want to subject my poor date to that, especially considering how patient he'd been this whole night even though he barely knew me or Adalyn.

Once Scott was out of sight I turned back to the door and pushed it open slowly. Not sure why I did that. It probably would have been smarter to make a loud noise so they knew I was there, but it felt rude barging in. Because you know...sneaking up and creeping on people while they're having sex is much more polite.

When I had pushed the door open far enough to see inside I saw Joe standing a few feet away from me, his head thrown back while a half naked woman was on her knees giving him a very enthusiastic blow job. They still hadn't noticed me, and right when I went to cough and make myself known, Joe came to orgasm and he let out a loud moan as he gripped the hair of Hooker McSucks-Alot, who had upped her rigorous tempo while he filled her mouth with his man juice.

I must have let out some kind of noise, probably a surprised gasp or some other noise that someone who accidentally witnesses her friend getting sucked off would make. My timing was indeed impeccable. If I wasn't so distracted from how stressful the night had been then the sight in front of me might have actually turned me on. Or made me crack up.

However, when Joe turned to look at me, finally noticing my intrusion, an entirely different noise came out of me.

A choked sob escaped my throat when I realized the face looking at me wasn't Joe, it was Chad.

I barely had time to register the surprise and embarrassment on his face before I bolted out of the door. I collided with Joe in the hallway, who grabbed me by my midsection as I tumbled over, partially from impact, but mostly because I was doing my damndest not to start retching all over his floor.

When he noticed the tears falling silently down my cheeks he pulled me up and tucked me into his side, ushering me down the hall and into the kitchen.

"I...I'm sorry...I shouldn't...I...Adalyn...She...But I should have...Oh my God…" I wasn't making sense and I was mortified at my lack of self control. I couldn't believe I was breaking down like that in front of someone. So many emotions came barreling forward as I stood in Joe's kitchen while he held me tightly in his arms, making soothing sounds.

Somewhere inside of me I knew I had no right to be so upset about Chad being with another woman. I had rejected him this last time, it was what I told myself I wanted. And despite how gutted I felt every time I thought about him, I was starting to feel like maybe it had been the right decision after all. That is, until I actually saw him with someone. Now...now I just felt like I was the biggest fucking idiot on the planet.

Later. I'd think about that later. Adalyn was my priority and I needed to get my shit together.

I pulled back, my tears finally starting to dry up, and seeing the look of sheer horror on Joe's face actually made a nervous bubble of laughter pop out. He still had no idea why I was so upset, and I was sure he had no clue what he was supposed to do to help me, but the confusion and fear in his eyes told me he cared. I shook my head, wiping my eyes and smiling apologetically. I'd been somewhat avoiding Joe since the fallout with Chad, needing to give myself some distance from the situation, but I had really missed him.

Realizing I'd wasted entirely too much time upset about seeing Chad, I quickly recapped the night's events to Joe. Like the flip of a switch Joe got serious, his entire body tensing up. Work Joe. Badass Joe. All business Joe was making an appearance, and though he was very intimidating when he got this way, knowing he was taking my concerns seriously calmed my nerves.

Chad appeared, pulling a shirt over his head and I turned back to Joe and buried my face in his chest, lightly shaking my head, hoping Joe would get the message that I didn't want to talk to Chad. His chest tightened, but he didn't say a word. He just grabbed my arm and led me in the opposite direction, away from Chad, and took me out front through the garage.

"Thank you, Joe. I'm so sorry for…"

"Stacy, stop," he cut me off mid apology. "You know I love you. No apologies necessary. I'm just glad you came to me. I'm sorry I wasn't able to help sooner; I didn't realize my phone was dead. Right now you need to go home and get some rest and let us look for Adalyn. I'm sure she's fine but she will probably be exhausted and emotional and will need someone to lean on, so you need to be rested for her."

His words were firm with no inflection, but I knew what he was doing. His confidence and commanding body language told me he was in control and everything would be fine. I threw my arms around his neck, even though he'd already switched over to cop mode, and when he didn't return my hug it didn't bother me in the least.

"Do you need me to take you home? I'm not sure you should be driving with how exhausted you must be."

"It's okay, I have a ride," I said, motioning to Scott standing behind me, holding the passenger side door open. Knowing we had reinforcements relaxed me enough to realize how horrible tonight had been and I felt terrible all over again that Scott had gotten sucked into such a mess.

Joe arched an eyebrow in question, but gave no other response other than a quick head nod as he turned back to the house. He yelled over his shoulder, demanding I get some sleep and promising to call me when they had found Adalyn. The fact that he'd said "when" and not "if" did not escape me, and the exhaustion that the adrenaline had been holding back finally fell over me like a heavy blanket. My limbs felt heavy and my eyes sagged, still burning from crying.

I made my way over to Scott and he drove me back to my apartment in silence. He offered to come in with me, but I politely declined, feeling like I had already taken advantage of his kindness long enough. I gave him a chaste kiss on the corner of his mouth when he walked me to my door. Right as I pulled away from him my phone rang and my hands were shaking so badly from lack of sleep that I dropped my phone when I tried to pull it out of my bag.

Scott answered it for me and I could hear Joe on

the other end, telling him they had found Adalyn and she was on her way to the emergency room. After hearing emergency room, everything else faded out. I took off running towards my car, but Scott caught up to me quickly, grabbing my hand.

"Stacy, let me drive you."

"No, it's okay Scott, you've been so great tonight. You should get some rest. I already feel horrible about how tonight has gone and you must be exhausted. I've put you out enough"

Scott shook his head and grabbed my hand, leading me back to his car. "That's nonsense, Stacy. I don't mind at all, I'm glad to be able to help. Once we know Adalyn is fine then we can both rest, but I'm fine to wait. In fact, I insist."

I wished so badly that I felt more for Scott than just kinship and slight physical attraction. He had been beyond amazing and anyone else would have fallen hard over someone as perfect as him, but my heart just wasn't in it. Maybe we could make it out of this and remain friends. We hadn't crossed any physical boundaries so keeping things platonic might actually work.

I may have dozed off a little on the way to the hospital, because suddenly Scott was gently nudging my arm. My eyes popped open as soon as I realized where we were. The brief amount of rest I'd gotten had actually made my body feel about a hundreds times more fatigued than before, but adrenaline kicked back in as I jumped out of the car and ran into the emergency room.

I halted abruptly, causing Scott to crash into the back of me, when I spotted Chad standing at the desk, speaking with a doctor.

CHAPTER 16

CHAD

A commotion at the doors to the emergency room caused the doctor to pause mid sentence, and I turned to follow his line of sight. Right there, a few feet away from me, was Stacy. She looked exhausted - her hair was disheveled, her eyes had bags under them and were puffy from crying, but mostly she looked absolutely stunning. I knew I'd fucked up back at Joe's, and I knew it would be best to just give her some space, but I so badly wanted to run to her and try to explain. And I almost did, until I saw the man standing behind her. The same one who I'd seen her drive away with as I watched out the window at Joe's. He slid his arm around her waist and whispered something into her ear. The gesture was so intimate, and all of the guilt I felt about Stacy walking in on my dumb ass getting a blow job went right out the window and was swiftly replaced with rage.

I knew I had no right to feel so possessive over her after I'd given up trying. But seeing another man with her was like having a bucket full of ice water doused over my head. I was a fucking idiot for accepting that she didn't want me, but no matter who the hell this guy was, Stacy was mine. Or at least, she would be, because despite how fucked up things were, there was no way in hell I was giving up again.

Stacy looked defeated and it tugged at my chest, but as soon as she saw the fire raging in me from the sight of her with another man, a fierceness overcame her. You could literally see her walls coming up and her face hardening as she geared up for a fight.

With his hand still on the small of her back, Stacy marched right up to the desk I was standing at and asked the nurse at the computer where to find Adalyn. She stood so close to me that I could smell her shampoo mixed with the light scent of her perfume, and despite how badly I wanted to punch the asshole that was touching her in the face, I wanted to wrap my arm around her and pull her into me that much more. I found my hand moving towards her, almost automatically, but as soon as my fingertip touched her arm she jerked away from me.

Never one to back down, Stacy looked me right in the eye and let me see everything she was feeling. Sadness, anger, betrayal and disappointment. If it hadn't been for the flicker of sadness, I would have thought she truly hated me. When she stormed past me in the direction of Adalyn's room I took off after her.

I started to call out for her, but she ducked into Adalyn's room, with her date still stuck to her side. Fucking asshole couldn't even give her two minutes of space to check on her friend?

Of course not, idiot, he's just being supportive. Unlike you who's being a giant dick.

Shit, I needed to get my act together. So Stacy had a date? What she had seen was much worse and I had no right to be angry. I was the one who kept pushing her away. I deserved the pain searing through me at the thought of another man touching her. I deserved worse, but it didn't stop me from desperately wanting to lay claim to her and tell that mother fucker to get lost.

"Dammit!" I yelled as I kicked a waiting room chair. A nurse ran up to me as I ran my hand over my face, asking me to calm down or leave. I just waved my hand dismissively, ignoring the huff she gave as she stormed back to where she'd come from. I needed to get ahold of myself before Stacy came back out. I had a lot that needed to be said, and saying it when I was pissed would only make things worse.

I paced back and forth for over a half an hour before Stacy and her date finally came out of the room. Her eyes locked with mine immediately, and I braced myself for her to walk away or scream at me, but instead she walked right up to me and wrapped her arms around me, pulling me into a gentle hug.

I was so stunned that I didn't move at first, but after a couple seconds my body relaxed and I pulled her tightly against me, all the anger I'd been feeling moments ago just melting away. After an entirely too short amount of time, Stacy finally pulled back, tears streaming down her face.

"Thank you for finding her, Chad. I'll never forget it," she whispered, then turned around and took her date's hand in hers and walked towards the elevators.

What. The. Fuck.

Why did that hug and her words sound so much like a goodbye? Why did I hear resignation in her voice, as if she knew those were the last words she would ever speak to me?

I took off towards her, determined to not let her pull away from me entirely like this, but the elevator doors closed right as I neared them. I just stood there watching the door close as she averted her eyes, each tear falling down her cheek proving what a worthless piece of shit I really was.

CHAPTER 17

STACY

Scott took me home to change and we finally parted, after having a brief discussion about staying friends. I was afraid to hurt his feelings, but he made it easy for me, saying he knew without me explaining that my heart belonged to someone else. I wanted to get angry at him for assuming shit, especially knowing he meant Chad, but he was right and I was fucking tired and he'd been a saint, so I bit my tongue instead.

I changed out of my dress, finally, and fell onto the bed. The doctors said when Chad had brought Adalyn in she was unconscious and would remain that way for a while, so I set my phone alarm to wake me in two hours.

When my alarm went off it felt like I'd been asleep for five minutes. Every muscle in my body ached like I had just ran three fucking marathons in a row. I had blisters on my feet from my shoes and all I wanted was to take a hot, relaxing bath, but I needed to get to Adalyn. I wanted to be there when she woke up. So I quickly tossed some of her stuff, along with mine, into a bag and headed to the hospital.

Ian was in her room when I got there, holding an extra cup of coffee for me.

"Thank you, but you need to get the fuck out." I

yanked the cup out of his hands and threw myself into the chair next to Adalyn's bed. She was still out cold and she looked so small and broken lying in that bed. My heart ached for her, knowing the kind of pain she was feeling, even if she wasn't conscious.

"I'm not going anywhere," Ian stated, stiffening his spine and crossing his arms like a toddler about to have a fucking temper tantrum.

"It's not a request. I get why you're here, Ian, I do. You feel bad and want to make sure she's okay, but when she wakes up she's not going to want to talk to you. At least not right away. I promise I'll keep you updated, but you can't be here right now. If you really want to make it up to her, then start by giving her some space."

Ian sighed and ran his hand through his hair, making me promise to let him know as soon as I had an update, and left, saying he'd be in the waiting room. I tried to sip on the coffee he'd brought me, but it just burned in my empty stomach and made me feel queasy. So instead I pulled my chair up next to Addy's bed and laid my head back, dozing off.

I woke to a scream, and shot straight out of my chair, lunging myself at Adalyn when I realized she was the source of the screaming.

"Ian...Maggie...hurts...why…" She wasn't making sense. Her words came out choppy and almost unintelligible, and I wondered if she was even aware of them coming out. Nurses rushed in as her heart monitor beeped off the charts, while I tried to calm her down. She never even looked at me, like she didn't recognize my voice. Then she was out again, dead to the world, after the nurses injected some kind of sedative into her arm.

Adalyn didn't speak again after that. When she finally came to, she was eerily calm. Honestly, it scared the shit out of me. She had done this after the rape, but it was different this time. Even in the quiet hours I'd spent sitting with her the weeks following the rape, you could still feel the emotions rolling off of her. This time, though, it was like she was dead inside. I tried to talk to her a few times, and the one time I said Ian's name, she freaked out again.

After sedating her the second time, I stepped outside with the doctor and gave him some background on Adalyn and what happened back in college. I gave the doctor her parents' phone number, who gave him permission to contact the psychiatrist who treated Adalyn after the rape. I was surprised to find out the psychiatrist was flying out, and it made me worry that things were more serious than I initially thought.

I felt like shit when I finally insisted Ian leave the hospital altogether. I knew he was hurting, and as much as I loved him, my loyalty was to Adalyn. Knowing Ian my whole life definitely added to my guilt, but Adalyn needed me more than he did. I knew he understood and wasn't angry with me, but it still killed me to see two of my best friends hurting so badly.

Weeks went by and Adalyn still wasn't speaking. I'd returned to work part time, only because I had bills to pay. I was so worried about Addy; I didn't want to leave her. I could tell my constant hovering was starting to make her crazy, though. Ian had been blowing up my phone constantly asking for updates, but I never had anything to tell him.

Then one day I got a call at work. One of the girls I worked with pulled me out of the operatory and said there was an emergency. My first thoughts went to Adalyn and I panicked.

"Fuck!" I ignored the gasp coming from the patient lying in my chair who had been startled by my outburst. I never in a million years could have predicted what would be waiting for me on the other line.

"Hello?!" I yelled anxiously into the phone.

"Calm your tits, Stacy."

"Adalyn?" I could hear her laughing on the other end of the phone. Fucking laughing. Bitch hadn't opened her mouth in weeks, then calls me out of the blue cracking up like she hadn't been out of her damn mind the last month. Was I in some sort of twilight zone? Did I huff some nitrous oxide and pass out?

"Yeah, it's me. Sorry, Ian's being ridiculous."

"Ian?! What is happening right now!?" The patients

in the waiting room were staring at me, but I didn't care. "What the hell is going on!? Why are you with Ian? When did you start talking? I feel like I'm losing my shit here, Addy!"

More laughing. "I'm sorry, Stacy. I promise I'll catch you up. But first, I need a favor…"

I called Joe as soon as I got off the phone with Adalyn and told him what happened between her and Maggie. I still couldn't believe Adalyn had run into her on the street and beat the shit out of her. It was so out of character for her, but I was so proud I could cry.

I knew it was a lot to ask, for Joe to be able to help if Maggie pressed charges, but I felt obligated to do what I could to protect Adalyn. There was no way in hell I would let Maggie cause her any more grief, not if I could help it.

Joe was not usually such a stickler for rules, but he was with Chad and said that there was no way Chad would let him go along with anything that would 'obstruct' an investigation. Fucking Chad.

"Put him on the phone," I demanded. I waited through several seconds of silence before yelling, "Now, dammit!"

"Stevens."

"Cut the shit, I know it's you. I told him to hand you

the damn phone. Now listen to me, you son of a bitch, you fucking owe me. I'm not the kind to hold grudges, but I haven't forgiven you for being such an asshat. So if you care at all about how you hurt me, then this is your chance to make it up to me."

I waited for him to say a smart ass comment or tell me to fuck off, but after a minute or so of silence, I took that as a cue to keep talking.

"Adalyn beat the shit out of that bitch Maggie who fucked up her life the night at the charity event. You saw first hand how messed up Adalyn was after that, so you have to understand why I can't let Maggie come after her, which she undoubtedly will. She's a psychotic whore with too much time on her hands and a propensity for drama."

I heard Chad sigh. "What do you need, Stacy? I won't break or bend the laws. If Maggie wants to press charges I can't stop her. I want to help, I really do, but I don't know what I can do for you."

"All I need you to do is make sure you guys are the ones who talk to her when she decides to file a report. I just need five minutes alone with her before you actually write it up, that's it. If she still wants to press charges after talking to me, then fine, I'll let it go. I drove by Maggie's place and she isn't home, and based on what Adalyn told me, she most likely went to the hospital. I doubt she's all that injured, but she'll want a medical claim on file if she goes after Adalyn. She'll be blowing things out of proportion and milking the situation. All I need is five minutes. Can you do that for me Chad?"

The silence between us was killing me. I glanced at my phone to make sure I hadn't lost him, but it was still connected. I was trying not to freak out and say something like 'I don't have all fucking day,' because I needed him on my side. Pissing him off probably wasn't a good way to get him to help.

So I waited for several minutes, which felt more like hours, then let out the biggest sigh of relief when Chad finally agreed. It wasn't even five minutes after we hung up when the text came in, saying they'd gotten the call and were going to the hospital to take Maggie's report.

The hell they were. Not if I had anything to do with it.

CHAPTER 18

CHAD

I shouldn't have agreed to go along with Stacy's request, but hearing her voice fucked with my head. I hadn't seen her or talked to her since the night I brought Adalyn to the hospital, and knowing I would see her again any minute made me nervous as shit.

Joe and I stood outside Maggie's door waiting for Stacy. When she finally stepped out of the elevators that were a few feet away from us, all of the air was sucked out of my lungs. She was more stunning than I remembered, and the determination on her face made my cock hard. It used to drive me up the wall how brazen and stubborn Stacy was, but knowing she was there to help her friend reminded me of how much I enjoyed sparring with her, even when I wasn't admitting it to myself.

I held my hand out in front of her as she tried to enter Maggie's room. "Five minutes, that's it. Whether you're done or not, we're coming in." She gave me a quick nod and walked past.

I should have walked away. I knew whatever was going to happen in that room was something I shouldn't be witness to, unless I wanted to end up arresting Stacy again. The girl had no shame and no fear. It was both endearing and fucking annoying. But I couldn't bring myself to walk away. Joe was distracting the nurses so they wouldn't go in and I had to make sure no one else would try to enter either. So I stayed glued to my spot, hoping to hell that Stacy would keep her voice down so I didn't actually hear anything.

I should have known better than to wish for Stacy to be quiet. She only had one level when she was angry, and it was somewhere between shouting and screeching.

"Listen, you stupid fucking whore, I'm only going to say this once, so you better shut your cum stained mouth and listen up. I'm not going to tell you not to press charges against Adalyn, that's your decision, but I should at least warn you. If you do that, then the beating you took from Adalyn will feel more akin to being licked by kittens by the time I'm done with you. I should have beat your nasty ass when you screwed over Ian, but I didn't per his request. I left you alone, and believe me when I say that it won't happen again. And if you for one second think that I won't actually track you down and make you fucking pay for hurting my friends, then you are in for a bitch of an awakening. Because I won't just kick your ass, I will torture you slowly and I will get sick pleasure out of it. And no amount of plastic surgery will be able to undo the damage that I do to your already ugly as fuck face. But I won't stop there. Oh no, I won't stop until I've made your reputation just as ugly to match. You will be a laughing stock and no one, not even the most desperate of people, will want to be near you. You will be all alone, like I know you've always feared. The facade you've worked so hard for, pretending to be better than you are, will be shattered, and people will see you for the piece of shit you truly are."

I slapped myself on the forehead with my hand, cursing at myself for not having walked away when I knew I should, while also fighting the urge to laugh at everything Stacy had just said. She was truly bat shit crazy, and any one who had overheard any of that would admit to you that it was awesome. I didn't know one other person in the world who would have been able to deliver such a ridiculous threat in such an eloquent way. It came out so naturally that you could tell Stacy was just speaking off the cuff and it wasn't rehearsed. That crazy shit was just pouring right out of her mouth, like saying those types of things was just a daily occurrence for her.

There was some mumbling, more words exchanged that I couldn't make out, and then Stacy emerged. Her chin was high and she was grinning from ear to ear. When we made eye contact her smile faltered a little, but not entirely. I had the sudden urge to fall on my knees, right in the middle of the fucking hospital hallway, in my full uniform, and beg for her forgiveness. But before I could, she muttered a "thanks" and was disappearing back into the elevator.

Two months. Two whole months after I made what was probably the biggest mistake of my life pushing Stacy away, I was still thinking about her constantly. Seeing her at the hospital, even briefly, was enough to gut me. I didn't know what the hell I was thinking that night at Joe's. I'd just been so fucking depressed, and it was screwing with my head. I didn't get depressed, especially over women. So when Leelah, the little brunette from Joe's party a while back, came on to me, my dick took over.

It was a piss poor excuse, but I just wanted relief from the ache in my chest. A brief moment in time to get Stacy out of my head and feel something other than resentment and loathing towards myself. As soon as it was happening, I knew it was a mistake. It didn't make me feel better, it made me feel like shit. It literally only took Leelah about two minutes to get me off because it had been so long since I'd had any kind of release. And picturing Stacy in my head the whole time made me feel like a dick, especially when she materialized in the room, as if conjured into existence by my pathetic thoughts.

I was giving Stacy space, and if I was totally honest with myself, I was too ashamed of myself to face her. I tortured myself constantly by wondering if Stacy was dating that guy she'd been with. If he'd had his hands on her and had her body underneath of him. It was bordering on obsession, how much Stacy consumed my thoughts.

Joe was barely speaking to me. He was cordial and professional, but we hadn't hung out outside of work since before the night I found Adalyn. I tried several times to get him to talk to me about Stacy, or anything at all, but he quickly changed the subject. I didn't have to ask; I could tell Stacy had told him what she'd witnessed. Sometimes I wished he would just fucking go off on me and tell me what a piece of shit I was.

After spending so many evenings alone in my house I was starting to go stir crazy, so I texted Joe asking him to hang out. I needed to figure out if I wanted to try and make things up to Stacy or move on, and I needed someone to talk it through with. Hours ticked by with no response and I started to get antsy, pacing back and forth in my living room.

I was never an especially cheery guy, even before all the shit that went down with my parents, but I'd never been a full out asshole to someone. I'd been nothing short of lucky when I got partnered up with Joe. For several years I'd had no one in my life. No friends, no family, just work. I'd become completely closed off from the rest of the world, but Joe hadn't given up. He'd pushed to get through to me no matter how much of a dick I was to him. So if he was upset enough with me to be completely blowing me off, then I had definitely gone too far this time.

I tried one last time to contact Joe and when he didn't get back to me, I decided it was time for more extreme measures. I would just have to track him down and hash things out. The thought of a heart to heart made me feel like a pussy, but I had to accept that I couldn't go on with the way things were. It was making my job miserable and as much as I hated to admit it, I missed my friend.

He wasn't at the gym or Petey's, so I drove to his house. He was coming out right as I was approaching, and I slowed almost to a stop when I saw Stacy following him. They were laughing and she looked so carefree and happy I almost turned the car around and left. There was a good chance that my presence in her life would only continue to hurt her, but I had to try. I was a selfish prick and knew Stacy would be better off if I just left her alone, but I couldn't do it.

I watched them get into Joe's pickup and like the stalker I was apparently becoming, I followed them. When they finally pulled up into the parking lot of a new dance club called Grind, the same one I'd initially met Stacy at, I had to seriously consider my options. To say I had no desire to step foot inside that place would be an understatement.

When Stacy climbed out of Joe's truck and I finally took a look at her, the decision was made for me. She was wearing a little black dress that was low cut in the front, perfectly showcasing her tits, tight around the waist and flowing at her hips then stopped midway down her thigh. She had on the highest heels I'd ever seen that did amazing things for her toned legs. The images running through my mind would have my mother rolling over in her grave.

I hung back a few minutes after they entered the club before I approached. The bouncer looked me up and down and it was then that I realized how I must look. I had on worn jeans and a tight black t-shirt and boots. Not that I looked like shit, but I'm sure I didn't look worthy to be going into some fancy ass dance club. When I realized he wasn't going to let me by, I flashed my badge. I hated doing that when it wasn't necessary, abusing my power like that, but it was for a good cause. I had apologies to make.

When I finally made it inside I immediately started scanning the crowd for Stacy. I couldn't spot her so I spotted a staircase that led up to a second level that overlooked the entire dance floor and figured I would have a better chance of finding her once I had a better vantage point.

It only took a few minutes once I was on higher ground to spot her and my heart rate picked up when I saw her dancing and swaying on the dance floor, her eyes closed and arms lifted high above her head. She danced like she was the only one in the club and it was breathtaking. I spotted Joe a few feet away dancing with some brunette little number and when I looked back to Stacy she had been joined by a man. Her back was to his front and she was shimmying down his length, rubbing her ass against his crotch. Then he turned slightly, and I saw that it was the guy from that night at the hospital. Her date.

By the looks of how close they were, they had to be together. The anger that coursed through my veins was almost paralyzing, and I had to take deep, steady breaths to gain some control over myself. I knew storming down there and starting a fight would only make it worse.

I saw Stacy lean in and say something in his ear, then she walked off the dance floor towards the bathrooms. There was my chance. Enough observing. Time for action.

CHAPTER 19

STACY

I was washing my hands when the door to the bathroom opened, and I could sense without looking that it was Chad. I don't know how I knew, but I could feel the air start to buzz with the same sparks I always felt when Chad was near.

I wanted to be angry, to turn around and yell at him and tell him to go fuck himself, but before I could do anything his hands wrapped around my waist. He dug his fingers into my hips and pulled me back so that I was flesh up against him, my ass the perfect level to his crotch because of the height my heels gave me.

I gave in to the lust that took over me from being held so close to his body and I tilted my neck to the side as I laid it back against his shoulder, inviting his mouth to taste me.

"Stacy," he moaned, pressing kisses to my neck. Someone emerged from one of the stalls and my eyes popped open. She gave us a dirty look and stormed out, and luckily the interruption was enough to clear my senses.

I pulled away and turned to face him, trying to remember why I was angry with him. I purposefully conjured up the image of him with that slut's mouth on him, but him being so close was making my brain foggy. Despite all the shit he'd put me through, I still had to fight not to reach out to him. My heart wanted to forgive him and feel his arms around me, but my head knew it would be a mistake.

"Are you with him?" He growled. It took me a second to realize who he was talking about. Part of me wanted to say yes, just to hurt him, but I couldn't. I didn't want to lie or play games anymore. I just wanted to move on.

"No, he's just a friend."

He nodded but looked skeptical, like he didn't believe me.

"I can't do this," I said as I pushed past him. He grabbed my arm and tried to stop me, but I yanked out of his grasp and headed back out to the dance floor. Scott was dancing with another girl and I didn't want to interrupt him, especially if Chad was going to follow me out to the dance floor. So instead I headed towards the bar, torn between hoping Chad would go the fuck away and wanting him to follow me.

"Stacy," he said from behind me right as the bartender approached. I turned away from the bartender to look at Chad. I couldn't do this with him. Not right then, and maybe not ever. But something in me wanted to feel him close to me one last time. So I grabbed his hand and dragged him towards the dance floor. "What are you doing?" He called from behind me.

"We're going to dance!" I yelled back over my shoulder as we pushed through the crowds of people, which wasn't easy because the dance floor was packed. I dragged us to a spot near the corner that was dark. Even though we would be surrounded by people, I wanted to feel like we had a little privacy. If this was the last time I'd be this close to him, I wanted to make the most of it.

We came to a stop and I turned to face him, throwing an arm over his shoulder and using my other hand to pull one of his arms around my waist, just above my ass. Some sort of tortured expression crossed his face, as if dancing with me were something he really had to think about, so I started to jerk out of his arms. Of course he would fucking reject me again. But I didn't get anywhere because as soon as I tried to pull away, he pulled me back tighter. His hands slid down from my waist to cup my ass and he growled in my ear.

"Quit walking away from me, Stacy. I'm not letting you get away this time."

I should have kept going, but I was pissed and wanted to hurt him. It was my turn to reject him. So I put my hands on his shoulders and shoved as hard as I could. "Fuck you!" I yelled as I turned to storm off, but he used both arms to grab me around my waist and pulled me back to him so hard it almost knocked the air out of my lungs. Hatred and lust warred with each other inside of me, turning into a storm of sexually fueled anger. I wanted to slap him, but instead I put my hand around his neck and yanked his face down to mine, kissing him as hard as I could. It was bruising and painful, but he kissed me back with as much fever, and soon the kiss turned from anger to hunger.

All the tension that had been building between us over the last few months was being let out in this one moment. The bodies closed in tighter around us as Chad broke our connection and started biting and sucking down my neck. I glanced around to see if anyone was noticing us groping each other like horny teenagers on the dance floor, but everyone was too busy dancing or too drunk to care.

Chad reached up and yanked the top of my dress down just enough to expose one breast, then he pulled the nipple into his mouth, sucking and biting on the tip. A moan slipped past my lips, but it was drowned out by the loud music. Chad reached around to grab my ass then using his hands on my hips he swung me around quickly, putting my back to his front. I pushed up against him, grinding my ass into his cock and he slid his hand down to my thigh, caressing his way back up.

Shivers shook me all the way from my neck to my core, and my clit started throbbing as he took ahold of my lace panties and yanked them off, throwing them down on the ground. I yelped at the flash of pain from the fabric ripping against my flesh and he bit down on my shoulder. My nipple was still exposed and he was twisting and flicking it between his fingers with one hand while the other made its way to my pussy. He inserted one finger, and I clenched around him while he sucked on my earlobe. I reached a hand between us and started stroking his hard cock over his pants.

I flicked his pants open with one hand and yanked down his zipper. Before I could reach into his boxers and grab him, he was pushing my hand away and bending me over slightly. Sweat started to drip down my neck and between my breasts, and feeling a crowd of people rubbing up against us as he pushed into me made me even wetter.

He was huge and he felt amazing. He moved both hands to my hips as he thrust into me in quick, hard pushes over and over again. The guy dancing in front of me felt my hard nipple brush against his arm and he turned around to see my exposed breast and the look of ecstasy on my face. Desire pooled in his eyes, but when he looked over my shoulder and saw Chad, he must have seen something on Chad's face that made him quickly turn back around.

Suddenly it felt as if everyone in the crowd was watching us, and dammit if that didn't make it even hotter. I closed my eyes and pretended everyone in the club knew what we were doing as I felt my orgasm building, clenching tightly around his twitching cock. Right as my orgasm overtook me, two other dancers looked in my direction and watched as I let out a moan that was more like a scream. Chad thrust two more times deep inside me and then I felt him still as he found his own release.

His cum was running down my leg but I didn't care. I turned to face him, pulling my dress back up to cover my breast. "Thanks for getting that out of my system. Now go to hell," I said coldly, pushing past him, through the crowd and found my way back to the bathroom. I knew he wouldn't follow me, I could feel the distance growing between us as I walked further and further away. I went into an empty stall and collapsed to the floor, my head between my knees, his semen still seeping out of me...and I cried. I don't know how long I sat there on the bathroom floor crying pathetically, but I didn't care. I just cried until there were no more tears, until the pain turned into numbness.

CHAPTER 20

CHAD

As soon as I came inside of Stacy a myriad of emotions flooded me. Guilt, anger, regret just to name a few. What the fuck was I thinking? I had come to the club to apologize, make things right, show her I cared and hopefully ask her out on a real date. Instead I fucked her in the middle of the dance floor with hundreds of people surrounding us.

I'd never done anything like that before in my life. Not only was it a stupid and reckless decision, but I'd used my badge to get into the club in the first place then committed several crimes once I was in the door. What if someone had recognized me? How many people knew what we were doing? I could lose my badge over this. I was nothing without it. My job was all I had.

I should have followed Stacy. I knew she was crying, she already had tears streaming down her face before she walked away. I still needed to apologize, but screwing her on the dance floor had made things a million times worse. If she didn't hate me before, she surely would now. What the hell would I even be able to say to make things better at this point?

I needed to think, get some air, figure out how to approach everything. I knew she wanted it as much as I did, but the thought that she may be regretting it or even worse, thought I had used her, made me feel like shit.

I was pacing back and forth out front, running my hands through my hair over and over and muttering curse words at myself when Joe came running out.

"What the hell, man? I saw Stacy past me crying and I tried to follow her but she went in the bathroom. When I came back to the dance floor I saw you looking pissed and storming outside. What's going on? Why are you here? What did you do?"

I wanted to be angry that he automatically assumed that it was my fault she was upset, but who the hell was I kidding? Of course it was my fault. All I'd done since I met her was treat her like shit. "I screwed up, that's what. I never should have come here. It was a mistake."

"Why are you here?"

"I wanted to talk to Stacy. I wanted to apologize, to her and you. When you wouldn't get back to me I followed you here."

"You fucking followed me? Wow. She really did get to you…" Joe trailed off and shook his head, looking down at the ground and laughing sarcastically. "I never in a million years thought…it's a good thing we dropped that bet." He was muttering under his breath and talking more to himself than me, but my head whipped in his direction at the mention of a bet.

"What do you mean bet? You bet something about

me?" I snapped at him, closing the gap between us.

"Nothing, it was just a joke." When I narrowed my eyes at him he threw his hands up in the air in surrender. "I'm really drunk man, just ignore me. I shouldn't have said anything." I would have let it go, but it was obvious he was hiding something and I was sick and tired of feeling confused about the whole situation with Stacy. So if Joe was keeping something from me that could help clear things up, then I'd be damned if I would let him get away with avoiding it.

"No, fucking tell me what you are talking about before I beat your ass for driving Stacy here and then getting too wasted to be able to drive her home."

"Look man, it's no big deal. It was innocent, nothing was meant by it," Joe defended as he backed away from me. I lengthened my strides and caught up to him, grabbing him by the collar of his shirt in one hand and pulling his face to mine. There was fear in his eyes and I knew it wasn't because he thought I would hit him; it was because he knew how angry I was going to get when he finally fessed up to whatever secret he was hiding. My heart was pounding, and as much as I knew I would be better off to drop it, I couldn't. Now I needed to know.

"Spit it out Joe," I growled between gritted teeth. The bouncer by the door witnessed our spectacle and started over towards us, but I flashed my badge - again - and he returned back to his station without so much as another glance. He was obviously used to looking the other way when shit went down.

"Okay, okay. Just let me go and I'll tell you." I let go of his shirt and shoved him in the same motion. He took a second to straighten his shirt out and regain his composure, then cleared his throat nervously before starting to talk.

"There was one day in the very beginning of all this shit with Stacy you when you acted like a giant dick to her. She was hurt and pissed and well, we got really drunk at my place and she was talking about wanting to get even with you. I told her that there was no way she would be able to get a rise out of you because you're always so controlled. One thing lead to another and we were making some dumb ass bet out of it. We dropped it and it stopped being a game a long time ago, I swear."

"So all this time I've been beating myself up over and losing my fucking mind over her, when it was all just a game for her? A game that you were in on? Are you fucking kidding me?!" I was yelling and seething, and out of the corner of my eye I saw the bouncer start to approach us again, but I turned to face him and shook my head. "Don't bother man," I said to the bouncer. "I'm not going to hit him. This fucker is already dead to me."

I stormed off to my car and I could hear Joe yelling for me, but I had already tuned him out. I didn't give a shit what he said at that point. Finding out Stacy had just been screwing with me and making a fool out of me when the entire time I was pushing her away because I was dealing with some serious demons only made the sting of their shitty betrayal even worse.

I couldn't believe my partner of two years, the same man who had stood by me at my dad's parole hearing, the one other person who knew everything about my past, would do that to me. Mostly, I couldn't believe I'd let myself believe for one fucking second that Stacy and I could be anything other than enemies. She played me, and she played me well. I felt like a fucking idiot and I knew what I needed to do first.

First thing the next morning, I was requesting a new partner.

CHAPTER 21

STACY

"Stace?" A voice called out, and I slammed my head back against the stall door. I figured Joe would come looking for me at some point, but I still wasn't ready to talk to anyone.

"Go away, Joe," I choked out.

"Stacy…" he whispered from the other side of the stall door. "Please tell me what happened, I'm really worried about you. I saw Chad leaving and went after him, but he didn't tell me anything, he just took off."

"Please, Joe, I can't…" The tears continued to pour out of me. It was embarrassing for Joe to hear me sobbing and all I wanted to was to be alone. I tried to hold in my sobs, but the pain in my chest was too strong to be contained and all it did was choke me. I took several deep breaths while Joe waited patiently on the other side of the door, and once I got my breathing back under control I managed to finally speak. "Please leave. I'll call you tomorrow. I'll get a cab home. Please, I'm begging you. Just leave."

I could tell by the way his legs were positioned that he was leaning his forehead against the door. He let out a heavy sigh, and without another word his feet moved away from the stall, and I listened until I heard the bathroom door close behind him. Once I knew I was he was gone I let the dam break once again, and didn't even fight the full body wracking sobs that followed.

It wasn't until at least a half an hour later that I realized I didn't have my purse. I'd left it in Joe's truck. It had my phone and my money in it.

"Dammit!" I yelled as I slammed my head back into the wall of the bathroom stall.

I pushed myself to my feet and went to the sink to run cold water over my face. I was a mess, my eyes puffy and bloodshot with mascara running down my cheeks. When I finally cleaned myself up enough to feel comfortable going back out into the club, I headed to the bar and asked to use their phone.

Of course I didn't have anyone's numbers memorized. They were all programmed into my phone. Luckily the bartender had a phone book behind the bar and I looked up the number to the police station. Damn, hadn't seen a phone book in ages.

Bill, one of the other officers at Joe's precinct, answered the phone. "Hey Bill, it's Stacy."

"Hey, Stacy! How are ya?"

"Not great. I was out with Joe but I left my phone in his truck and he's already left. I was going to get a cab home but he's got my purse too. Can you patch me through to him so I can ask him to come back? I don't have his number memorized and I'm using the bar's phone."

"Sure thing, sweetheart. Hold on a sec." The line went quiet for several seconds and then Bill came back on the line. "Sorry, hon, he didn't answer. Want me to try Chad? They're probably together."

I didn't want to talk to Chad. He was the last person on earth I wanted to talk to. But I was stranded and didn't have much of a choice so I told Bill to go ahead and put me through.

"Stevens," Chad barked when he answered the phone.

"Chad?" The line was silent for several seconds and I wondered if he'd hung up.

"What the fuck do you want?" He said in a calm, cold voice that sent chills through my body. I figured he was pretty pissed at me for walking away like that, but he callousness caught me off guard. After all, I was the one who'd been treated like shit up to that point.

"Um, actually, I was wondering if you might be able to come get me or call…" He cut me off before I could finish.

"No."

"No?"

"If Joe bailed on you, that's not my problem. I'm sure you can manipulate some unknowing prick at the club to take your home. Don't call me again."

The line went dead and I stared at the receiver in

shock. What the fuck just happened?

I thanked the bartender and walked outside. I had no idea what to do. I saw Joe's truck at the end of the parking lot and started to run toward it, thankful he hadn't left yet. Only when I reached it he wasn't inside and I assumed he must have taken a cab home since he'd had several drinks.

I took a chance and pulled on the door handle, hoping maybe he left his truck unlocked like he did his house, and thankfully I was right. I grabbed my purse and pulled out my phone but it was dead.

"Dammit!"

"Trouble, sweety?" A gravelly, cold voice said from behind me that most definitely wasn't Joe's. I spun around to see who it was, regretting having not moved my pepper spray into my clutch before we left. I figured I wouldn't need it when Joe was with me.

"Um, no. I was just waiting for my boyfriend. He's a cop. He should be here any second." I was hoping that would scare him off, but suddenly two other men emerged from both sides of him, both with the same devilish look in their eye. They were all stalking towards me and I debated trying to run, but I knew I wouldn't get far with three of them chasing after me in my six inch stilettos.

Just as I went to scream for help, the first guy punched me square in the stomach, knocking the wind out of me. Now that he was closer I could see his teeth were rotted and he smelled of booze and cigarettes. I tried to stand up but he kicked me, and I fell back down to the ground. My purse flew out of my hand and one of the other men picked it up and started rifling through it.

"Please," I whispered, still unable to talk from the blows I'd taken.

"Shut up, bitch," the man still hovering over me yelled as he kicked me again. I heard a snap and hoped he hadn't broken a rib.

"Alright, man, we got her purse, let's take off before someone sees us," one of the guys said to the man still hovering. It would have been a good idea to just shut up, but I had never been good at making good decisions. And since tonight had apparently been the night for making the worst mistakes of my life, I figured, may as well go out with a bang.

"Feel free to use my credit card to buy a toothbrush and body wash." I made a gagging motion, which he took to mean I was making fun of him, but it was just bad timing because I was literally gagging. I was having to take deep breaths to recover from the blows, and pulling in so much of his stench at one time combined with the pain was making me nauseous.

"Oh you think you're so much better than me, huh princess? Maybe someone needs to teach you a lesson in manners. Lucky for you, I'm up for the job." The evil dripping from his words caused me to recoil, and I had to fight not to gag again as he slid his tongue over his rotted teeth slowly. I started to try and scream again but he kicked me again, this time in my face, and immediately blood started to drip into my eye and down my cheek. My lip was already starting to swell and my mouth filled with blood.

He grabbed me by my hair and started dragging me across the parking lot towards a back alley where they could do whatever they wanted with me and not be seen. His grip on me was so tight it felt like he was going to rip my hair right out of my head, but my hair seemed like a small price to pay if it meant I could escape, so I continued thrashing and kicking, trying to break free. I dug my nails as hard as I could into the arm gripping my hair, but he backhanded me square across my cheek, effectively ceasing all movements from me.

Blood continued filling my mouth so quickly that I started choking on it, and when I saw my attacker get irritated with the blood splattering in his direction as I coughed, I looked up and tried to spit it in his face. He quickly swiped it off his cheek and yelled before jerking his knee up and slamming into the underside of my chin. I heard a snap as my head flew backwards on impact.

He let go of my hair suddenly and I collapsed to the ground, still sputtering and coughing up blood. I tried to lift my head to see what was happening, but my vision was blurry with the unshed tears I refused to let go of. One eye was swelling almost completely shut, and for a second I thought I was hearing things when I heard someone yelling for the men to get off of me.

My vision in my one good eye cleared enough for me to see Joe running towards me, gun in hand, and then all three men go scattering. When Joe reached me he knelt down and cradled my head in his hands, muttering apologies over and over.

"Hang on, Stacy, hang with me. I'm going to get you out of here, okay? Are you okay to move? Maybe I should call 911 and have you taken to the hospital in an ambulance."

"No!" I yelled, but the exertion sent stabbing pains through every inch of my body and I bent over, clutching my stomach. "Please, I just want to go home. I just need cleaned up." There was still so much blood pouring into my mouth, and my lip was so busted that the words came out muffled. I watched the struggle in Joe's face as he debated whether or not to take me to the hospital against my will.

"Okay, I'll take you home, but if your injuries look really serious once we get all the blood cleaned up then you are going to the hospital whether you like or not Stacy. I should force you to go right now anyway, but I know it's been a rough night. Let's just get you home for now."

Joe cradled me in his arms and carried me to his truck. The adrenaline from chasing off my attackers had completely sobered him up. The drive to my apartment was quiet and felt incredibly long, and when we finally pulled into the parking lot, Joe came around and scooped me up again and carried me inside.

Adalyn wasn't home and I was thankful, I didn't want her seeing me like this. There would be too many questions and I couldn't deal with having to answer any of them right now, both mentally and physically drained. Joe gingerly sat me on my bed then disappeared into my bathroom, re-emerging with towels, antiseptic and bandages.

It took a good twenty minutes to get all the blood cleaned off of my face, but once he was able to take a look, none of it was serious enough to warrant a trip to the emergency room. The worst of my injuries were my ribs, but they weren't broken, I could tell. Maybe fractured, but there would be nothing they could do for that. Joe begged me to go to the hospital anyway.

"I'm just too exhausted, Joe. The only thing they can do for me is prescribe pain meds but I don't want them. I just need to rest."

I was emotionally spent and hanging on by a thread. Between what happened with Chad and then being attacked, I didn't think I could handle strangers poking and prodding me. As much as I wanted to just put the whole thing behind me, Joe all but had a meltdown when I told him I didn't want to file a report, so I reluctantly agreed to go to the station with him in the morning.

Joe helped me into the shower and sat right outside on the toilet in case I needed any help. Neither of us spoke as I let the hot water run over me and tried to keep the tears from resurfacing. I was still in too much shock to fully absorb what had just happened to me and too stunned to worry about modesty, so I let Joe towel me off and help me get dressed since I could barely raise my left arm because of my ribs. He laid me on the bed and went to get me ice for my lip and eye, which were swelling more and more by the minute.

He took off his shirt and pants, but left his boxers on, and climbed into bed next to me. He pulled me into his arms and I snuggled into his chest and finally let the tears come out as I let the weight of everything finally sink in. Joe just held me, whispering soothing words into my ear, rocking and cradling me until sleep finally came over me.

CHAPTER 22

STACY

When I woke up the next day in Joe's arms the first thing I noticed was the pain. The excruciating pounding in my head, the stabbing pain on my left side and the tenderness of my cheek, lip and eye on the right side of my face. The second thing I noticed was Joe's morning wood.

"Well, helloooo soldier," I dragged out in a teasing way. I felt Joe chuckle beneath me and the movement made me groan in pain.

"Sorry, you must be pretty sore. Let me get you some pain meds before we go to the station." Joe moved me out of his arms gently and laid me back on my pillow then he stood up and started to put his pants back on.

"Joe I really don't want to go to the station."

"Dammit, Stacy, you are going with me to the station!" He yelled, whipping around to give me a death glare. "You're getting some pain meds in you and then I'm taking you to the station and you will file a damn report and you won't argue with me about it. You may not want to face what happened Stacy, but if you filing a report can get these guys caught before they hurt someone else then it's worth it."

I winced, partially from pain and partially from the harshness of his words. He was right, I knew he was right.

Filing the report wasn't really the issue. I just didn't want to see Chad. As if he could read my mind, Joe's face softened and he sat down on the edge of my bed and put his hand on my ankle, rubbing in slow, soothing circles.

"I'll go in first and make sure Chad isn't in there if that's why you don't want to go. But tell me what happened, Stace. What went down between you and Chad?"

"I don't...how did he even know I was there? He came storming in like he knew I would be there."

"He followed me."

"What!?" I yelled and jerked upright, immediately groaning as a searing pain sliced through my abdomen.

"We haven't been on the best of terms. I didn't want to tell you because I knew you would think it was your fault. We haven't really talked other than work stuff when we're on the job since that night you ran out of his house. He tried to reach me last night and I ignored him, so he came by my house. He wanted to find you and apologize, so when I wouldn't answer he followed me."

"Joe...you're right. I do feel like it's my fault. You shouldn't punish him because of me. I appreciate it, really, but as much as I hate Chad, I don't want to come between you two. He may be an asshole, but he needs you, and he's one of your best friends. Why won't you just talk to him? It's not like you to shut people out."

"Because I didn't want to hear his shit. I've always known Chad was an asshole, but I never thought he would treat you the way he did. Whenever he's tried to ask about you I changed the subject. I was hoping he would just let it go, let you go, if I never let him talk about it. At first I kept hoping he would change, especially once I saw you getting through to him, but instead he just proved over and over again that he was never going to change. At least that's what I thought, last night at the club, seeing how upset he was...I've never seen him so worked up like that. So...lost. It just came out; I didn't even think about what I was saying. I may have accidentally mumbled something about our bet, and he heard and sort of went off the deep end."

"What!?" I shot up, then let out a long string of swear words. I seriously needed to quit moving around so quickly, I was in excruciating pain.

"It slipped! I was just talking out loud, I didn't mean for him to hear anything. But when I realized what I'd said and he saw how panicked I got, he wouldn't let it go. I tried to tell him it was nothing and it hadn't been a game for a long time, if ever, but he didn't believe me. Honestly, this whole time I thought it was more of a game for him than it was for you, but seeing the betrayal on his face when I mentioned that damn bet...I seriously screwed up, Stace, I'm sorry."

"That explains why he was such an asshole to me when I called him...well that and because... never mind."

"When did you call him?"

"At the club. I thought you'd left and I didn't have my phone, so I asked to use the bar's. I didn't have anyone's number so I called the station and asked Bill to put me through to you. When you didn't answer they put me through to Chad, but when he answered he just said some really nasty shit to me and hung up."

"I'm sorry, Stacy. I never left the club. I wouldn't have left you there like that. I don't know how you even slipped past me without me knowing. I went back to the bathroom to check on you, but when you weren't in there, I panicked. That's why I was in the parking lot. This is all my fault…" Joe hung his head and shoulders slumped. I ignored the pain radiating throughout my whole body and scooted my way down the bed to put my arm around him.

"It's not your fault, Joe. If it's anyone's fault, it's mine. Chad isn't the only one at fault for everything. I did want to screw with him and I was too busy trying to figure out how I felt about him to come clean and just lay it on the line for him, so it makes sense that he flipped out like that."

"He was mad before I told him, Stacy. Did something happen in the club between the two of you?"

I didn't answer at first. I'd done crazier things than have sex in the middle of a packed dance floor, but I was ashamed about everything that led up to it. At some point during all the shit that's transpired between me and

Chad I had started to actually have feelings for him. I never should have let that happen between us, I should have listened to him when he wanted to talk. I'd messed everything up.

Even though every word that came out of my mouth made me feel like shit, I told Joe every detail of what had happened at the club. I had confided every detail to him about everything else and he was the only one who really knew what was going on with Chad and I didn't want to start shutting him out now.

Joe's fists clenched and his body tensed as I told him the story. Joe was your typical protector type, so if it came down to who he would blame, he would always blame Chad.

"Joe, please, I am just as much at fault for this as he is. We've both been assholes and should have just been real with each other from the beginning and none of this would have happened."

"No, Stacy, don't you dare take the blame for his behavior. Chad is fucked up but that doesn't excuse his actions. He should have controlled himself better and insisted you guys talk. You are not some random whore he can screw in the middle of a club. You deserve better than that, and the fact that he has the nerve to even be mad about the bet or anything else is bullshit."

"I know, you're right, but I should have just told him how I felt a long time ago. Maybe if I would have come clean about how I was falling for him then he could have at least made a clean break instead of this game we keep playing."

"I'm sorry to say it, Stacy, but that would have only made it worse."

That made me jerk my head back in surprise. "Why would it have made it worse?"

"I told you, Chad has a shitty past and it's not my place to tell you his story, just trust me on this. All of this is his fault, he should have manned up and found some self control."

I wanted to keep asking for more information, but I sensed it wouldn't do any good. Joe was loyal to a fault, he would never tell me something if it wasn't his secret to tell, no matter how angry he was at Chad. So I let it go and made my way over to the bathroom to brush my teeth. Joe had to brush my hair for me because I was in too much pain to lift my arm that high. After helping me get dressed and make it down to his truck, he took me to the station.

He stood by my side the whole time, held my hand when I cried as I told the story of what happened, and I knew I'd never be able to repay Joe for all the ways he'd helped me in the short time we'd known each other.

Two hours later we were finally finished with the report and I was exhausted. Joe started to lead me out of the building but his supervisor stopped him. Joe sat me down in one of the chairs by the door, my pain meds were starting to wear off and I couldn't stand for too long.

When Joe came back out about twenty minutes later his face was completely drained of all color and his fists were clenched.

"What's wrong Joe?" I jumped up to go to him, but immediately fell back down in the chair because of the pain.

Joe stopped in front of me but never looked down at my face while speaking.

"Looks like I've been assigned a new partner."

It took all the strength I had left not to break down and cry in the middle of the station. I had fucked things up for everyone and Joe didn't deserve this. I hated myself and the guilt consumed me. I wanted to push Joe away; to tell him he's better off without me. I knew now with Chad shutting him out, that he needed me. So instead of being selfish, I took him in my arms and let him walk me to his car. We'd get through this together.

When we got to my apartment Carrie was waiting inside for me. When she took in my beaten and bruised face she winced, but didn't seem shocked. I looked over at Joe who smiled sheepishly.

"I called her this morning with your phone before you woke up. I knew you'd need some help but would be too stubborn to accept it."

I wanted to glare at him and mouth off about not

needing anyone, but the puppy dog look Joe was giving me just zapped the anger right out of me. He walked me over to the couch and said his goodbyes, then Carrie walked him out. They went into the hallway and closed the door so I couldn't hear them.

A few minutes later Carrie came back in, avoiding eye contact with me.

"What was that about, Carrie?" She shrugged and started working her way around the kitchen, picking up, then getting something out of the freezer for my face when she saw me wince.

"We're not talking about me. Not until you tell me what the hell happened."

CHAPTER 23

CHAD

I fucking hated my new partner. He was too old to be out in the field and I wondered why he hadn't been put on desk duty yet. Our first day patrolling together, I swear to God, he fell asleep. I drove his ass around all over town while he napped. And once he was out, he was out. There were several times that I almost checked his pulse to see if he'd died, but then he'd start snoring. Yeah, he snored loud and a lot. I should have just dropped him off at the retirement community and picked him up at the end of the day.

Three weeks. Three fucking weeks being stuck with this guy. Three weeks of avoiding Joe every time he tried to talk to me when our paths crossed. Three weeks of spending every waking minute of every damn day trying not to think about Stacy. Three weeks of obsessing over the betrayal eating away at me.

It made sense, really. I'd finally gotten to the point where I considered Joe a friend and could admit that I had feelings for Stacy, then I find out they were fucking with me the whole time. Of course.

I hadn't been to Petey's or the gym in three weeks, not wanting to risk running into Joe or Stacy. My life was getting pretty lonely and I needed to either find new places to hang or just face them. Both options sounded exhausting.

So one day after a particularly annoying day with my new corpse of a partner, I said fuck it and went to the gym. I needed to pound out some anger and if I didn't do it on the bag soon, it would end up being my new partner's face.

I took a quick look around and didn't see Joe, so I went to work wrapping my hands before I started in with the punches. I was out of shape, I'd waited too long to work out, so I was rusty at first. My muscles screamed at me and my hands ached, but I pushed through the pain and pretended the bag represented my life and beat the shit out of it.

I didn't stop until there was blood running out of the tape wrapped around my knuckles and my lungs threatened to explode from lack of oxygen. I made my way over to the drinking fountain and spotted Joe out of the corner of my eye on one of the mats to the right. He had his arms wrapped around some blonde, showing her how to throw a punch. Typical Joe pick up technique.

For a second I considered going over and talking to him. I missed my friend, even if it made me feel like a pussy to admit it. I even took a step towards him, but then he pulled away from the blonde to give her room to try out the moves he'd just taught her and I froze in my tracks. It was Stacy.

I stood there frozen in place, trying to remember all the reasons I was pissed at her. She wore tiny running shorts, which could probably be considered underwear as opposed to workout clothes they were so small, and a tight fitted tank. Her skin was glistening from sweat and her arms and legs looked more toned than I remembered as if she had been working out since I'd last seen her.

I wanted to look away. I needed to find a way to make myself stop staring before one of them noticed me, but before I could, her body shifted slightly and I got a look at her face. It looked...bruised? What the fuck?

I moved closer to see if I was imagining it, but the closer I got the more I could make out the injuries to her face. Her cheek was slightly puffy and her face was covered in bruises that were starting to yellow, indicating it had been a while since she'd gotten them. There was a cut with stitches over her right eye and her lip was scabbed over in the corner like she had busted it. She punched the air and her shirt lifted a fraction and I could see the bruises snaking around her entire torso.

Without thinking I ran towards her and gripped her shoulders with my arms. When she flinched I let go and winced, hoping I hadn't hurt her.

"Stacy, what happened to you? Were you in an accident?" I searched her eyes, my brow furrowed, my mouth turned down in a frown. Though her injuries looked mostly healed I could tell that however she had initially gotten them had to have been extremely painful. She looked shocked to see me, but then her face clouded over. Her eyes darted down to her wrist, where I had wrapped my fingers around without even knowing.

"Fuck you," She growled as she yanked out of my grasp and stormed off. I started to follow her but Joe grabbed my arm, preventing me from running after her.

"Get off!" I yelled as I pulled away from him. I turned to go find Stacy but he pulled me back again. "Do you have a death wish, Joe?" I growled.

"Leave her alone, Chad. She doesn't want to talk to you."

"What, are you her fucking keeper? If she doesn't want to talk to me then she can tell me herself."

"I think her saying 'fuck you' and storming off was her way of telling you that."

"Yeah, well, that's not what I heard so she needs to try again." Joe had moved in between me and the direction Stacy had walked off in, blocking my path to her. I started to shove past him, but Joe shoved me back as hard as he could. I stumbled one step, but recovered quickly. I was at least twice Joe's size when it came to muscle mass. I was bulkier while Joe was lean.

I had to remind myself that beating the shit out of Joe right now wouldn't make things any better. I wanted to be angry, but honestly, I was kind of impressed at his bravery. He knew I could easily take him but he pushed me anyway.

"Joe, I'm trying not to get really pissed off at you right now for getting in my way but you're making it very difficult. So before you end up getting hurt, please move out of my way, or I'll just move you myself."

"Fuck you, Chad," he spat out calmly. "Don't threaten me like I'm the problem here. You can beat the shit out of me if you want because that's what it's going to take to get to Stacy. She doesn't want to talk to you. Do you think kicking my ass is going to change that? If you really care about her then you'll let her go."

"You don't know how I feel about her. Don't act like you know anything about me."

Joe laughed sarcastically and shook his head. "I do know you, Chad, that's the problem. You're your own worst enemy and if you don't start taking the blame for your own shit then you're going to be alone for the rest of your life." I started to argue but Joe kept going. "You can avoid me, request a new partner, threaten to kick my ass and harass Stacy, but it won't change anything. You really fucked up this time and forcing your way into her life isn't going to fix anything. If you really want to make things right, then find a better way to do it. In my opinion, you don't deserve her forgiveness, but that's up to her. But I'll be damned if I let you go after her when you're still pissed and over reacting. She's put up with enough of your shit and until you're ready to treat her with the respect she deserves then you'll have to go through me first."

I wanted to be pissed. I wanted to punch Joe in his fucking face and tell him he was wrong and to mind his own business, but I couldn't. He wasn't wrong. As much as I hated to hear it, he was a hundred percent right. I had no one to blame but myself and I couldn't go after Stacy right now. I needed to get my own shit together before I tried to talk to her.

I tried to remind myself that I hated both of them, that they had fucked with me, but at that point it didn't matter. I had missed Stacy. I'd missed both of them, and even if it had started out as a game, at some point it had become more. I was still angry, but running was the wrong thing to do. I should have stuck around and fought harder instead of hiding like a coward.

Joe stood in front of me, poised to attack if he needed to, but he wouldn't get a fight out of me right then. I needed to figure out where my head was and talk to him when we were both calm. He needed to go after Stacy and make sure she was okay. I wanted to be the one to go after her and comfort her, but I was the one who had hurt her in the first place. I didn't deserve to have her in my arms, to be the one kissing away all of her pain.

"Thanks for taking care of her, man," was all I said as I walked away from Joe and headed to the locker room, not bothering to wait for a response. I didn't know at what point I had completely derailed my own life, but I needed to find a way to get it back on track. Just ten minutes ago I was convinced I was totally done with Stacy, but seeing those bruises and knowing something bad had happened when I wasn't around...it put into perspective just how badly I wanted her in my life.

CHAPTER 24

STACY

Seeing Chad hurt more than having the shit kicked out of me in the parking lot of Grind. I'd spent three weeks recovering and doing everything I could to avoid thinking about him. Joe swore he hadn't seen Chad at the gym and convinced me to go learn some self defense moves. As soon as I was able to move comfortably I had started running. It was seriously horrible at first, but Carrie and Joe took turns running with me and it was easier with someone encouraging me.

I still hadn't told anyone what happened to me. I didn't want to be alone, though I was pretending like everything was fine. I ended up admitting to Carrie that I'd been jumped, but I left out all the rest. The only person who knew everything that was going on with Chad was Joe. Carrie and I argued for at least an hour over me not wanting to tell Adalyn or Ian. I felt bad asking Carrie to keep it a secret, but I knew telling them would just cause them to worry and they were working hard on Adalyn's new comic about Ian and were still in the honeymoon phase of their relationship. Adalyn had pretty much moved in with Ian as soon as they'd made up.

I knew Adalyn and Carrie would be furious with me for not telling them if they ever found out about all that had gone down with Chad, but I was so ashamed I couldn't bear to tell them. Shame was a new emotion for me. I'd done my fair share of activities that the general populace would consider more than shameful, but it had never bothered me before. This was different though.

This was different because I actually had feelings for Chad. I had been denying them and fighting to pretend they weren't there, but they were. I didn't know if Joe was right or not. Maybe being honest with Chad only would have made things worse, but now I'd never know. He hated me and honestly, I was okay with that. It made it easier for me to be angry with him instead of just angry at myself.

I had reason enough to be angry with Chad, I wasn't some weak minded woman who blamed herself when the guy acted like an asshole. I wasn't blind to how much of a douche he had been to me over and over again, but the blame was as much on me as him because I kept coming back for more. I made excuses for it and pretended it was an attempt to get even or whatever bullshit seemed right at the time, but it was a lie. A facade. Me pretending it was all a game because I was too afraid of getting hurt.

A lot of good all that shit did me. Not only did I get hurt anyway, but I'd hurt others in the process. I had been lying and keeping things from my friends, and I had so many secrets that I couldn't even keep them straight. I wasn't good at holding things in and it was eating me up inside.

Knowing I had ruined Joe's friendship with Chad was chipping away at me slowly. I thought about going to Chad and pleading on Joe's behalf, trying to explain what happened and see if I could repair the damage I'd done, but I knew that was a mistake. Joe was a grown man and if he wanted to fix things with Chad then he could handle it himself, and I wasn't going to use Joe as an excuse to see Chad again, which let's face it, was really the reason I considered contacting him.

I missed him. I missed fighting with him. I missed the angry tension between us. I missed the rare moments when we let our guards down and could be ourselves around each other. I missed the way my heart would stop when I heard him laugh and I missed the fire that burned in my chest when we touched.

He didn't want me though, and I needed to accept that. Obviously the physical attraction was there, but he didn't want more. He had every opportunity to try for more and he walked away every chance he got. It's part of why I'd walked away so quickly on the dance floor. I couldn't bear to watch him push me away again.

No matter how I looked at it though, nothing about this situation compared to any other I'd ever been in, because I'd never had feelings for any of the other men before. I never wanted any of them to stick around, to want more with me than a quick lay. Finally wanting more with someone and knowing they didn't want me back was so painful I actually would prefer another kick to the ribs. This feeling was exactly why I'd never let anyone in before.

Working out had helped a lot. It kept my mind busy and the endorphins, as Carrie had explained as "nature's reward for taking care of yourself", were most likely the reason I hadn't fallen into a depression. As much torture as it was, I was getting stronger, and that made me feel better about myself. Joe was helping me train. I wasn't looking to become some exercise nut, but I wanted to be able to defend myself, at least a little.

Joe kept trying to talk me into moving since the guys who stole my purse had my ID with my address, but I loved where I lived and I refused. He stayed over every night the first two weeks but his dick eventually got tired of being in bed with a woman who wasn't putting out and I insisted he spend some time at his own place and get laid. I couldn't stand his constant bitching and if I walked in on him jerking off in my bed one more time I was going to lose it. One time I even woke up to him rubbing one off right next to me. It was one huge fight when he got some of his spooge on my face. Even though hot, naked Joe beating off his massive dick was an extremely sexy sight, it didn't matter how wet my panties got because he was my best friend. We both knew it wouldn't work.

After three weeks of taking off work to recover I finally had to go back, but after four straight days of not seeing Joe I was getting really lonely and wanted to go see him, so I drove by his house but his truck wasn't in the driveway. I was really tired of being home alone so I decided to just drive around for a while. I drove until my eyes started to get heavy and decided I had to call it a night, so I headed toward my apartment. I'd never in my life spent so much time feeling sorry for myself, but there wasn't much I wouldn't give to not have to go home to an empty apartment.

CHAPTER 25

CHAD

I couldn't quit thinking about Stacy since I'd seen her at the gym. Aside from the bruising and cuts on her, she looked amazing. The anger and hurt in her eyes when she looked at me was looping through my mind and I kept having to talk myself out of reaching out to her. Joe was right with everything he said to me at the gym and I was determined to get through to her, but I needed a plan first.

I'd still been avoiding Joe but I really needed to face him and apologize. I resolved to do it the next time I saw him, but that plan backfired on me. Four days after seeing Stacy at the gym I was coming in for my night shift as Joe was on his way out. I started to walk over to him and ask if he'd talk to me for a minute, but Bill, one of the other officers beat me to him.

"Hey, Joe. I was getting ready to come find you. We got a lead on Stacy's case."

I stopped mid step, caught off guard from hearing there was a case about Stacy.

"We had another person come in and report an attack. Muggers fit the same description Stacy gave. We think we know where they are operating out of and we are going to head over there. I'll let you know as soon as we have some more information."

"What the fuck! Stacy was attacked?!" Joe and Bill jerked their heads in my direction as I stormed over to where they were standing. "Why didn't someone tell me?!" I knew I needed to tone it down a notch, but I was too angry to calm down.

"Because it was none of your fucking business, Chad."

"Like hell it isn't! I could have been helping!"

"Helping!?" Joe got in my face. "Like you helped her when she called you for a ride?"

"What? When? I haven't…" I trailed off as I thought back to that night at the club. "She called me from the club and asked me to call you but she didn't..." My mind spun a mile a minute, trying to recall our conversation that night. It was brief and I'd blocked it out, but now that I really thought about it, I think she did ask me to go get her.

"Yeah, because you fucking cut her off and said some dickhead shit to her before hanging up on her."

"Wait…so this happened that night at the club?" Son of a...

"Yeah, she didn't have her phone or any money and needed a way home so she went outside trying to figure out what to do. She was jumped by three guys who stole her purse and beat the shit out of her before I stopped it."

"How is that my fault!? Where the fuck were you,

Joe? Why would you leave her there!?"

"I didn't!" Joe was screaming at me at that point. "I was waiting inside while she fucking cried her eyes out for over an hour in the bathroom. She slipped outside when I went to take a piss for two seconds and I panicked when I couldn't find her. But she never would have been crying and freaking out if it weren't for you and she wouldn't have gone outside if you hadn't hung up on her. So back the fuck up, Chad. Now!"

I fell backwards a few steps. Not because Joe had pushed me, but because I was so stunned I felt like I could fall over. She'd been crying in the bathroom? She got jumped because I wouldn't give her two seconds of my time to explain why she was calling?

Screw this waiting around shit. I had to find her. Things were even more messed up than I imagined and I needed to make things right. As soon as I heard them say her name, I felt like something was wrong. Maybe it was all in my head, but it felt like gut instinct. Even if she were fine, she didn't need to be alone. Joe should never have let her be alone until those asshats were caught.

I shoved past Joe and ran out the door to my patrol car. I could hear Joe yelling and running after me, but I hopped in the car and threw on the lights. We weren't supposed to drive the cars out of uniform or use our sirens to run every fucking light in the city, but I didn't give a shit. I had a bad feeling that Stacy was in trouble, and nothing else mattered except getting to her. I had to see her and make sure she was safe.

CHAPTER 26

STACY

I was exhausted by the time I got back to my apartment. I'd been driving around for hours and it was late. I got out my keys and phone as I trekked up the stairs and didn't even notice my door was cracked open until I went to push my key in the lock. The door pushed open and before I could process what was happening something made contact with the back of my head, sending me flying to the ground.

I rolled over and moaned, and when my eyes started focusing I recognized the same three men who had attacked me at the club. Two of them were tearing apart my apartment. They were pulling out drawers and dumping the contents on the floor, ripping shelves and pictures off my walls and yanking everything out of my cabinets. When I turned my gaze to the man standing over me I saw a tongue slide over the same rotted teeth that taunted me that night of my attack and knew this time I wouldn't be so lucky.

Everything Joe taught me over the last few weeks came flooding back and before my attacker could do anything else, I rolled away and quickly stood up, crouching to a defensive position. My head was pounding and I felt blood trickling down my neck, but I was hyper aware and knew I at least wouldn't go down without a fight.

My attacker laughed at my stance, mocking my attempt at protecting myself. I took the offensive approach and tried to bring my knee to his groin, but just before my knee made contact, his fist collided with my face. The same place on my lip that had been split just weeks before cracked open again and blood dripped down my chin. I wiped it away with the back of my hand and did my best to stay upright, determined not to show any weakness.

I was outnumbered, though. As soon as his buddies realized I was fighting back they lunged at me. I got an elbow to the jaw from one of them just before the other one tackled me to the ground. The guy I'd gotten a hit in on bounced back quickly and held my legs down while the other held my arms. I was completely restrained but I was thrashing my head and fighting as hard as I could to get free. My muscles felt heavy and fatigued but I pushed through the pain, praying that this was just a dream and I would wake up any second.

Rotted teeth man started to undo his pants and I tried to scream out but he covered my mouth with his dirty hand. I tried to bite him but his palm tasted like grease and filth and my stomach rolled from the disgusting taste that filled my mouth. He continued to remove his pants with one hand and tears started to fall down my cheeks. One of my legs broke free and I got a good kick in to his groin.

He jerked away and cursed at me, then turned back to spit in my face and punched me as hard as he could in my stomach. The scream I was about to let out got ripped away from me as I choked harshly with the blow from his fist. He landed another punch, this time to my face and my head snapped to the right and blood sprayed out onto my floor. I was gasping for air and choking on blood, thinking to myself that this must be what it felt like to drown as I continued to cough up blood.

He landed two more solid blows to my stomach before he jerked my pants down. Pain and fear threatened to paralyze me, but I refused to give up so easily. So I went still long enough to make him think I'd given up, and when his grip on me loosened slightly, I yanked my leg free and kicked him as hard as I could, making him fall backwards. As soon as he was in my line of vision again I knew it had been a mistake, because he no longer looked like he was enjoying himself, but rather like he wanted to get this over with quickly.

He grabbed my head between his hands and slammed it down onto my wooden floors once, twice, and then on the third time everything went dark. I couldn't have been out long because when I started to regain consciousness he was yanking down his pants and mine were around my ankles, but knowing he hadn't penetrated me yet gave me hope. When he removed his pants the rest of the way and gripped his erection in his dirty hand a cry slipped from my mouth.

He backhanded me and I lost count of how many kicks to my stomach and punches to my face I took before I blacked out again, but only for a second that time because when I opened my eyes I saw my attacker being pulled off of me. One of my eyes was completely swollen shut and the other was blurry with tears, but I could see that the man who had pulled my attacker off of me was Chad.

Chad threw him across the room with ease, causing my attacker to slam into my kitchen cabinets before falling to the floor. I tried to scream out and warn him when the other two men jumped him, but I couldn't get any sound to come out. Chad shrugged them off, and one of them went down after one hard hit to the jaw. The second got one hit in on Chad, but Chad was seemingly un-phased as he gave the man three hard hits to his face before he joined his friend on the ground.

Chad turned to look at me and the rage in his face quickly melted away to worry as he took a step in my direction. Chad started to reach out to me, but I saw my attempted rapist regain consciousness and lunge for Chad. In that moment I realized I was more scared about Chad getting hurt than I had been the whole time I'd been being attacked. Such a strange time to realize that Chad meant more to me than my own life, but before I could really process that startling revelation, Chad turned and gripped my attacker by his shirt and began punching his face over and over and over again.

As Chad knelt over the man, unrelenting in the blows he delivered to his face, I knew without a doubt he was going to kill him. Blood was spraying everywhere and the guy had gone completely limp. They were close enough to me that even with my severely impaired vision I could see the fire in Chad's eyes, and as badly as I wanted to get up and stop him, I couldn't move. I just watched and cried, worried not for the man on the ground who deserved what he was getting. But instead for Chad, whose life would end right along with the man he was going to kill, because he would lose his job and his freedom and it would all be my fault.

Suddenly as Chad's arm was pulled back for another punch, Joe came flying into the room and lunged at him, ripping him away from my attacker. I heard them yelling at each other but couldn't make out what they were saying. Knowing Joe was there and Chad would be safe relaxed me and it was getting harder to keep my eyes awake.

I tried to call out for Chad, but it came out a strangled gurgle, drowned out by the blood still filling my mouth. I didn't know why he was there or how he knew to come, but I was so grateful to see his face. I lost the battle to keep my eyes open, but when I felt Chad's hand on my face I forced myself to look at him, needing to see his face. Only when I opened my eyes, it wasn't Chad's face I saw, but my attacker's.

I panicked and started trying to scream. If my attacker was okay, then that meant Chad wasn't. Did I imagine Chad saving me? Why did my attacker look perfectly fine? Was I just dreaming Chad pummeling his face while I was blacked out? I started shaking and convulsing and felt on the verge of vomiting. My attacker slowly backed away and suddenly Joe was kneeling beside me and yelled for Chad to call a medic.

Chad? If he was talking to Chad, then that meant he was okay.

"Chad! Chad!" I tried to yell, but I was starting to hyperventilate and choked again, while I heard Joe whispering in my ear that I was safe and going to be okay. He sat next to me rubbing my hair and telling me to stay awake, that help was on the way, but I couldn't fight any more. Chad was okay, I was okay. Everything was going to be okay. And once I realized that, it all went dark again.

I drifted in and out of consciousness when the paramedics arrived. I vaguely remember being loaded onto a stretcher and pushed out of my building into the back of an ambulance. I could hear Chad arguing with one of the medics about demanding to come with me and I could hear Joe trying to calm him down, but I couldn't find the strength to open my eyes or move any part of my body. I worried briefly if I was paralyzed, but was out again before I could think about it any further.

I didn't come to again until I was in the hospital, being led down a hallway where all I could see were the bright lights on the ceiling. It was like the scene out of a movie and for a minute I prayed that it was and that this wasn't really happening. I could hear voices talking quickly and yelling, and it sounded like it was most likely the hospital staff. I wanted to call out for Chad, but an oxygen mask was being forced down over my mouth so my words came out mumbled and unintelligible.

When I felt the mask lift, I reached out blindly and grabbed the shirt of whoever was standing to the right of me and yanked down. Everything was blurry and I didn't know who it was, but I had a message I needed to get out. If I was going to die, and based on the pain I was in I was pretty sure I was, then I needed Chad to know.

I told the person to tell Chad I loved him and that I needed him to know that, but I was fairly certain that my words only made sense in my head and weren't coming out right. I tried again to speak but the mask was quickly placed back over my face and my grip on the person's shirt loosened as I was pushed through a set of doors, only to be greeted yet again by darkness.

CHAPTER 27

CHAD

The drive to Stacy's apartment took fucking forever despite how recklessly I drove the whole way there. When I finally made it to her parking lot I didn't bother parking, instead I just got as close to the building as I could and jumped out of the cruiser, barely taking the time to put it in park before taking off for the stairs, not willing to waste the time it would take to turn off the car or close the door.

I took the stairs two at a time and my heart felt like it was going to beat out of my chest. I couldn't tell you how I knew something was wrong, I just did. Like a beacon calling out to me, pulling me to Stacy like a magnet, I just knew in my gut that whatever I'd find when I got to her would be bad. I hoped to hell I was wrong.

Despite the premonitions that had been flooding my brain since I found out about Stacy's attack back at the station, nothing could have prepared me for the scene before me when I finally made it to her door.

Three men, two of them holding her down, one of them holding his dick in his hand. Stacy's pants were around her ankles and her top was torn, exposing her stomach and a black, lacey bra. There was a pool of blood surrounding her head, and there was so much of it on her face and in her hair that she was almost unrecognizable. Stacy was unconscious, completely still and unmoving.

I saw red. I didn't just see red, I saw a fucking inferno of rage consume my vision and something inside of me snapped. All the years I'd spent swearing I would never raise my fists like my father went out the fucking window. When I pulled the guy with his pants around his ankles off of her, years and years of pent up rage came barreling out all at once as I threw him like a rag doll across the room, watching as he slammed into the cabinets and fell to the ground.

It didn't matter if I was releasing demons that I'd kept hidden and locked away all my life. If killing these men with my bare hands for hurting Stacy like this would ruin my life, then I truly didn't give a shit. It would be worth it if it meant these motherfuckers would never be able to lay a finger on her again.

I felt the other two men approach me and took one down with a hard hit to the jaw. The other one got a swing in, but it felt like getting punched by a toddler. These thug drug addicts were severely malnourished and so doped up that they stood no chance against me.

All three of them were unconscious, and I found I was disappointed that they'd gone down so easily. I still had rage boiling in my veins, and the desire to release my anger on their lifeless bodies was almost impossible to reign in. But when I looked back at Stacy and saw her beaten and bruised body, all my rage was zapped out of me and worry took over. I knew it wouldn't be a good idea to pick her up and pull her into my arms like I desperately wanted to without knowing where and how severe her injuries were.

I just wanted to make sure she didn't have any injuries that needed immediate attention before calling for a medic and some back up. I didn't get the chance to check, however, when the first asshole I'd thrown off of her tried to jump me.

He would have fucking raped Stacy if I hadn't walked in when I did and with that thought, all reason and rational thought left my body and my fist started making all of the decisions. I punched him over and over, feeling his bones crunch beneath my knuckles, the cracking of his jaw echoing through the apartment. Blood was spraying everywhere every time my fist made contact with his face, but I couldn't stop. I knew if I didn't stop I was going to kill him, but I also punched that little voice telling me to stop in the face, and just kept on swinging.

It wasn't until Joe appeared, yanking me away from the bloody mess in front of me, that I was able to truly take in what I was doing. Before I even had a chance to worry about the son of a bitch's limp body lying on the floor in front of me I ran towards Stacy.

I would rather have taken a dozen dull razor blades to my sternum than have to feel the pain that tore through me when Stacy panicked at my touch. She was terrified of me. I tried to reason with myself and argue that she was just traumatized and maybe she couldn't see clearly, didn't know it was me, but when Joe knelt down beside her she instantly calmed. I backed away, the weight of the situation crashing down on me, but Joe tossed his radio at me and snapped me back into reality. I called for a bus and tried to convince myself to check on the assholes I'd knocked out cold as we waited for the medics to arrive, but I couldn't bring myself to care. I knew there would be hell to pay for what I'd done, and part of me didn't give a shit if he died, but the other part of me wanted to finish what I'd started and make damn sure the asshole wouldn't live another day.

Joe moved out of the way for the paramedics, giving them room to check Stacy's vitals and assess the situation. Joe rattled off some information to them, but the voices around me were muffled and everyone aside from Stacy become a blur. I couldn't tear my eyes away from her.

I pushed my way out of the apartment and followed the medics, trying to climb in the ambulance behind Stacy, but they wouldn't let me. I threatened their lives, became hysterical and irate, but Joe stepped in between me and the ambulance and convinced me to let them leave and do their jobs.

I raced over to the cruiser, still running with the

door still wide open and I hopped in and took off before anyone could try to stop me. I actually beat the ambulance to the hospital and was waiting when they started to unload Stacy. I tried to decipher what they were saying about her condition but there was so much commotion and they moved too quickly for me to hear enough.

I flashed my badge at anyone who dare approach me, abusing my authority over and over again, but I didn't give a fuck. If I had my gun on me I'd pull it and shove it down anyone's throat who tried to keep me from Stacy. I sidled up beside her as they rushed her towards an OR, ignoring the doctors and nurses yelling at me to get out of the way. Stacy fisted my shirt in her hand and was trying to speak, so I pulled the oxygen mask away from her face.

Somewhere in the background I heard them threatening to throw me out of the hospital if I didn't stop interfering, but I ignored them and kept my focus on Stacy. Her eyes were glassy and unfocused, and she was struggling to speak. I tried to reassure her, but as soon as I spoke, she said my name. I wanted to think she was calling out to me, wanted me there, but it came out so pained and tortured that it sounded more like she was begging for me to stay away.

Hearing the fear in her voice as she said my name was enough to break me. As Stacy let go of my shirt and the nurse put the mask back on her face, I fell backwards and watched as they wheeled her into the OR.

I was pacing back and forth in the hallway outside of the operating room when Joe arrived, playing the last hour over and over in my head. Why had Stacy been so terrified of me at her apartment? Was it seeing me almost kill that man? Was she terrified of me now?

"Nice of you to fucking show, Joe!" I yelled as he approached. I knew I was taking out my fear and frustrations on him, and really I should be thanking him for jumping in and keeping me from murdering that son of a bitch back there, but I was too worked up to think clearly.

"Fuck you! Not all of us are maniacs and act like selfish assholes all the time."

"Selfish!? I'm here for Stacy! How is that selfish?!" I was seething with rage and my adrenaline was still coursing through my veins.

"How about abusing your authority and driving like an asshole in your cruiser, nearly killing a man with your bare fists, making a scene which caused the medics to not be able to leave right away with Stacy, and then driving like a maniac on the road again on the way to the hospital, endangering yourself and everyone around you. What, in all of those actions, sounds selfless to you, Chad? Don't you ever think? If you really care about her then you would think more about what you're doing. I've never seen you so out of control. You need to get it together."

I pushed up into Joe's face, our chests bumping, but he stood his ground. He looked just as angry as I felt and I knew fighting with Joe wasn't going to fix anything, wouldn't make Stacy better. I couldn't help myself, though.

"Yeah, well, I wouldn't have had to do any of those things if you had protected her like you should have, Joe. It's your fault she is in that operating room right-"

I was cut off when Joe's fist connected to my face. He'd hit me dead center and I knew I would have a black eye or broken nose, or both. Instinct told me to hit him back, or in the very least, get in his face. But instead I froze, staring down at my hands that were covered in blood. Stacy's blood, her attacker's blood, and now my blood. So much fucking blood.

My chest started heaving up and down and I was trying desperately to control my racing heart as I gasped for air when suddenly, without notice, my knees gave out and I crumbled to the ground.

I sat kneeling in the middle of the floor, a grown ass man, a fucking cop, having what I assumed was a panic attack. Joe leaned down and put his hand on my shoulder, crouching next to me where I sat on my knees. I buried my head in my hands and tried to focus on breathing. I could feel the tears threatening the back of my eyes and I truly couldn't fucking care less. I'd spent my whole life holding in all of my emotions and where had it gotten me? I was in the middle of a hospital, covered in blood, having a melt down while the best thing that ever happened to me was fighting for her life in the operating room.

It was like my heart was a pressure valve, building and building for the last thirty years, finally about to implode with every pent up emotion at the worst possible time. Joe was right. I should have been stronger for Stacy. Not just tonight, but in every way since the day we'd met. I had been trying so hard to deny how I felt for her that I'd completely lost sight of myself and the things that were important.

I'd lost my partner, who was my only friend, and I was most likely going to lose Stacy for good. It was all too much to accept. It would have been so much easier to have someone else to blame in that moment. My dad for making me a violent bastard just like him, or Stacy for pushing all my buttons, throwing me over the edge, or even Joe for getting involved and treating my life like a game. But none of that mattered. I was the one who had lost control and I was the only one to blame.

I was shaking violently, hunched over in a useless heap in the middle of the hallway with a grown man next to me, holding me in a bear hug. I should have been embarrassed or ashamed, and I was, but not because of that moment. I was ashamed of what had led to the moment that had completely broken me. Finally taking responsibility for my actions and admitting to myself that I had fallen in love with Stacy was the most freeing moment of my life.

Chapter 28

Stacy

When I'd finally gained enough strength to open my eyes I was met with a cold, empty hospital room. It took several minutes to remember what had brought me there and the realization that I was alone hit me like a ton of bricks. No one except Joe even knew the whole truth of what had been going on the last couple of months and I couldn't expect Joe to be with me instead of working or living his life. I didn't even know how long I'd been in the hospital or if anyone knew I was there.

I pressed the call button for the nurse and within seconds a woman came running in. She immediately started checking my vitals, helped me drink some water and asked me a few questions. She told me I had been in the hospital for three days and had suffered some serious injuries, then she left to get the doctor.

I sat there for several minutes in the silence of my hospital room, trying not to cry. I didn't want to cry until I at least had all the pieces of the puzzle. I wished desperately that someone, anyone, was there to help me through this. Why had I been so stubborn and retreated so far inside of myself lately? Everything was still a blurry mess and not having all the details made me feel like someone was sitting on my chest.

I heard foot steps, which I assumed belonged to the doctor, and I didn't bother lifting my head. I sat in the bed, my head hung with regret, and waited to hear just how bad my attack had been. I just prayed they hadn't actually raped me. I couldn't even begin to imagine how disease ridden my poor vagina would be if that had happened.

"Stacy," I heard my name come out as a hoarse whisper, so quiet I almost didn't hear it, but I still recognized the voice. Chad.

I hesitated for a beat, almost too ashamed to face him, but when I finally looked at him and took in his appearance I literally stopped breathing. He looked horrible. His eyes were red and puffy like he'd been...crying? His hands were shaking and his clothes were wrinkled and worn like he'd been wearing them for days. He looked utterly miserable, and the desire for him to hold me flooded over me, and I mentally willed him to say that he wanted that, too.

The last time I'd seen him I'd been such a bitch. So many things had gone wrong between us, and I didn't realize just how terrified I'd been of having to face him again. I would have assumed Chad would be yelling at me, telling me what an idiot I was for not being safer and blaming me for getting attacked. Instead, he looked at me with longing and regret, and I knew he blamed himself.

I wanted to reach out to him, but when I went to lift my arm I realized I was shaking almost violently, as if I were having a convulsion. The pain that shot through my arm and into my chest from trying to move forced a choking sob from my throat, and tears pooled in my eyes as I gripped my chest, suddenly feeling like I was having a heart attack. I heard an alarm on my heart rate monitor go off as the stabbing pain pierced through my chest. Seconds later I was surrounded by nurses and a doctor. They shoved a needle into one of the ports attached to my arm and my eyes instantly grew heavy as I drifted off to sleep.

When I woke up for the second time I was instantly flooded with relief at the sight of Joe sitting in a chair next to me, his feet propped up on my bed and the remote in his hand as he flipped mindlessly through channels on the TV in my room.

"This isn't a fucking hotel, Joe," I grumbled, barely audible with how dry my mouth was. Joe immediately pulled his legs down and gripped my hand in his, reaching over me to grab the cup sitting on my bedside table and lifting the straw to my lips. "At least you're useful. I guess I'll keep you."

Joe chuckled and I saw how tired he looked, his eyes weary and heavy lidded. "I've been so worried, Stacy.

You have no idea how happy I am to hear your smart mouth right now," he teased as he shook his head and looked away briefly. When he spoke his words sounded cautious, like he was afraid of my reaction. "Do you remember anything?"

I stared out the window at my lovely view of the side of the building and tried to recall the details. "Pretty much everything, I think. There are pieces missing, but I think it's from when I kept passing out. Some of it's blurry, but unfortunately my memories of the attack are crystal clear." I thought for a second and realized I had no recollection of getting to the hospital, so apparently I was missing some parts. "Did they catch the guys?"

"You don't remember that part?"

"No," I said with a frown. "What happened? Please tell me those assholes are in jail. Or dead." Joe winced when I said dead and I briefly felt guilty for joking if one of them was dead, but then I remembered the assholes attacked me and tried to rape me, so screw them. If they were dead, it was there own damn fault.

"Ummmm…" Joe rubbed his hand over the back of his neck, looking everywhere except directly at me.

"Cough it up, pretty boy. What aren't you telling me?"

"Well, yes they were caught. No they aren't dead, but one of them is in critical condition and it could go either way."

"Okay…awesome. Why didn't you want to tell me that?" He hesitated again and I was starting to get impatient. What the hell wasn't he telling me?

"Chad is the one who put him in the hospital." He winced as he watched me react. I don't know what he was expecting me to say or do with that information. I was in a fucking hospital bed, beaten and bruised, and he looked like he was afraid I was going to attack him.

Flashes of Chad in my apartment flooded my mind. Of him pulling my attacker off of me, knocking out the two other men, punching my attacker over and over, blood spraying everywhere. My eyes darted back and forth while my thoughts tried to keep up with the memories coming back in waves. I remembered Chad coming to me when I was on the ground, putting his hand on me, and how badly I wanted him to pick me up and hold me and tell me everything was going to be okay.

But then I remembered seeing my attacker in my face and Chad was suddenly gone. How much of this was real and how much was I just imagining? It was all choppy and didn't make any sense. Joe was sitting patiently next to me, holding my hand and not saying a word.

I told Joe everything I could remember about Chad being there, which apparently wasn't all of it.

"You freaked out when he touched you, Stacy. Like you were terrified of him." Joe's eyes looked pained as he said that, and I wondered why me being afraid of Chad would hurt him.

"I wasn't afraid of him. I remember him coming to me and I was hoping he would pick me up and carry me to safety, but then he was gone and my attacker was in my face. I wasn't thinking rationally; I was literally out of my mind. Of course now I realize that I was probably hallucinating, but I was in shock then. Did he really think I was afraid of him?"

Joe didn't have to answer, his face said it all. "There was also the scene in your room when they had to sedate you after you saw him."

That part was blurrier, but I still remembered it. "Yeah, he came in after the nurse walked out. I don't think I've ever been happier in my life to see his fucking face. He was a hot mess, though. I felt like shit that he was obviously having a hard time because of me. I expected him to yell at me and tell me what an idiot I was, but he just looked so...broken. So I tried to reach out to him, but my body was shaking violently. Suddenly I felt like I couldn't breathe, and next thing I know the entire fucking hospital runs in and drugs me again. Assholes," I muttered the last word, shaking my head.

When I looked back at Joe his face had gone completely pale and he looked panicked.

"What, Joe? Why do you look like that? What am I missing?"

"Shit!" Joe yelled as he stood and tugged hard on his hair. "I've gotta find Chad."

"What? Joe!" I yelled after him as he took off towards the door to leave my room. "Where are you going? Please tell me what's going on?" A tear escaped and rolled down my cheek. Joe made it back over to my bed in three easy strides.

"I have to talk to Chad. I promise you'll find out everything soon. Now that I know you're okay, I have to make sure Chad is too. It can't wait."

Joe was gone before I could argue for more information, but shortly after he left Adalyn and Carrie came strolling in. Not strolling...storming is more like it. They. Looked. Pissed.

"Hello, ladies. What can I do for you today?" I joked. Deflecting an intense situation by being sarcastic and intentionally obtuse was kind of my forte.

"Shut up, Stacy. I'm just here to tell you that as soon as you've healed, I'm going to kick your ass," Carrie barked at me.

"What the hell did I do to you? And injured or not, I could still take you Carrie. You weigh like 80 pounds. You'd fit in my pocket."

"Stacy!" Adalyn yelled, looking angrier than I'd ever seen her. It didn't last long, because she immediately burst into tears, collapsing at the foot of my bed.

"Uhhhhh...there, there?" I gave Carrie a look and

mouthed 'what the fuck' as I stroked Adalyn's hair. I had no idea what was going on, or why she had gone from screaming at me to crying in two seconds.

"Holy shit, you're pregnant," Carrie whisper-shouted. Adalyn's head jerked up and through her tears her lips curled up and she smiled. Holy shit, this emotional train ride she had me on needed to slow the fuck down. I was getting dizzy.

"Ooooh, will you name it Stacy?" Adalyn narrowed her eyes at me. "What? I'm laying in a hospital bed after having the shit beat out of me, almost being raped, being in a freaking coma for three days and you two bitches come in here yelling at me, then crying, then trying to make it all about you with your unborn fetus and what not? Seriously, I can't get like, five minutes of attention over this?"

Adalyn's lip pouted and started to quiver and I could see the tears pooling in the corner of her eyes again. "Shit, Addy! I'm sorry. Please stop crying, it's seriously freaking me out. If you're going to cry constantly then I'm never going to survive this pregnancy." I reached for her and she shockingly took my hand. Adalyn was big on boundaries.

"What the fuck!" I yelled when she put her hand in mine. "Is that an engagement ring!?" Adalyn blushed and looked down sheepishly while mine and Carrie's jaws dropped. "What the hell is happening in the world!

I'm gonna lose my shit!"

Adalyn laughed and Carrie came over to hug her. "I'm sorry guys. Ian proposed the day before Stacy's attack and we didn't want to tell anyone because of the timing. I knew I should have taken it off before I came here, I just couldn't bring myself to do it. And no one knows yet about the baby, except Ian, of course. And before you ask me if he's marrying me because he knocked me up, Stacy, the answer is no. I didn't tell him until right after he proposed. I had planned on telling him that night anyway."

"Shut up, whore, you know I don't give a shit. Ian is bat shit crazy about you." I started jamming my finger on the 'call nurse' button over and over again incessantly. When the nurse finally appeared in my room she yanked it out of my hand. "What the fuck? What if I need something?"

"Do you need something?" Snotty McNurseBitch asked me with her lips pursed and arms crossed.

"Yeah, I need a bottle of champagne because we bitches have shit to celebrate. I also need some freaking food. I haven't eaten in like a month. Do you guys even feed people around here? And not that nasty hospital food, I want something good so you'll probably need to make a run somewhere. Also, I need someone to take this tube out of my vaginal parts so I can go take a shower and piss on a toilet like a normal human being. And while you're at it, do you guys carry these gowns in any other color? This pukey green color really does not look very good with my skin tone. I'd prefer to see it in a deep purple or fuchsia if you have it. Oh, and these blankets are scratchy. What are they made of, sand paper? Don't you have anything softer?"

The nurse cut me off before I could keep going. "This isn't the Hilton, it's a hospital. I'll start from the top. Yes, I'll get you some food. Best I can do this time of night is Jell-O and crackers. No one is going to go get you anything, I'm a nurse, not a butler. You can't have your catheter removed until the doctor comes in for his rounds in the morning and clears you to get out of bed. We only have one type of gown and those blankets are made of cotton and are your only option as far as supplies from the hospital. Once you get moved from ICU, which will most likely be tomorrow, then your friends may bring you some of your things from home. Until then, what you see is what you get. Now, would you like some Jell-O or crackers? I may even be able to scrounge up a popsicle for you."

"Jell-O and a popsicle? I'm sorry, do I look like a toddler or an elderly person?" I moved my tongue around, counting all my teeth. "Nope, I still have all my teeth, they didn't get knocked out in the attack. That means I can chew things. Please fetch me something that does not melt or turn to mush in my mouth, please." I waved my hand dismissively, earning an eye roll as the nurse walked out, not even bothering to say anything else. Rude.

"Hey! You never gave me back my remote thingy so I can bug the shit out of you all night!" I yelled after her. I figured if I annoyed them long enough then they would get me out of here more quickly. Of course, they also controlled the pain meds so maybe I should back off...

Carrie and Adalyn let out the laugh they were trying to hold back and I joined in, but only for a second because, dammit! Laughing hurt.

"Okay, help me yank some of this shit out of me because I don't need permission to use a toilet. Last I checked it's a free country and the constitution says I have the freedom to piss wherever I'd like. You guys can catch me up while I wash the hospital smell off of me. Joe bolted before I got any details."

"Um, Stacy, I really don't think that's a good idea. You don't know how bad your injuries are. What if you fall and make it worse?"

"That's why you're going to stand behind me, Carrie, so that you can break my fall if I go down. Duh. If it makes you feel better, you can get in the shower with me. It's pretty small, but you're tiny, you'd probably fit."

Carrie narrowed her eyes at me, then shifted her gaze just over my shoulder. I realized at the last second that she was going for the call button to tattle on me. She bolted around my bed, but before she could grab it I threw my water pitcher at her, effectively soaking her and stopping her in her tracks.

"You bitch!" She yelled as she picked it up and ran over to the sink to fill it back up. Adalyn jumped out of the way right before Carrie dumped the pitcher over my head, then we all fell into a fit of giggles. Every inch of my body ached, but I didn't care. The love and gratitude I felt for these crazy bitches overshadowed everything else.

CHAPTER 29

CHAD

I didn't know what to do when I left the hospital. Stacy had panicked again when she saw me. No matter how many times I tried to reason away her reaction, I kept coming back to the same conclusion. She had seen the monster in me that day in her apartment, and as much as it killed me, maybe she was right to fear me. I wanted to go to her and make things right and prove to her that I would never hurt her, but isn't that what I'd been doing all along? Hurting her? No, not with my fists, but with my words and actions. Isn't that just as bad?

I drove around mindlessly and found myself at a home improvement store. Before I knew it, I had new locks for Stacy's front door, a reinforced deadbolt, chain and a security system. Apparently I was headed to Stacy's to do some security upgrades.

Stacy's place was a disaster. I thanked my subconscious for bringing me unknowingly to her apartment, there was no way she could come home from the hospital to this mess. I pushed past the crime scene tape and took in the room. I had to block out the images that assaulted my memory when I saw the outline of Stacy's body where she had been laying on the ground.

I found her cleaning supplies under the kitchen sink

and got to work scrubbing the floors first. There was so much blood everywhere and there was no telling who's it was. Probably a little bit of everyone's. I was able to get all the blood out of her hardwood flooring, but her carpet was destroyed. I was down on my knees pulling up the carpet several hours later when Joe walked in.

"Uh, whatcha doin', buddy?" Joe asked casually as he strolled in with his hands in his pockets. He'd always had a way of looking at ease even in a tense situation. It calmed those around him and added to his appeal. I'd missed his annoyingly calm persona.

"What's it look like?" I replied sarcastically. He smirked at me and I couldn't help but return his smile with my own. It felt good to smile. I wasn't sure my lips could even move in that direction anymore, but it was nice to lose the perpetual frown I'd been wearing. "Well? You just gonna stand there, pretty boy, or are you gonna help?"

Joe chuckled as he made his way over to my tool box and got to work.

Two days later Joe and I had finished replacing the flooring and started working on the walls. There were several holes from where things had been yanked violently off the walls or where bodies had collided with the drywall. Joe made me go home the day before to shower and change. Only then did it dawn on me how horrible I must have looked and smelled.

When Joe and I wrapped up the major part of the repairs on the third day, Adalyn, Ian and Carrie showed up with pizzas and beer. A pang of guilt came over me at the thought of Stacy sitting in the hospital recovering while we were in her apartment, but the girls assured me that Stacy was more than fine and was enjoying torturing the nurses.

It was remarkable to see everyone come together to get things ready for Stacy's return. The girls finished the cleaning while the men worked on installing the security system. All of Stacy's furniture and decorations all throughout her living room and kitchen had been destroyed, so the girls went on a little shopping spree and the men carried all the heavy furniture up the stairs and helped hang things on the wall.

By the fifth day we were completely done. It looked like an entirely different apartment by the time we finished with it. Despite the new paint color, carpet and furniture it still felt like Stacy. Her friends knew her well and every change we had made was well thought out with Stacy's preferences in mind.

Joe and Ian had gone to pick up Stacy from the hospital and the girls had hung back to finish up getting everything ready. I had been debating with myself all day as to whether or not I should be there when she returned. I wanted her to be excited and happy to see her new apartment, not panicked from the sight of me. It felt like a hand was literally gripping my heart and threatening to pull it out of my chest, still beating, at the thought of never getting to be near her again. But if the only way for Stacy to be happy and feel safe again was for me to keep my distance, then that's what I would do.

The whole week I could tell something was on Joe's mind. He always looked like something was on the tip of his tongue and I didn't know why he was holding back, but I'd made myself so busy with fixing Stacy's apartment that I'd been able to distract myself enough not to badger him about it. It felt like everyone was walking on eggshells around me, and they were treating me with a kindness I knew I didn't deserve. At least I could be thankful in knowing that Stacy had people in her life who truly loved her and would watch after her, even if I couldn't be one of them.

When the time came for Stacy to return I tried to leave, but the women quickly trapped me in, insisting I stay. I tried to argue, but not for very long because they both made it obvious I didn't stand a chance. I was growing increasingly nervous about seeing Stacy, seriously doubting whether or not I could keep my composure if she reacted to me again the way she had the last two times. My palms were sweaty and my knee bounced up and down as I sat on the couch, staring at the front door.

The girls kept stealing glances at me and whispering, and I knew they could see how nervous I was. I considered being embarrassed about it, but quickly got over that. Maybe if they could see how much I cared about Stacy then they could help me plead my case. The time for holding in emotions and hiding from the world was gone, and the only way I would be able to get through to Stacy would be to expose myself entirely, no matter how much I hated the vulnerability.

Just when I thought I couldn't possibly sit still any longer, the door opened and Joe walked in first with his hand around Stacy, with Ian following close behind. Stacy's eyes widened in surprise and her jaw dropped, the happiness clearly reflected on her face as she took in her new and improved apartment. She looked fragile and smaller somehow, her left arm in a sling and a crutch under her right. A tear slid down her cheek when she spotted Adalyn and Carrie in the kitchen as they ran toward her, helping her hobble further inside.

Stacy still hadn't noticed me, and I didn't even realize I had stood up and taken a few steps towards her. It was as if my body was literally drawn to her and I had no control over it. Stacy shifted, her movements stiff, as she looked around and took everything in. When her eyes landed on me she froze and I felt my breath hitch. Suddenly exhaling was a forgotten luxury, my mind afraid to breathe for fear of setting off any kind of reaction from her.

This was it. This was the moment where she would

freak out and I would walk away, because I couldn't hurt her any more. As much as I wanted to tell her everything, about my past, how I really felt about her, my fears and hopes for the future - no matter how badly I wanted that, if she wanted me to leave then I would.

The entire room fell silent and everyone stared, their eyes darting back and forth between the both of us. It felt like time stood still and when her eyes widened just a fraction, I braced myself for the worst.

CHAPTER 30

STACY

Joe and Ian babied me all the way from my hospital room to the car and then up to my apartment. It was pissing me off and if I could have lifted one of my arms without wishing I were dead then I would have smacked them upside the back of their heads. I had some injuries, albeit pretty bad ones, but I wasn't entirely crippled or an invalid. I could fucking walk without them feeling the need to cling to me.

I was in the middle of ranting to Ian about how controlling he was being when Joe opened my apartment door, and what I saw effectively shut me up. For a second I wondered if I was even at the right place. Everything looked brand new. I had expected to come home to a disaster and though I hadn't admitted it, I was seriously dreading it. As badly as I wanted out of that hospital, I wanted to be at home even less. I couldn't put out my friends, though. They'd already done so much for me and if they sensed hesitation in me even a little bit, then one of them would insist I stay with them and I couldn't do that. I just needed to find my big girl panties and go back to my apartment.

I never in my wildest dreams expected to come home to this. Freshly painted walls, each alternating between a coral and a teal. Long curtains with an abstract design hung from my windows. A new couch and armchair sat catty corner to a new flat screen TV. Every inch of my apartment from the lighting to the appliances was literally brand spanking new. I knew it had cost them a fortune and as much as I wanted to bitch and complain about them spending money on me, what they had done was truly touching and it was their way of supporting me. I knew that as much as it made me uncomfortable to not use sarcasm in this moment, I needed to choke it down and allow myself to just feel grateful.

When my eyes landed on Chad my heart, mind and body stilled completely. I had missed him so much and my need to have him close was all consuming. It literally stole every breath, every thought, every heart beat right out of me and they all drew together and formed a massive ache in my chest that begged me to run to him.

Chad hadn't been back to see me at the hospital, and once I remembered how I'd reacted to him I really couldn't blame him. He saved my life in the most literal form of the expression and I owed him more than I could ever repay him.

I faintly registered that everyone was staring, waiting to see what my reaction would be. And like a scene out of some cheesy Lifetime movie, I dropped my crutch and despite how incredibly painful it was, I lunged at Chad and threw myself in his arms. He caught me easily, but as he tried not to grip me too tightly while also not letting me fall, he lost his balance and fell back on to the couch.

He quickly scooped my legs up with his arm under my knees and cradled me tightly to his body. I snuggled my head into his chest and pressed myself up against him as much as I could, needing to be closer. Knowing I would never be close enough. I took in a deep breath through my nose and smelled the familiar scent of soap and manliness that was uniquely Chad.

I turned my head and glanced back over my shoulder to see everyone staring at us, the joy from our reunion showing on their faces. I smiled at them with as much genuine, heartfelt love I could muster. Then told them all to get out.

"I love you guys. Thank you for what you did here. I will properly thank you later, but right now I need to catch up with my man, and you don't want to be here for what I have planned."

With one collective groan they all waved goodbye and left the apartment. I turned back to face Chad, still clinging to him as if my life depended on it.

"Stay with me," I begged, pleading with my eyes.

"Always," he whispered as he stood and carried me to bed.

Chad carried me into my bedroom, cradling me in his strong arms, and gently laid me on the bed. Never letting go, he managed to lie down next to me, still keeping me in his embrace. I stared directly into his eyes and said his name as sweetly as possible.

"Yes, Stacy?" He replied with the same tenderness in his voice.

"I'm hungry." Chad let out a full belly laugh. "What? Did you think I was going to say something all sappy or loving?"

"Not even a little bit." He grinned from ear to ear and then kissed me on the tip of my nose. "We have a lot to talk about," he said, his expression growing more serious. I let out a heavy sigh to show just how exhausted I was. It didn't work. The look on his face told me that the talk was happening now, whether I liked it or not.

"I know. Where should we start?"

"How about you tell me about the bet."

"I don't know what to tell you, Chad. It was dumb, and mostly a joke. We were wasted when we talked about it and we never even decided what we would win at the end of it. I didn't realize it at the time, but I was just using it as an excuse to be near you. You made me so angry and most of the time I wanted to fucking kill you, and by the time I realized the only reason you made me so angry was because I liked you so fucking much it was too late. Things had spiraled out of control."

He kept one arm still wrapped around my waist, lifting the other to brush my hair out of my face. Chad was always serious, but the intensity I felt as he stared into my eyes caused shivers to run down my spine.

"I was doing the same thing. I was…I was afraid."

His confession caused my head to jerk back so I could see his face better, but the sudden movement caused pain to spike down my shoulders into my lower back. Chad saw me wince and immediately shifted, putting himself a little further underneath me so I could see him better without having to strain.

"Afraid of what, exactly?" I knew what I hoped he would say. I tried to tell myself not to get my hopes up, because if he didn't say what I was hoping for, I did not want to be disappointed. I did not want him to see that on my face. We were finally together and communicating in a way that was not yelling or part of a game. Whatever he chose to confess to me, I had to be happy. It had to be enough that he was willing to confide in me about something that was clearly difficult for him to say.

I held my breath and watched him struggle. I wasn't sure if he was struggling with the right words to say or with whether or not he was going to say anything at all, but I hoped after everything we'd been through that he was at least to the point of giving me some honesty. I may not have been innocent in all of this, but I felt I at least deserved to know some truth behind his actions.

"Honestly? A lot of things," he said as he let out a deep breath. He stared at the ceiling and I lay still, my chin in his chest, studying him. The seriousness of the situation made me feel vulnerable and the urge to make a joke made me want to squirm, but I was afraid to move. The intimacy that lingered in the silence between us was intense, and while normally it would have me running for the hills, I found it was strangely comfortable. "I don't even know where to start. There is so much I need to tell you. Things I've never told anyone, and I'm not sure how to do it."

I lifted my hand to his cheek and tried to will him the strength, hoping he could feel through my touch that no matter what, I wasn't going anywhere. To see such a strong, sure man be so insecure about himself was killing me. I knew without him telling me that whatever it was that he was keeping locked so deep inside must be overwhelming. I bit my cheek and forced myself to remain quiet, giving him the chance to tell me at his own pace instead of trying rush him.

"I know you're exhausted, but would you be up to going somewhere with me?" I wasn't sure if where we were going was related to what he needed to say or if he was just trying to avoid the topic, but he was the one who had wanted to talk. As much as I wanted him to just get it all out before I went out of my mind, I wanted him to tell me on his own terms. I didn't want him to regret sharing his demons with me.

"I'd go anywhere with you," I whispered, melting even further into him as I watched relief flood his face.

"Do you want to take a shower first? Or get something to eat? Maybe this is the wrong time. It could wait. You should rest, it's selfish of me to take you somewhere right when you get home from the hospital." His words came out so quickly and a giggle escaped my lips before I could stop it. Seeing him flustered made him less intimidating and so much more endearing. It was adorable.

"Chad, stop. I won't be able to do anything until we clear the air about everything, anyway. But so you know, if you're not ready to put everything out there right now, I'm okay with that. I can wait."

"No!" Chad shouted quickly, causing me to startle. "I'm sorry, I didn't mean to yell. I just...I need to get this out. It can't wait. You deserve to know everything. I appreciate you being so understanding, but this is what I want. I want you to know me, Stacy. Really know me."

We were both quiet as Chad helped me change into clean clothes, then helped me down the stairs and into his Jeep. I felt like a fucking grandma, wobbling down the stairs at snail speeds. Every movement made pain ripple through my body. I was trying to be badass, and I thought I was doing a good job of hiding my pain, until I heard Chad chuckle. I glared at him, which only made him laugh harder.

"I'm sorry, you're just so adorable when you're trying to be tough. It's okay to be in pain, Stacy. Trust me, no one is going to think you are weak for hurting after what you went through. The fact that you're up moving around and not huddled up in the corner crying puts you a hundred steps ahead of most people."

"Quit reading my fucking mind. Are you some kind of witch or something?"

"Warlock."

"What?"

"A male witch is a warlock."

I stopped mid step and stared at him in shock. "Holy shit, my boyfriend is a nerd."

He raised his eyebrows at me briefly before setting us back in motion down the stairs. "Boyfriend, huh?"

"Yep. Well, maybe. I don't know how I feel about you being a closet nerd."

"I'm not a nerd, that's just common knowledge."

"Yeah, for nerds."

Chad continued chuckling all the way down to his Jeep. He looked like the happy, laid back Chad I'd seen that night at the bar when we'd played darts. He was a naturally sexy specimen, but when he smiled it made me want to tear my clothes off. I restrained myself, though. Wherever we were going was serious business, I could tell. Well, and also I couldn't lift my arms above my head so I'd most likely just get stuck in my clothes if I tried to remove them.

Neither of us spoke while he drove us to a still un-disclosed location, but he twined his fingers with mine and gently rubbed the pad of his thumb over my knuck-les as he drove. Gone was the laughing, carefree Chad from moments ago. His face was tight and focused, and I knew he was somewhere else. I grew more and more antsy the longer we drove, and when Chad noticed me start to fidget he gave me a reassuring smile that instantly calmed my nerves.

I tried not to let my mind wander, dreaming up pos-sible secrets he could have that would be upsetting him so much. I wanted to be strong for him, to be able to show him that he could open up to me without me crum-bling or freaking out, but things had been so uncertain since we'd known each other that mustering up that kind of courage was difficult.

I must have dozed off for a bit, because when I opened my eyes the Jeep wasn't moving. I looked over to Chad, who was staring out the windshield looking fro-zen. He didn't even notice me sit up and shift towards him, so when I gently placed my hand on his knee he jumped, but quickly regained his composure.

"How long was I asleep?"

"Not long, maybe twenty minutes. I didn't want to wake you." He wasn't looking at me while he talked and him avoiding eye contact brought back the nerves I'd felt before drifting off to sleep. I finally looked out the window and saw that we were in a cemetery.

"Um, I'm trying to not be weirded out that you brought me to a cemetery. I mean, if I had a million guesses I never would have thought you'd bring me here. Look, if you try to bury me alive then you bet your ass I will dig myself out and come after you."

Chad laughed lightly as he climbed out of the Jeep and rounded to my side, opening my door.

"We don't have to walk far, but I can carry you."

"I may walk like an old bitty right now, but I'm perfectly capable of walking on my own." Truthfully, I was in a shit load of pain, but I didn't want to complain.

"Okay...but I know you're in a shit ton of pain, Stacy. You keep refusing my help and I'm going to force you to use a walker."

"You know, if those Back To The Future movies had been right, then I could just use one of those badass hover boards. Damn you Marty McFly, for getting my hopes up!" I yelled, shaking my fist in the air.

Chad laughed and continued to let me pretend he wasn't holding almost all of my weight as we walked. Luckily when he said we didn't have to walk far he was telling the truth, because soon we were standing in front of a very large headstone.

"Mariam Stevens," I read aloud before I remembered Chad's last name. "Is this...are you related to her?"

"That's my mom." His eyes were downcast and I expected to see them holding sadness, but instead I saw anger. I stood there next to him, unmoving, waiting for him to continue. Quite honestly, I wasn't sure what to say. Finding out it was his mom coupled with the unexpected anger he was obviously feeling had completely thrown me.

"My dad killed her." He winced at my gasp and I inwardly chided myself for not being able to control my reaction.

"Where is he now?"

"Prison," he answered without hesitation, as if he expected the question.

"Will you...if you don't want to tell me what happened, it's okay." I meant it, I would be okay with him not telling me, but I really hoped he would. His entire body was tight and you could feel the rage radiating off of him. I reached out to put my hand on his arm, and he flinched, but after a few seconds he slowly started to relax. Finally, he turned to face me, looking me in the eyes for the first time since arriving at the cemetery.

"When I was little, he was my hero. He was a cop, and I wanted to be just like him. People admired him and respected him, and he just had this confidence about him that made him seem untouchable. It wasn't until I was a little older that I realized the admiration and respect I thought I'd seen in their eyes was fear. He was abrasive and demanding." Chad broke our eye contact, looking down at his mother's grave again.

"I don't know what happened. I don't know if he was always like that or if something changed, but I know at some point things were good. I can remember him teaching me how to ride my bike and throw a football. He would take me fishing all the time, just us. He never lost his temper, he was always patient with me. Maybe I was just blind to who he really was because of my age. I've wondered a lot if maybe I just saw what I wanted to, but it felt real either way." He paused and took a deep breath, holding it for several seconds before releasing it.

"I was twelve years old when I got my first glimpse of the bastard he truly was. I'd always been a good kid. Made good grades, never got in trouble. But when I started junior high I was nervous, fell in with the wrong crowd. The other kids decided to break into an old ware-house one day after school. I needed to be home and I didn't want to get in trouble, but I was afraid of being made fun of." He kicked a rock with the toe of his shoe, mumbling curse words under his breath.

"It was so dumb, I should have just followed my gut and went home. Instead I tagged along, and when I didn't come home my mom called my dad, worried. He got in his patrol car and came looking for me and spot-ted my bike out in front of the old building. I was around back, just sitting on the grass, but the other kids were throwing rocks into the windows. I heard his loud voice yelling and watched the other kids skitter away, and I just sat there, frozen in place. The look in his eyes..."

"I'll never forget that look. It was the first time I saw true disappointment, and I hated that I'd let him down. I started to apologize, but he cut me off. He didn't like excuses. He drove me back home in silence and told me to go to my room as soon as we got back. I figured he was deciding my punishment with my mom, and even though I was in trouble already, I couldn't stand sitting around waiting. So I snuck out of my room and tip toed down the hall, trying to hear what they were saying." He was physically shaking at that point, and I was desperate to comfort him but I knew nothing I said would take away the pain of whatever he would say next. So I stood there, watching the amazing man in front of me crumble as he relived a story of his childhood.

"I heard him yelling, but I couldn't hear my mom, so I went down a couple of steps. When I made it far enough down to be able to see them, I saw my mom kneeling on the ground, pleading for him to calm down. She was whispering, probably so I wouldn't hear, but the more she pleaded the angrier he got. I watched as he lifted his hand and swiped it across her face, her head jerking to the side. I didn't mean to, but I let out some kind of sound and he turned to see me. Then all at once, his anger was aimed at me. I turned to run up the stairs. I was terrified. I'd never seen my dad so angry."

"He put his foot in the door frame right as I tried to close the door, then shoved it open so hard it threw me back with it. I thought he would apologize for knocking me down, but instead he walked over and grabbed me by the neck of my shirt and lifted me into the air. He was screaming at me about being irresponsible and how my mother was an idiot and how he was the only one who could do anything right. Then just like he had done to my mom, he backhanded me, letting go of my shirt and I flew halfway across the room. I was a scrawny little kid and I was no match for him."

Chad slipped his hand through mine and led me over to a bench by the side of the road where we had parked.

"Everything changed after that. For a long time, I thought that incident was what made him start beating us, but as I got older and thought back on things, I realized he'd probably always been hitting my mom. Just after that day there was no longer a need to keep it a secret, so he did it openly. She took the brunt of it, and as long as I didn't interfere he would only yell at me instead of using his hands. I hated myself for not standing up to him. I knew I was young and it wouldn't have done any good, but watching him beat my mom like that..." He trailed off and his face grew cold, his hand tightening in mine.

"One day he beat my mom so bad she blacked out.

She should have gone to the hospital but she knew if she did people would find out what happened and she didn't want anyone to know. I begged her to tell someone. I couldn't understand why she was protecting him. It made me angry, not just at him, but at her. I begged her constantly to just take me and run away, to go to anyone who could help us, to just get us out of that house. But every time she would shut me down, telling me it was not an option. Sometimes she would make excuses for him, blaming herself for his actions. Other times she just walked away, completely avoiding the topic."

"After that, several weeks went by with no violence. He was working a lot so we rarely saw him. I actually felt myself start to relax a little and my mom even managed to smile a time or two. I saw what it would be like for us without him, and it hurt me to know she wouldn't leave him. It felt like she was choosing him over me. I know that's not fair, but I was a kid."

I wanted to tell him it absolutely was fair. She should have done whatever she could to protect her son. My body started to shake with rage, but Chad took that to mean I was chilly and he went to retrieve a jacket from his Jeep, then wrapped it around my shoulders.

"Anyway, one night he came home drunk. He must have gone out after his shift and he was angry before he ever walked in the door. I knew before he hit her that it would be bad, so I ran and grabbed the phone and hid in my closet and dialed 911. I heard loud thuds and knew he was knocking her around. I just prayed the cops would get there in time before he killed her. After what felt like forever, I still hadn't heard anything and I started to worry the cops weren't coming. So I climbed out of my closet and tip toed down the stairs. When I got down there…"

Chad stood up and started pacing. My stomach clenched in fear, but not because I was afraid of Chad, but afraid for him. No young boy should have to witness such vile acts from their parents. The fact that he turned out to be so noble and strong was a miracle at best. My heart expanded even further and my admiration towards him grew.

"He was standing at the door, laughing with the cops. Fucking laughing! My mom was lying on the floor behind him, a bloody heap, not even moving, and the cops did nothing. He wasn't even trying to block them; they could see her. It was in that moment that I knew, just knew, that there was no hope for us. He was the police for Christ's sake, of course they would stick up for their own. Fucking pricks." He mumbled the last part as his chest heaved up and down harshly.

"They left and I watched as he walked back over to my mom and kicked her in the stomach, over and over again. He yelled, accusing her of being the one to call the cops. Of course she couldn't have, he'd been beating the shit out of her the whole time. But he was drunk and wasn't thinking and he just kept kicking and kicking. Eventually she stilled entirely and I knew...he'd finally done it. He'd killed her."

Chad stopped pacing and instead stood still in the middle of the road, staring straight up at the sky.

"He looked directly at me and there was nothing in his eyes. No remorse, no guilt, no sadness. Just...nothing. Without a word he walked right past me and up the stairs and into his bedroom, then slammed the door behind him. I took off running towards my mom, shaking her, crying and begging for her to wake up. She didn't, and I didn't know what to do. I'd already called the police and a shit lot of good that did me. So I ran out the front door. I ran and ran, barefoot and in the middle of the night. Finally, when I was too tired to run anymore, I just laid down in the grass. It wasn't until someone was shaking me awake the next morning that I realized I'd ran over five miles to my school. My teacher was the one who found me."

"She looked worried and it came back to me all at once what had happened. I started screaming the words "he killed her" over and over again. I was kicking and flailing, but she wrapped her arms around me tight and held me until I calmed down. She took me to the police station, even though I begged her not to. I was afraid my dad would get even more angry and would come after me. Only this time when they went to my house, my mom was dead, and they couldn't look the other way."

"My dad was arrested and two months later was sentenced to twenty years in prison. The cops that had overlooked him beating us were let go from their positions and put on probation. Apparently they had ignored several situations similar to that one. That's how I found out he'd been doing it longer than I thought, and that my mom had tried to fight back at first. She knew though... she knew what I didn't. That the police wouldn't help. If only she had told me. I wouldn't have called them and she might…" He choked on his last words and turned his back to me, and I knew he was on the verge of tears and trying to shield them from me. I whispered his name, a plea for him to come sit with me, and he did. When he sat back down, I leaned into him, resting my head on his chest.

"I didn't have any other family so I went into foster care. The teacher that found me ended up adopting me and it was the best thing that ever happened to me. I wouldn't have made it without her. She got me counseling so I could work through my issues from the abuse and my mother's death, and she was always patient with me when I would have these freak outs where I would start screaming and breaking things. It was mindless, just a way to unleash the pain pent up inside me. She never got mad or yelled or scolded me. She just kept her distance until I wore myself out and then held me while I cried."

"She sounds amazing."

"She was. She died of breast cancer two years ago."

"Oh." I had no idea what to say, so I just sat quietly, waiting for him to continue.

"The only thing I'm grateful for out of that whole mess is that I became a cop. I knew not all cops were bad, but I also knew they needed more good ones. I would never push aside something like that, no matter who it was, and I was determined to make a difference so that the same thing didn't happen to someone else. It took a lot of therapy to help me see straight, and I still don't think I'm completely healed. Maybe I never will be. I hated my mom for a long time, blaming her for what happened. Then I had to deal with the guilt of hating her for so long. I tried not to be angry at my dad. Not because I wanted to forgive him, but because when I let myself feel angry about what he did the rage would consume me. I was terrified I would end up like him, so I worked really hard to never show anger. Never lose my cool. It's too risky and I just couldn't let myself repeat his mistakes."

"Chad," I said gently, my hand cupping his cheek and pulling his eyes to mine. "You are nothing like him. That may not mean much coming from me since we really don't know each other that well yet, but I know, Chad.

I just know. If there was at all a possibility that you were even a tiny bit similar to him, then I wouldn't...I wouldn't care about you like I do. I see the good in you. So don't question my judgment or I'll get pissed."

Chad gave me a light smile. I so badly had wanted to tell him I loved him. I knew I cared deeply for him, despite how hard I'd been trying to fight my feelings. But it wasn't until that moment when the words almost came out so easily that I realized I really was in love with him. It just didn't seem like the right moment. We were sitting in a cemetery while he told me a horrible story about his childhood. When I told him I loved him for the first time, I wanted it to be a happy memory.

We sat there quietly, the only sounds were our breaths mingling in the air as the sun started to go down. My body felt heavy with exhaustion, but I wasn't ready to stop talking. There was so much more I needed to know.

"You know how else I know you aren't like him?" He didn't answer, just raised one eyebrow at me, like he already knew what I was going to say. "You've never once hurt me, and if anyone deserves an ass whooping, it's me." I nudged him with my shoulder, and gave him a small smile.

"But seriously, thank you for sharing all of that with me. I know how hard that was. It means a lot to me that you trust me enough to talk about that with me. I just...I wondered...How does that story relate to what is going on with us? Are you just sharing because you want to be open with me? If so, then that's great, but it feels like there's more reason behind why you brought me here to tell me all of this."

Something in his expression caused a cold dread to course through my veins. Suddenly I was terrified it would be something I didn't want to hear, but I couldn't bring myself to regret asking. Whatever he said wouldn't push me away, I was there to stay. As long as he was honest, we could make it through anything.

CHAPTER 31

CHAD

I wasn't sure how to answer, knowing whatever I said would come out wrong no matter how I tried to word it. I just hoped she would understand the meaning behind my words. I thought telling her the whole story would be hard, but it felt freeing. No one knew the whole truth, not even Joe. It felt good to not have to hold it in after so many years of feeling weighted down by the guilt of it all.

So I took a deep breath and faced Stacy, ready to bare my soul.

"It's been a long time since I struggled to maintain control over my emotions. Something about you just really pushed and pulled at me. At first, I thought it meant I should avoid you. I thought you were toxic." She winced at that last part, and I hurried to keep going, wanting to reassure her of how wrong I'd been. She was exactly what I hadn't known I needed.

"I was wrong Stacy. You didn't do anything wrong. You were perfect. I just...I hadn't felt anything for anyone in so long. I mean, yeah, I have emotions and I feel sad or happy, but not really. It's all surface level. Even with sex, it was just a release, never anything intimate. I knew getting close to anyone meant the chances of me getting angry and lashing out at them were higher, so I avoided anything meaningful for so long."

"All that anger I projected on to you, I was really just angry at myself. I was constantly warring with myself over my emotions. I was an idiot, trying to talk myself out of what I felt for you. I constantly went back and forth between trying to shut my emotions off and trying to give in to them. It wasn't until I realized I couldn't fight it anymore, when I finally accepted that my feelings for you weren't going anywhere, that the anger finally stopped. I was trying to protect myself, protect you, from pain, but all I was doing was hurting us both. And when I found those guys attacking you at your apartment, I just lost it. Then you were afraid of me and…"

Stacy jerked her hand away, and I thought maybe I'd finally made her angry and she was going to leave. Instead she climbed onto my lap and wrapped her arms around my neck, pressing her cheek against mine.

"I was never afraid of you, Chad," she whispered, and I could hear the sincerity in her voice. "I was in shock and not in my right mind. The only thing I was afraid of that day in my apartment was of you getting hurt. I wouldn't be able to live with myself if something had happened to you because it would have been my fault." She pulled back and put both of her hands on either side of my face and I could tell by the way her eyes searched mine that she was making sure I knew she meant what she was saying. "I hallucinated my attacker when you knelt down beside me, I wasn't freaking out because of you. I even tried to cry out for you at the hospital before they took me in for surgery. When you showed up in my hospital room, I was so fucking happy, but in so much pain. I tried to move and it hurt so bad, I can't even describe it. But I was never, never afraid of you. I could never be afraid of you, Chad."

She gently brushed her lips against mine before pulling back again. "Wait..." she said, furrowing her brow in confusion. "Is that why Joe freaked out at the hospital?"

"What do you mean?"

"He said you thought I was afraid of you. I explained it to him that I wasn't, and he said he had to take off and see you and that he would explain later. When I saw him again he seemed perfectly fine so I didn't press it, but is that why he ran out?"

"I don't know, he never said anything to me. I did think it was strange when he found me at your apartment and just started helping me. He didn't say a word, actually. If I had to guess, I'd say yeah, that's why he took off. He knew how much it was killing me that you didn't want to see me. Based on how out of my mind I'd been over you, he probably thought I was on a rampage, destroying the town or something like fucking Godzilla."

She laughed and then pulled my mouth onto hers

roughly, tugging at my lower lip with her teeth. She gently ran her fingers through my hair, and the contrast of her touch and her almost painful kiss lit a fire in me. I stood with her in my arms and carried her to my Jeep, somehow managing to find the willpower to pull away from her to open her door. If I didn't get some distance from her fast then I would end up taking her right there in the cemetery, and that would be all kinds of levels of messed up.

After I had her settled into the seat and buckled in, I rounded the Jeep and climbed into the driver's side. When I started the ignition and turned to face her, I could see everything I'd hoped for reflected back at me. Compassion, understanding, love, desire.

We drove in comfortable silence back to her apartment, and I carried her as quickly as I could up to her apartment while trying to be as careful as possible not to jostle her. I wasn't sure how she'd made it the whole three hours at the cemetery without once letting on that she was in pain, but I knew she had to be. Stacy was undoubtedly the strongest and most stubborn woman I'd ever met, and she'd put on a brave face for me.

I laid her down gently onto her bed and stood over her, looking down at the woman who had so quickly and completely changed me, made me a better man. Her face was still freshly bruised, a bandaged cut above her eye and her arm in a sling. She looked fragile and it reminded me that despite how strong Stacy was, she was still capable of being hurt. And I swore to never be the one to hurt her, physically or emotionally.

"Chad," Stacy whispered, her voice low and husky, laced with need. I wanted so badly to be inside of her, feel her wrapped around me, showing her how good I could make her feel. I had a lot to make up for, and once she was healed, I would treat her body with the love and care she deserved. But it wasn't about me, I just wanted to make her feel good. So I slowly started to peel her yoga pants off of her legs.

Despite being in the hospital for a week, Stacy's skin was silky smooth and perfect. I sucked in a harsh breath when I realized she didn't have panties on under her pants, and that she was waxed almost bare just like her legs. I climbed onto the bed, kneeling over her, as I dragged one hand up her right leg slowly, stopping just before her sex.

She arched her back, trying to get closer, but I continued to trail my hands up and down her legs, over her stomach, around her hips. She felt so soft, the perfect contrast to my calloused hands. I took special care around all the places she was hurt, placing soft kisses over every bruise and cut.

"Please," she begged, her eyes hooded and full of desire. I wasn't done memorizing every inch of her, but I decided to give her what she wanted, and I slid my hand over her thigh and back up. My finger traced the outside of her sex and I could feel how wet she was already as I slowly dipped one finger lower and flicked it across her clit.

Stacy gasped and arched her back off of the bed, in what I was sure had to be a painful motion, though she showed no trace of pain, just pleasure. As she continued to tremble and writhe underneath my touch, completely surrendering to me, I knew without a doubt that it was the most beautiful and erotic sight I'd ever seen.

CHAPTER 32

STACY

God, Chad was going to kill me. My pleasure was build-ing slowly. So slowly that it was almost painful. And yes, I was in a lot of pain elsewhere from the attack, but I could barely feel it. I was so consumed with Chad's hand massaging me in the place I wanted him most that a fucking tornado could have ripped the top half of my apartment building off and I would have been too caught up in pleasure to even notice.

I was begging for more, rolling my hips trying to gain friction, needing to feel more of him. Finally, when I thought I would lose my mind from the slow and gentle torture he was inflicting, he started to pick up his pace and his movements sped up. When his mouth joined his hand it was only a matter of seconds for my pleasure to course through me, and I cried out his name, my whole body convulsing as I rode out my orgasm. Chad contin-ued his assault, ignoring my plea for him to stop. Instead he kept on devouring me, licking and sucking until the pleasure bordered on pain until I was screaming.

Chad finally slowed down, gently bringing me down from the aftershocks of my orgasm, before scoop-ing me up into his strong arms. My body was completely limp, partially from being sated and also from the day's events.

Chad carried me into the bathroom and sat me down gently on the edge of the bathtub. I watched intently as he turned on the water and checked the temperature, making sure it was just right, then taking the time to pour in some of the bath salts I kept on the edge of the tub. Then he turned to me and very carefully helped to undress me until I was completely bare before him, and he held me up and eased me into the bath.

I expected him to take a seat next to me, or leave me to myself, but he started to pull off his own clothes. Before I knew it, Chad was climbing in behind me, pulling me into his arms. I could feel his erection stiff against my lower back, but he made no attempt to make it known. He seemed perfectly content to just hold me as he casually grazed his hands up my arms to my shoulders where he started to gently knead the knots in my shoulders.

It felt amazing, soaking in a hot bath with a beautiful man as he massaged all my worries out of me. I let my head roll back and let out a moan.

"I'm trying to be a gentleman here, Stacy, but if you keep making sounds like that then I won't be able to control myself." His voice was low and husky in my ear. It sent shivers down my spine, spreading goose bumps all down my arms and legs.

"Maybe I don't want you to be a gentleman," I teased. Despite how tired I was and how much pain I was still in, I wanted so badly to feel Chad inside of me, but I knew he wouldn't give me what I wanted. He would put my comfort before his, even if it meant having blue balls for weeks.

To pretend I wasn't at least a little shaken up from the attack would be total bullshit, but nothing got under my skin more than some assholes interfering with my sex life. Just thinking about it made me want to kick puppies. Chad must have felt me tense because his hands stopped and he pulled away to look at my face.

"What's wrong? Are you in pain? Did I hurt you?" The worry in his voice was so sweet, and I couldn't believe how freaking lucky I was to have him there, taking care of me.

"No, you didn't. I was just thinking about the pricks that attacked me."

"You're safe now, Stacy. I won't ever let anyone hurt you." I bust out into laughter, and the sudden movement sent a searing pain through my ribs, but I couldn't stop. Chad looking at me like I'd lost my damn mind only made it worse.

"No, no. That's not what I mean," I managed to say in between laughs. "I don't care about that. I'm just pissed that we can't have sex because of my stupid injuries."

Chad looked confused at first, but then joined in my laughter.

"You are so amazing, Stacy. Truly." His words were heartfelt and I knew he meant them, so I sank further into his arms and finally let my entire body relax. Chad gave me a lingering kiss on my temple, and I slowly drifted off to sleep in his arms.

When I woke, I was tangled in my sheets, still naked. Chad must have carried me from the bath and dried me off. I looked around the dark room but didn't see him anywhere. Glancing at the clock I saw that it was two in the morning. Where did he go?

CHAPTER 33

CHAD

After Stacy drifted off to sleep I carried her to her bed and gently dried her off with a towel, careful not to wake her. Though she was so exhausted that a Mack truck probably could have driven right through her bedroom and it wouldn't have woken her.

I bent to slip under the covers with her when I heard my phone vibrate on the table next to the bed where I'd sat it when we first got back. A quick glance showed a missed call and voicemail from the precinct. I was tempted to ignore it and catch up on some sleep, but after lying awake several minutes, still wondering what was on my phone, I finally caved and listened to the voicemail.

It was my captain, asking to see me first thing in the morning. He didn't elaborate, but his tone told me enough. He was terse and his voice tight, and it was apparent something was wrong. The last time I'd heard him speak to me that way was the day before my dad's last parole hearing, but he wasn't up for another one for at least a few years, so it had to be something else.

After the attack on Stacy it had been strongly recommended that I take some "vacation" time. I knew there was a possibility that there could be repercussions to my behavior the day of Stacy's attack, but I hadn't heard anything since so I thought maybe my captain had handled it. I was due to return to work in a few days, but based on the way his voice sounded and him asking me to come in tomorrow, I had a feeling things weren't as "handled" as I'd hoped.

"Chad," I heard Stacy whisper from behind me. She was hunched over and clutching her side, looking drowsy and confused. "I woke up and you weren't in bed. I got worried."

I rushed to her side and wrapped one arm around her, gently grabbing her elbow with the other and leading her back to the bedroom. "I'm sorry, I had a voicemail from my captain. I stepped out because I didn't want to disturb you."

"Is everything okay?"

"Yeah, everything is perfect," I half lied. I knew Stacy would feel responsible for getting me in trouble, and I didn't want to add to her stress, especially since I didn't have all the facts yet anyway.

I helped Stacy climb back into bed and then joined her, pulling her back to my front and wrapping my arms around her lightly, careful not to hurt her. Only a few seconds later I heard her breathing slow and even out, telling me she had fallen asleep. I laid there awake and let my mind wander, replaying everything that had taken place since meeting Stacy.

I was surprised at how right it felt to have her in

my arms, but not in an alarming way. My whole life I hadn't allowed myself to even entertain the thought of having a real relationship with someone, and Stacy had swooped in and changed everything. I found that all the tension and anger I'd felt around her when I was fighting the connection between us had dissipated, and in it's place an overwhelming calmness took hold. Whereas I would normally be stressed and worried about my job and what may happen when I went in the next day, instead I was completely at ease. Whatever happened, I would get through it now that I had Stacy. Nothing and no one could come between us, I'd make sure of it.

CHAPTER 34

STACY

Chad had to go into work so he dropped me off at Carrie's. I really wanted to bitch about him treating me like a child who needed a fucking babysitter, but I knew he was just trying to take care of me so for once in my life, I shut my mouth.

"Fetch me a beverage, wench!" I yelled at Carrie as if she were my servant.

"Oh my gosh, you are driving me nuts, Stacy. When will Chad be back to pick you up? I hope it's soon or I'm going to lock you in a closet."

"Will you lock me in your 'special closet'?" I asked, wiggling my eyebrows up and down.

"Shut up, Stacy! You will not speak of my special closet ever again." Carrie didn't embarrass easily, but her closet was a sensitive subject. She blushed as she threw a water bottle at my head.

"Careful, slut! I'm injured here. You can't just throw shit at me!" I winced as I picked the bottle up off the floor. I'd just barely blocked her throw with a pillow or it would have drilled me in the face. Carrie dramatically plopped down on the other end of the couch and laid her head back, staring at the ceiling. "What's on your mind, sugarplum?"

She turned her head to look at me, and I knew without her speaking exactly what she was thinking about. I gave her a knowing smile and she threw a pillow at me.

"Quit reading my mind, Stacy. It's annoying."

"I wouldn't have to if you'd just tell me what's going on. I'm assuming it has to do with Joe. Don't think that just because we haven't hung out much lately that I don't know you've been spending time with him." Her eyes widened and I couldn't help but laugh, causing her to throw another pillow at me.

"Dammit, woman! Quit throwing shit at me! He didn't tell me; I can just tell by the way you guys are around each other. Joe is harder to read, but you can't hide anything from me Carrie, you know that. So are you going to fill me in?"

"Not yet," she mumbled, fiddling with a loose thread on the blanket she had draped over her lap. I felt like a shitty friend for being so wrapped up in my own stuff lately and not knowing what was going on, but Carrie didn't share easily, so I didn't push her. Joe was a good guy, so whatever was going on, I trusted him to take care of her. Truthfully, I worried more about Joe than Carrie. Although, if anyone could handle Carrie's issues, it would probably be him.

"Why did Chad have to go to the station? Isn't he off for another couple of days?" Carrie asked as she flipped through the channels on the TV, trying to find something for us to watch.

"I don't know, he said he had a meeting with his captain, but he was acting kind of weird. Something is up and he didn't want me to know."

Carrie looked at me like I'd just told her that my vagina was the pot of gold at the end of the rainbow.

"What?" I asked her, my words mumbled as I chewed a big mouthful of popcorn.

"You didn't make him explain?"

"No, if he wants me to know, he'll tell me." Carrie's jaw dropped open. "Stop looking at me like that," I said, throwing a handful of my popcorn at her. "I'm capable of being patient and reasonable."

Carrie scoffed but didn't say anything. She just shook her head and turned her attention back to the TV.

"I have to go to the bathroom," I announced. Carrie's phone chirped and she just nodded her head at me as she checked it. She turned her head and tried to hide her smile, but I caught a glimpse of it. Yep, something was definitely up.

I walked down the hall but instead of going left into the guest bathroom, I made a right into her bedroom. Carrie's place was fairly small even though she could afford a mansion if she wanted. Between the money her dad had left her and her successful dance studio, she made more than enough to live somewhere at least twice the size of her current house. Carrie had always been pretty modest, though.

I wandered across the room, trying to be quiet as I went for her special closet, only it was locked. "Dammit!" I yelled, jiggling the handle.

"What's wrong? Are you okay!?" Carrie yelled. "Dammit, Stacy, stop trying to get in my closet."

"Why is it locked?"

"Because last time you got in it I couldn't get you to leave. You're such an addict, it sucks you in like a vortex, and as much as I love you, that was a very disturbing week for me that I really don't want to relive."

"Ugh, you are such a prude," I whined before plopping down on her bed. Carrie rolled her eyes at me but laid down next to me. We both stared up at the ceiling, neither of us speaking, lost in our own thoughts for several minutes.

My thoughts drifted to Chad and I couldn't help but wonder what was happening and why he'd acted so off this morning. I didn't get to think about it long, though, because soon both Chad and Joe came barreling into Carrie's bedroom.

"Sup, guys?" I asked as Chad came around and pressed a kiss to my temple. I caught a glimpse of Joe's smirk and snuck a look at Carrie, and much to my surprise, she was blushing. The urge to embarrass her was strong, but I fought it. Thankfully, Joe did it for me.

"Well, well, well. What have we walked into. Two

beautiful women lying in bed. Only you ladies have entirely too many clothes on. Here, let me help you with that," he joked as he went for the hem of Carrie's thin silk cami. I expected her to flip out, but instead she laughed and then fell into a fit of giggles as Joe tickled her.

"Alright, you two, wait until we get out of here," Chad said, scooping me up into his arms. I was going to forget how to use my legs if he kept carrying me everywhere, but it felt too good being in his arms for me to complain.

Joe was straddling Carrie as she laughed hysterically, neither of them noticing us leave the room. Hmmmm... very interesting.

I turned my attention back to Chad as he carried me out to his Jeep. "Everything okay at work?"

"Actually...not really," Chad said as he lowered me onto the seat. "Let's go grab a bite to eat and I'll explain."

"This is such bullshit!"

"Keep your voice down, Stacy. It's fine."

"Like hell it is! I can't believe they are doing this. You're suspended? For saving me? On what planet does that make sense? Would they have just preferred I died instead of you kicking some guys' ass? What the hell?"

Chad took my hand in his, rubbing circles with his

thumb, an effort to calm me down that would most certainly not work. I was riled up.

"It's not that. They are claiming it was police brutality. I was off duty and beat the man within an inch of his life. That combined with my dad's criminal history puts the department in a tough spot."

"What does your dad have to do with anything? He beat his own family, not criminals who were trying to rape innocent victims. This is such bullshit," I huffed, pushing my plate away, wishing I could chuck it across the room.

"Stacy, you need to eat. You haven't touched your food," Chad said, letting go of my hand and gently pushing my plate back in front of me.

"I'm not hungry. I lost my appetite," I said, crossing my arms. I was so fucking livid. "I'm sorry Chad. This is all my fault."

"It's really not, Stacy. If I could do it over again, the only thing I would do differently is I probably would have finished the job. That asshole deserved what he got for trying to hurt you. I will never regret protecting you. So don't you for one second think this is your fault."

I couldn't help but feel guilty, but looking at Chad's face, the stress and exhaustion clearly taking a toll on him, I knew I had to keep that guilt to myself. I needed to be strong for him, not turn the situation around to be about me. Guilt wouldn't accomplish anything.

"So what do we do?" I asked, forcing myself to take a bite of my food. It had gotten cold a long time ago, but forcing the disgusting eggs down my throat was worth it when Chad's shoulders visibly relaxed a little just because I was eating. He should be worried about himself and his career, not my damn appetite. Stubborn, selfless man.

"Nothing we can do. There's a hearing in a few weeks where I'll get to plead my case, but it most likely won't do any good. Once they make up their mind, there really isn't any changing it."

"So what could happen? Could you lose your job?"

"Possibly, but most likely if they don't just drop it then I'll just be forced into early retirement."

"Well, this just sucks," I pouted, making Chad chuckle. "I just…" I trailed off, wondering if I should even voice my concern. It was a selfish thing to worry about, but things with Chad were still so new and I was terrified something would screw everything up again.

"What, Stacy?" Ever since coming home from the hospital, Chad was almost an entirely different person. He was patient and gentle, always calm and in control. The loose cannon I'd become accustomed to seeing was gone and I almost wondered if I'd just imagined it all. His voice held so much tenderness and love when he spoke to me that it made me question my sanity.

"I know it's selfish, but I'm afraid if you lose your

job you will resent me for it. Maybe not right away, but eventually. I know how much your job means to you, and you might not do it intentionally, but there could come a day when you end up regretting me." I hung my head, embarrassed and feeling vulnerable. I knew he would re-assure me, but he couldn't know the future. He couldn't know if his feelings would change down the road.

"You're in my life for good now, Stacy. Now that I have you, nothing is going to change that. Of course I can't promise you that I'll never get angry with you. I will undoubtedly get angry and frustrated and just flat out pissed at you, probably daily." I narrowed my eyes at him and he laughed, taking my hand in his. "We're both too stubborn and temperamental to not fight all the time, but I'd rather fight with you every day the rest of my life than go back to the hollow, lonely life I lead before I met you. You bring me to life, Stacy. So even when you're obnoxious and annoying as hell, I wouldn't have you any other way. And nothing will ever make me regret saving you that day. My job isn't what makes me happy, you are. I just cared so much about my job because it's all I had, but not anymore. It doesn't matter what I do for a living, as long as you're with me."

My heart expanded just like the Grinch, and I felt warmth spread through me. A solitary tear escaped my eye and I quickly swiped it away. "That was some really sappy shit, Stevens," I teased, internally blaming my pain meds for making me so damn sensitive. I was turning into quite the crybaby.

Chapter 35

STACY

The next two weeks passed by in a blur. Every day I regained some energy as my injuries healed. As much as I loved my newly decorated apartment, it made me too uneasy to live there. Not because I was afraid, it just brought back the memories of the attack, so I'd been staying with Chad. He constantly complained about all my "girly shit" taking over his house, but he didn't hide his grin as well as he thought he did when he was whining. He loved having me there, girly shit and all.

A few days after I got home from the hospital the dentist I worked for asked me to come in. He sat me down and told me he was retiring. I wasn't surprised. He should have retired years ago. But that also meant I didn't have a job to go back to. The stress of both Chad and I not knowing where we stood with working was there, but we were able to ignore it. Chad had bought his house with cash, fixing it up after it had gone into foreclosure. My lease with my apartment was almost up and Chad hadn't asked me to move in, but considering I was pretty much living there anyway, I thought maybe he would soon. I hinted about the subject, but he never took the bait. It was difficult to not just come right out and ask him, but for once in my life I was going to be a girl about things and let him take the lead. It was driving me nuts, but I was managing.

It took some coaxing, but about a week after returning from the hospital I finally convinced Chad to have sex with me. It didn't do wonders for my self esteem that I had to practically beg him, but I knew it was just because he was afraid of hurting me. I was enjoying all the hand and mouth play, but I was ready for the real thing. So one day when he ran to the store to get some household items we were running out of, I put on a tiny little scrap of a teddy that Adalyn had brought me. She whined the whole time about not wanting to be involved in my sex life, but being the good friend she was, she finally caved and went to VS and got me some slutty lingerie.

When Chad came back and saw me spread eagle on the bed in nothing but ridiculously high stilettos and my sheer, lacy teddy, he was finally unable to resist. He was gentle and sweet and completely opposite of our first time at the club, and I found the intimacy made it better. I'd never 'made love' to a man before, but that was definitely what we were doing. He loved my body over and over, until I was so loved I fell into a love induced coma.

After that we weren't able to keep our hands off of each other. We spent days not even getting out of bed except to shower and eat, and while I was loving every minute of it, I knew it was going to end soon. Chad's hearing was coming up, and eventually I needed to start looking for another job. Most of the time we were both able to pretend those issues weren't weighing on us, but every now and then Chad would start to close off and shut down, and I had to force him to come back to me.

He was used to holding things in and fighting his demons alone, but I wasn't going to let him do that anymore. I was prepared for a fight every time, expecting him to push me away, but after some gentle pushing he would finally confide in me. I felt horrible hearing how stressed and worried he was about his job, but I did my best not to show it. I knew he needed me to be strong for him, and so I forced myself to have a positive attitude and not let him know how incredibly guilty I felt for getting him in this shitty situation.

We still fought almost constantly, but what would start out angry would turn into play. One minute we'd be screaming at each other over who gets to control the remote, the next minute we'd be rolling around on the ground tickling each other and laughing. One morning I tried to cook breakfast, which of course went over horribly because I'm a terrible cook, but when he tried to take the spatula from me I refused to relinquish control of the kitchen. Our physical struggle over the spatula turned into a food fight, and a half hour later we were wearing our breakfast instead of eating it, and ended up having to shower and go out for food. Which of course didn't even happen until lunch time because we got a little distracted in the shower.

Time passed both painfully slow and sickeningly fast. So many things were up in the air, and the one stressing me the most was my living situation. I hadn't brought it up in a while, mostly because I was afraid he would tell me he didn't want me in his house once I was healed, but I'd become so comfortable that it felt like my home. Several times I opened my mouth to ask him about it, but quickly bit back the question, not wanting to add to his stress with his deposition in only a few days.

Adalyn had cut back to part time at work because her pregnancy made her so sick and miserable, so she would come visit with me while Chad would go to the gym to work off some nervous energy. Carrie would join us as much as she could, and it was a nice break from the constant testosterone surrounding me day in and day out staying with Chad.

I'd never seen Addy so emotional, but everything made her cry. I felt bad for Ian, I would go crazy if I had to deal with her ups and downs constantly, but I knew he didn't mind. Carrie was distant in a way I couldn't put my finger on, and every time I tried to ask her about it she just brushed it off or changed the subject. If I had any idea at all what was causing her behavior I would have pried answers out of her, but I was clueless and it was pissing me off. Lucky for her there was so much else going on in my life that I let it go, but I was determined to figure it out once we got through Chad's work crap.

Finally, the day came for Chad's deposition and I could shit a brick I was so nervous.

"Stacy, you're making me nuts with all your bouncing around. You're like a Chihuahua on crack."

"I can't help it! I'm losing it, man!" I'd been dressed and ready to go since six in the morning and his hearing wasn't until four in the afternoon. I was literally losing my mind.

"You sure you want to wear that?" I looked down at my outfit and looked back at Chad inquisitively.

"What's wrong with what I'm wearing?"

"Well your dress is a little short and your heels are pretty impractical. I don't want you to be uncomfortable."

"What do you think I'm going to do while you're in there? Run a marathon? No, I need to look my best and this is my 'hot shit' outfit. I figure if all else fails I can either seduce one of them into letting you go or I can stab one in the heart with the spike of my heel. Either way, this outfit is necessary."

Chad rolled his eyes at me and continued to struggle with his tie in the mirror. I smacked his hand away and did it for him, earning a grunt from him.

The drive to the hearing was only about ten minutes but it felt like ten hours. Chad kept reaching over to squeeze my knee, trying to get my legs to quit bouncing, but I felt like I was going to jump out of my skin, so as soon as he pulled his hand away I started bouncing again. I thought my nerves would add to his, but instead he found it humorous and laughed at me and shook his head.

Joe was already waiting for us at the city building where the hearing was taking place, but I had told everyone else not to come. If it went badly, I didn't want Chad to have to face anyone. I knew he would need space.

Chad sat me down in a bench in the hallway and I watched as he and Joe entered the room together, while I had to sit there and helplessly wait.

A half an hour later I'd about worn the heels off of my shoes from pacing the ground. I was losing my mind waiting out in the hallway for the ridiculous bullshit behind the closed doors to come to an end. Finally, the double doors slowly started to open and I ran up to Joe to ask him how his deposition went, but the solemn look he was wearing did nothing to ease my anxiety.

"It's bad, Stace. They want to make an example out of him. He's sitting in there listening to them blame all of his dad's sins on him. It's horrible. I did what I could, but I don't think it's going to make a difference." Joe looks completely defeated as he runs his hand over his face and looks down at the ground.

I didn't even think. I didn't have to. I was already

moving towards the doors, practically running, but Joe grabbed my arm right when I reached for the handle.

"Stacy, no. You can't go in there. It will only make things worse and you'll end up getting arrested."

"Shut up, Joe, I don't care. I'm not going to stand out here and let the man I love's life fall apart because he saved me. They can throw me in fucking jail, I don't care." I shrugged out of his hold and burst through the doors.

The room immediately went silent as all the heads turned to look at me.

Chapter 36

Chad

My captain was in the middle of giving his statement on my behalf when the doors flew open at the back of the room. Every officer in the place immediately turned to see what the commotion was, and of course, it was Stacy. To be honest, I'd expected to see her sooner. I knew my girl well, and she was not the type to sit on the sidelines while shit went down. I probably should have jumped up and tried to stop her, but the whole scene before she even bust through the doors was bullshit. There probably wasn't much she could do to make it worse.

"Alright, you limp dick mother fuckers," she said in a cool, collected voice, a complete contrast to the fury in her eyes. She was geared up for the battle of a lifetime and the men in the room with us had no idea what was in store for them. I tried really hard to control myself, covering my mouth to hide my smile, but a chuckle slipped out anyway. Luckily no one noticed. Everyone just sat stunned, frozen in place from the bizarre spectacle Stacy was making.

"I'm here to set you all straight so that Chad can get back to his job and you can all find better ways to spend your time instead of harassing honorable men like the one sitting over there," Stacy said, pointing at me, but not looking my way. "Plus my feet are fucking killing me from pacing around the lobby for over an hour in these five inch stilettos. I know, I know, it's not your fault I wore these killer shoes, but you can't deny they make my legs look fabulous," she said as she pointed the toe of her shoe, showing off her long legs. I couldn't help but chuckle as several of the men actually leaned up out of their seats to get a better look at her.

Finally, one of the IA officers gained his bearings and stood to address Stacy. "Ma'am, I don't know who you are but you can't be in here. You need to leave right now before we have you arrested." He squared his shoulders and it was practically hysterical when the shock of her response registered on his face.

"You want to know who the fuck I am? I'm the woman he saved from getting raped and killed, dumbass! Do you even know anything at all about what happened? Surely you've seen my picture in the reports. They took plenty at the hospital where I spent a week of my life being treated with some pretty sick injuries. Though you didn't hear me complaining, because I was just thankful to be alive. You know WHY I'm alive? THAT man, right there!" Stacy yelled, pointing at me.

For the first time since entering the room Stacy glanced in my direction, and despite the anger still evident all over her, she managed to sneak a wink at me. Even when going bat shit crazy, she was still so goddamn adorable.

"Yes, of course, I know who you are. I was just caught off guard. I'm terribly sorry for what you endured, but you still can't be here. This is an official and private matter."

"Uh, yeah, I know. Don't you think it would make sense though to have me here considering this whole crock of shit is happening due to something that involves me?" Stacy looked at the officer like he was the biggest idiot she'd ever encountered. He crumbled just a little bit under her glare, but quickly recomposed himself.

"I understand, but that is not how the law works, ma'am."

"Fuck the law!" Stacy yelled, interrupting him. His patience was waning, but if Stacy was affected by his annoyance, she didn't show it. "If the law means you're going to strip a good man of his badge for saving my fucking life then the law is fucking stupid." Suddenly Joe was at Stacy's side. I thought he was going to try to remove her or calm her down, but all he did was stand next to her and stare straight ahead, his expression stoic. What the hell was he doing?

Another officer entered the room and tried to grab Stacy's arm and pull her to the doors, but she shrugged out of his grasp and quickly moved away from him. She was only a few feet away from the people deciding my fate, and she turned back to face them. My girl may have been crazy, but no one could call her weak. She was the bravest person I knew.

"I'm not going to tell you how to do your jobs. I'm assuming you've been doing this long enough that if you're too stupid now to see you're ruining a man's life for no reason, then nothing I say is going to help. So instead, let me explain what's going to happen." She paused to look each one of them in the eye, and a couple of them even flinched.

"I'm going to walk out of this room and I'm going to call every news station that will hear me out. And you know they will, because everyone likes a scandal. They will see my bruises and cuts and I'll give them copies of my hospital records. I'll tell them how Chad rescued me and saved my life, and how he got fucking punished for it. I'll tell them how the city apparently condones violence against women. I'll make sure they know that you would apparently prefer that I had been raped or killed than have some piece of shit criminal get his face bashed in. And I'm willing to bet that there are enough people out there who will agree with me when I say that the assholes who did this to me deserved a lot worse. They will join me as we unite against you. The higher ups will have to cower down to public opinion, because you know they can't risk not getting re-elected. So what will happen? They'll need someone to blame. And who is that going to be? Should I pause here for dramatic effect while it all sinks in? Because yep, the sorry asshats who are going to take the fall for this will be all of you. So not only will you have cost the city one of it's finest police officers, but you'll also cost yourselves your jobs."

I was fucking impressed. I leaned back in my chair, crossing my arms, giving a smug smile. They all sat quiet for a few moments, and when one of the IA officers started to speak up, Joe joined Stacy. He walked up and took her side again, and it hit me all at once what it was they were doing for me. Yeah I knew they were risking getting in trouble to help me, but they were doing it to help *me*. I had no idea what the hell I'd done to deserve such amazing people in my life, but I'd never been more thankful than that moment for the stubborn dumbasses standing at the front of the room who refused to let me shut them out of my life.

"If you take his badge, you may as well take mine. Because I will stand by Stacy's side, telling everyone the truth about what happened. I was there and I'll make sure the right story gets told."

"You know it's a federal offense to threaten law enforcement, right?" It was a rhetorical question, because of course Joe knew that, but it was intended to intimidate them into backing down.

"No shit, fucktard. He's a fucking cop, of course he knows it's against the law. Any idiot who watches Law and Order knows that. And guess what? We don't give a shit. You know why? Because we aren't the ones in the wrong here. You don't like what we're saying, then do something about it. If you think throwing us in jail is going to right the wrongs of this bullshit hearing then by all means, take me away." Stacy held her hands out in front of her, offering herself up as a sacrifice. They all hesitated too long though, and she dropped her arms and laughed. "Yeah, thought so."

Stacy turned on her heel, gave me one last wink, and stormed out of the room as quickly as she'd entered it. The entire scene only lasted about ten minutes, but it felt much longer, and once her body disappeared behind the doors, I exhaled a deep breath. Only once Stacy was out of the room my confidence faltered and I started to worry about the repercussions of what just happened.

CHAPTER 37

STACY

As soon as the doors closed behind me, I collapsed onto the bench sitting against the wall directly in front of me. My chest was heaving up and down as I bent over, gripping the edges of the bench. I was taking deep breaths, trying to slow my pounding heart.

I didn't know how I managed to keep it together in there. It was almost like an out of body experience, like I was someone else in the room watching some crazy person threatening a room full of cops and city officials.

The adrenaline was starting to wear off and I felt panicked. What had I done? I probably just made it so much worse for Chad. Of all the times to lose my mind and go off the deep end, I'd picked the worst one. Chad would hate me. In a matter of just a few minutes I'd managed to ruin everything.

I felt tears streaming down my cheeks but I couldn't lift a hand to wipe them away. My body started shaking uncontrollably, the fear of losing Chad consuming me. Even during my attacks, I didn't feel so scared, so helpless. I finally had him, the man that I love, back in my life. I had his love and I just flushed it down the drain with my outburst, which I was sure he wouldn't be able to forgive. His job was everything to him and I knew my irrational, idiotic self had just ruined his chance of keeping it.

I felt an arm on my shoulder and jerked my head up in surprise, greeted with Adalyn's sympathetic face. She sat down beside me just as Carrie took the seat on the other side, and they wrapped their arms around me and hugged me tightly while I finally let go of the little control I still had and let the loud, angry sobs out. I was faintly aware that Joe and Ian were also there, but the hatred I felt for myself for being so stupid was consuming me, and the sound of my wailing cries drowned out any other noise.

It wasn't until I felt the loss of Carrie and Adalyn's arms around me that I started to pull out of my melt down. I was still crying and shaking, but I started to calm down. I felt an arm around me again, but it was heavier and bigger, so I looked up expecting to see Ian or Joe. But it wasn't either of them.

It was Chad.

I could barely see his face through my tear filled eyes as I wrapped my arms around him tightly, burying my face in chest, muttering apologies over and over again. I expected him to push me away, to yell at me and tell me what a fuck up I was and everything else I knew I deserved. But he didn't. Instead he hugged me back, smoothing my hair and whispering soothing words.

I was so surprised by his reaction that for a second

I almost forgot what I'd done and allowed myself to feel comforted, but then reality came back to me and I pulled back, expecting to see anger or even hatred in his face. Instead, all I saw was love.

"I'm so sorry, Chad," I hiccupped. "You should hate me. I ruined everything. I'm so stupid. I know better, I know I can't just run around saying and doing whatever I want and not expecting there to be consequences. And I hate myself. I know that this time you are the one who will be suffering from my idiocy. I know I don't deserve it, but I'll do anything Chad, anything to make this up to you. I'll do whatever I can to show you how sorry I am and maybe one day you can forgive me. Please say you'll give me a chance. I'm so sorry."

I was rambling, my words coming out frantic and rushed, wanting to get it all out before he had the chance to stop me. To give me the rejection I knew was coming. I'd done so much stupid, regrettable shit in my life, but costing Chad his job was unforgivable. Even if he managed to forgive me, I'd never forgive myself. Chad had already lost so much in his life and his job was so important to him and selfishly all I could think was that I hoped I was maybe more important to him than his job and that maybe we had a chance.

I couldn't look at him. I couldn't bear to see the resentment and anger he must be feeling towards me. I wouldn't survive losing him again, especially knowing this time the only person to blame would be me. So I just sat there, staring at the ground, waiting for the inevitable. He was shaking with rage, his whole body trembling. But when he was shaking so hard it was rocking the bench, I finally looked up at him.

What the hell?

He was laughing. Like full out belly laughing. When he saw me finally looking at him he really let go, and for a minute I just sat there confused as hell, but his laughter was contagious. I'd never heard him laugh this hard. I couldn't help myself, so I gave in and joined him. I didn't know if it was one of those our-lives-are-fucked-so-there's-nothing-to-do-but-laugh-about-it laughs, but it felt good to laugh either way.

When our hysteria started to die down, I saw everyone staring at us. Adalyn looked confused and sad, Ian looked indifferent, Carrie looked happy and Joe looked amused. It was then that I realized I still didn't know what exactly happened after I left the room.

"They let it all go, Stacy. I get to keep my job," he said as if reading my mind. My jaw fell open and I tried to find words but I couldn't speak. I couldn't believe it. How was it possible that I hadn't screwed everything up? "Apparently your little outburst in there scared some sense into them. I thought for sure I'd be bailing your ass out of jail right now, but after a few minutes of whispering amongst themselves, they just dropped it, said I could go."

"Oh my God, Chad, that is so great!" I flung myself onto his lap, straddling his legs and kissing him over and over, covering every inch of his face with my mouth. I didn't care where we were or who was watching, I was just so relieved to know everything was going to be okay. Although...I couldn't help myself. I had to know. So I pulled back and looked him in the eye and asked a question I was afraid I'd regret.

"Chad...I'm so so happy that everything worked out. It was a big risk going in there like that, and honestly, I didn't even think about how stupid it was until afterward. I just...I have to know. If you had lost your job because of me...would you have been able to forgive me?"

His smile fell completely and his eyes narrowed. He was angry. Like, really angry.

Dammit. I knew I shouldn't have asked. I just couldn't leave well enough alone, could I? Like I was determined to fuck up my life somehow.

I tried to pull away but he put his hands on my waist and held me in place.

"There would have been nothing to forgive. I can't believe that after everything you still don't realize what you mean to me."

"I didn't mean, I just...I know how important your job is to you. And I know how irresponsible it was of me to do that. I wouldn't blame you for hating me, that's not why I asked. I just...I don't know. I need you to know I'm sorry."

"Don't." His face was still angry but he softened a little around his eyes. "Even if what you did had cost me my job, I would still be thankful. You weren't being careless or spontaneous Stacy; you were acting out of instinct on my behalf. You saw me in trouble and you jumped in. It wasn't crazy, it was brave. No one has ever fought for me like that. Even when my mom would take my dad's hits so I would be spared, she just took them. She never fought back. You, Stacy, are a fighter. You are strong and brave and amazing."

His hands moved to my face, his thumbs wiping away my tears. The anger was gone and all that was left was love.

"I don't know what I did to deserve you, Stacy, but I'll spend the rest of my life trying to prove that I'm worthy. I don't want you to change. I don't want you to be serious and cautious like me. I want you to breathe your life into me. When you're with me, it's the only time I feel alive. I don't care about my job. I don't care about anything but you Stacy. I would give up my whole life if it meant I could keep you by my side forever."

If that wasn't a declaration of love, then I didn't know what was. I went in to kiss him, but he gently pulled me off his lap and sat me back down on the bench. The loss of his body touching mine was almost unbearable, and I started to stand up, wanting to reclaim him, but he stopped me by dropping to the ground in front of me.

Before I could figure out what he was doing, he was holding out a box. He was on one knee, I realized, not crouching. And he was holding a fucking jewelry box. A little square one and I swore to all things holy that if there was a ring inside I was going to kick him in his nuts. It's not that I didn't want to marry him, but we could barely make it through a meal without walking away covered in half of it. Marriage just seemed a little...no... ENTIRE-LY...too soon of a decision. He had lost his damn mind.

"I was going to plan a big gesture for this. You deserve amazing things, Stacy, and I want to be the one to give them to you. I can't stand seeing you unsure about us, about how I feel. That you would ever think I would choose anything over you, that I would leave you for any reason at all, tells me that now is the time to do this. No matter what happened today, this was going to happen. You could have gone in there and stripped naked and gave the city manager a lap dance as a bribe to let me off and I still would be here on my knee."

"Dammit, why didn't I think of that?" Chad glared at me, but I could see the smile he was hiding. It was going to hurt like a mother fucker when I had to tell him no. I contemplated just interrupting him and saving him the effort, but I was still a little too stunned to think.

"I love you, Stacy. I know I haven't said it yet, but it's not because I didn't feel it or because it's hard to say. The words just don't do justice to the way I feel about you and every time I started to say them, I knew it just wasn't enough. It will never be enough, Stacy, but I'll say them anyway. I'll tell you I love you a hundred times a day, so many times that you'll hate the words, and then I'll say them anyway. Even when you're pissing me off and making me so angry I could strangle you, I'll still shout from the rooftop how much I fucking love you."

I wasn't sure what to say to that. He still hadn't asked the question, and I couldn't quit staring at the box, still unopened. I didn't want to hurt him. I was terrified that saying no after he put himself on the line like that, in front of all our friends, would cause irreparable damage, but it was too soon. I didn't have any doubts that I wanted to be with Chad for the rest of my life, but adding that kind of commitment so soon was going to put a lot of strain on our relationship. I wished he had done this in private so the let down would have been easier to handle. I felt trapped and I hated myself for not feeling as sure as he did that we were ready for this next step.

I was doing my damndest to hide my doubts, but I was so overwhelmed that I knew my resolve was slipping. I looked around at all the faces staring at us. Carrie and Adalyn's jaws were wide open, while Ian and Joe were smirking. I was going to punch them in their nuts later for finding this humorous.

I turned back to Chad expecting him to get irritated with how long it was taking me to say something. Finally, I managed to find my voice and squeak out a response.

"Chad, I... I don't know what to say. I mean...I love you, too, you know that. More than anything, and I'm so happy with you, even when you're being a grade A asshole. But I just..."

"Stacy," Chad interrupted me. "Before you say anything else, just let me get this out okay. I have a really important question to ask you, and I can't think of a better time or place to do it than now, in front of all our friends who are staring at us like any of this shit is actually their business." Everyone snickered and his lips quirked up into a grin. I reached my hand out to stop him, really not wanting him to finish his thought, but he just ignored me and kept going.

"Stacy, would you please make me the happiest man in the world and please..." he paused, slowly opening the box and I held my breath, fighting the urge to close my eyes and losing. I squeezed them shut and told myself that if I didn't see the ring, then the question wasn't real and we could go back to pretending this whole scene never happened.

"Stacy," Chad said gently. "Open your eyes, Stacy."

"Huh uh," I whined like a toddler, knowing I was

acting like an immature asshole, but still too afraid to see the disappointment in his face when I said no.

"Stacy..." Chad growled, sounding less patient but still with a hint of teasing in his voice. "You can't sit here with your eyes squeezed shut forever. Just open your damn eyes and stop acting like a five-year-old, or I'll take you over my knee right here in front of everyone."

I snapped my eyes open at his threat, and my eyes drifted to the box of their own volition.

"You fucking asshole!" I yelled, slapping Chad over and over and trying to kick him as he dodged my hits and fell back on his ass, laughing hysterically. "You made me think you were proposing!"

Inside that damn jewelry box was a key, and I assumed it was to his house.

"You're such a dick!" I pounced on him and straddled his waist. He was laughing so hard he was wheezing and I took advantage of his weakened state and pinned his arms above his head.

"Stacy, get up, you're making a scene," Adalyn chided from behind me.

"I don't give a shit! That was so messed up, Chad!" I could hear the guys chuckling beside me, but I tuned them out and focused on the jackass underneath me. Chad finally started to calm down and I pushed off of him, tempted to kick him in his nuts.

He climbed to his feet and took my hands in his. I tried to jerk them away so I could pout, but he held on tight and looked me in the eye. I tried to look away, but he barked my name so loud it made me yelp and my attention immediately snapped back to him.

"I know you aren't ready for a proposal, Stace. We're still figuring things out and we're both so messed up that taking things to that level so soon would just scare one or both of us off. I want you to move in with me, but you should know that I do plan to propose one day. You're it for me, Stace, so you better start preparing yourself now because one day there really will be a ring in this box and I'd prefer for you to marry me willingly. Though I'm not above cuffing you and dragging you to a JOP if that's what it takes."

I yanked the box out of his hand and opened it back up and looked at the key.

"What, you couldn't even spring for a pretty key chain or something?" Chad just laughed and pulled me in for a deep, delicious kiss that took my breath away and had the guys cat-calling and strangers that walked past us whistling. When he finally pulled away, my vision was hazy with lust and all my anger shifted to the spectators who were preventing me from being able to strip the man in front of me naked so I could do naughty, naughty things to him.

"Well, Officer Juicy Jizz, let's go make sure my key

works for our house. I can think of a few places that still need some christening." I stifled a giggle when everyone collectively groaned behind us.

"One thing's for certain. Life will never be dull with you in it, Stacy."

Acknowledgements

There are so many people that I need to thank, and I'll get to them, but I think for this book in particular I should probably start with Stacy.

I'd love to take all the credit for everything in this book, and while the situations and exact events were a hundred percent fictional, they most likely would never have existed, even in my imagination, if it weren't for my best friend, Stacy Adams.

Let me first give you a little background on Stacy and her involvement in my life. If you were to meet us in real life, you would automatically assume we'd been friends since the beginning of time. You would also be wrong. As I write this, Stacy and I have known each other for all of five months. Stacy and I are basically the same person, only she is *a lot* mouthier and a much bigger fan of hugging than I am.

RL Stacy (or Real Life Stacy, as we now refer to her) didn't just inspire the persona for book Stacy. They are essentially the same person. Throughout the entire process of writing this series, Stacy would constantly joke that it was like I crawled up inside of her brain and stole her thoughts. I have no doubt that if any of these scenarios were to actually happen, then RL Stacy would react the exact same way.

Stacy has been my biggest supporter since I made

the decision to try my hand at writing. I didn't set out to write a book about her, but once she requested I name a character after her, the story took on a life of it's own. I also didn't expect Stacy to become such a beloved character. I guess spending so much time with her day in and day out makes it harder to see that she's actually pretty funny and not just incredibly annoying. (Although in my defense, you try spending as much time with her as I do, and then tell me you still love her as much as you did when you were just reading about her.)

In all seriousness though, I *could* have done this without her, but I wouldn't have enjoyed it as much. She has spent countless hours listening to me bounce ideas off of her, yelling at her when she made suggestions I didn't like, and then reading and rereading my books a hundred times before I was happy with the finished product. On top of all that, she's also spent countless hours listening to me complain and drone on about my relentless obsession with author NA Alcorn, not to mention all the insecurities that come along with stepping out of your comfort zone to try something you have no idea if you are even good at.

Along those same lines, I'd also like to thank her husband Chad. (Yes, I also chose that name per her request. RL Stacy is a demanding and bossy little hussy.) RL Chad used to be a cop and has been somewhat of a consultant for the book, and his input was priceless and much appreciated.

Next I'd like to thank again all the other authors out there who continue to inspire me and bring me hours of joy through their words and characters. The author I should thank the most would be NA Alcorn, who not only put up with my stalker-like tendencies, but actually encouraged them, earning her my undying love and devotion. My level of affection for her is beyond what's considered socially acceptable between two friends who have yet to meet in person, but that doesn't stop me from going all fangirl at the mention of anything that has to do with her.

Massive thanks for my talented and patient husband, who has done so much behind the scenes to make these books happen for me. Everything from formatting, to editing, to cover design, website development and publishing... there isn't a doubt in my mind that without his help, my books would not exist.

Thank you, thank you, thank you to my supportive family! Missy Coyner - my beautiful and sharp witted mother who made me who I am today. Susie McCarter - my aunt who never fails to deliver a laugh every time I see her! Monica Buettner - my pain in the ass future sister-in-law who I've come to love like she's always been a part of the family. Thank you to all of you for helping with the proof-reading and editing part of this series. You've been a huge help and your support and encouragement mean the world to me. I love you all.

Finally, thank you to my readers! Those of you who took a chance on Adalyn and made it to Stacy, you rock. My ARC readers who took the time to read my books and give me your honest feedback, I couldn't do this without you! Especially Jenny Thompson-Rowlands - you finding my book was by chance, and through GoodReads you have become a dear and valuable friend. As soon as you finish teaching me how to speak all your cool Brit slang, don't be surprised if I show up at your door to test it out!